D1742952

Artful Designs

by Sharon Bill

Artful Designs

by Sharon Bill

www.SharonBill.com

This book is a work of fiction and, except in the case of
historical fact, any resemblance to actual persons, living or
dead, is purely coincidental.

Cover Illustration by Billy
www.BillyArt.co.uk
© Billy 2018

To Becky,
  Your stitching is beautiful, in all respects x

Chapter One

Beth closed the door after saying goodbye to her last pupil of the evening. She'd been giving piano lessons since the close of school that day and it was usual for her husband, Drew, to have the kettle boiling ready to make a cup of tea as soon as she'd finished. The kitchen was unusually quiet and no steaming kettle greeted her as she walked through the door. She carried her search on through the kitchen and walked into Drew's art studio, looking for signs of life. Maybe he'd got carried away with his work - but no husband was to be found there either. A thorough search of the house was unfruitful and led her to look outside. Adjoining the garage, which was now converted into the art studio, was a large shed which usually housed garden tools, bicycles and the expected desultory bric-a-brac. A recent bout of spring cleaning meant that it was now relatively empty, but subdued noises could be heard emanating from within the structure. A strange sight met Beth's eyes as she opened the door. Opposite the entrance two figures stood facing the long, interior wall. Both were clad in thin plastic overalls and gloves. Hoods covered their heads and their faces were concealed behind goggles and dust masks. One figure was taller than the other and the broader back and shoulders hinted at middle age. The shorter apparition was of a slimmer build and moved with the agility of youth. Both were wielding aerosol paint cans. The younger protagonist was dextrously brandishing a can in each hand and was too absorbed in his current occupation to notice the unexpected audience. On hearing the door open the taller figure turned to face Beth, nodded and extended an upturned palm towards her. It was to be supposed that this was in fact her husband who was signalling that he'd be with her in about five minutes. Beth shook her head and walked back to the kitchen smiling. Setting three mugs of tea onto the table Beth pottered around the kitchen waiting to find out what her husband was up to - although the evidence of her own eyes when she'd opened the shed door made this quite apparent. She wondered who the other mysterious figure was, who seemed so adept with spray cans.

Beth had met Drew when they were both eighteen. At that time she was studying for the Oxford Classical Music syllabus and Drew was part of the Art Department on the same college campus. Despite the many social taboos that dictated that classical music and fine art students shouldn't mingle they'd spent long hours chatting next to the vending machine in the shared refectory. He'd introduced himself as Andrew (that being his name) but Beth had quickly named him Drew in reference to his field of expertise. She'd thought it the height of hilarity then and still smiled even now as she thought of the aptness of the nickname. Beth had retained a love for cheap vending machine coffee ever since then and, in addition to the joint tea breaks that were still an integral part of their working day, they'd sometimes extend their morning break to visit their local motorbike dealership to drool over any new additions to the showroom whilst nursing a plastic cup of automatically vended instant coffee.

Crinkling and shuffling soon signalled the approach of the graffiti artists and muffled chatter became more clear as dust masks were removed and the door into the kitchen opened. Drew was in animated conversation with a young man who looked to be in his late teens. Both men hindered the progress of removing their overalls with much gesticulation to explain particular aspects of their discussion. Beth added a plate of home made oatmeal cookies next to the mugs of tea and the three of them sat around the ancient pine table.

'Beth, let me introduce you to Scott. He's on placement at the Whitworth Art Gallery. This is the young man who keeps me sane while I'm locked away cataloguing paintings in the basement.' said Drew.

Suddenly all became clear to Beth. Drew was being optimistically polite when he referred to Scott's time at the Whitworth as a placement. From a previous conversation Beth knew that Scott was completing a period of Community Service after being prosecuted for vandalism and getting slapped with an ASBO after repeated graffiti offences. The Judge had shown an inspired logic and dictated that, if Scott was so passionate about art, he should use his time to serve the community in a genre that he obviously had a passion for. If he needed to vent his creativity, then let it be in an appropriate channel. From the reports that Drew brought back with him from his days at the museum, the Judge's wisdom had proved to be insightful and Scott was flourishing under the guidance of like minded, if somewhat more conventional, enthusiasts. It was becoming apparent that Scott had a lively intellect and a natural eye for art in many forms and he was becoming a real asset to the work that was underway at the gallery. The Whitworth was currently closed to the public as it underwent a major refurbishment programme. An awful lot of heavy manual labour was required as priceless works of art had to be lugged into storage. Some of the exhibits were of massive proportions and the hefty frames required back breaking efforts to move them to safety as work got underway. Scott was proving more than equal to the task; in fact his exuberance and willingness were causing him to become a valued and respected member of the team.

Drew had gleaned a reasonable resumé of Scott's background from Theodore Hunter, the gallery Curator. Of course it was necessary for the police to give Theo a full account of Scott's background if he was to accept Scott as a part of the team. Theo hadn't seen any reason to hide the information from his colleagues and Drew in turn had chatted about the situation over various meal times with Beth at home. Sometimes Beth's twin brother had also been party to the conversation and had given extra insight into the situation as he was a Detective Chief Inspector at Winsford Police HQ. What was obvious from all of these discussions was that Drew was becoming genuinely fond of Scott. According to Drew, Scott lived at Cherry Hill Court, a block of flats in one of the least salubrious areas on the edge of Manchester city centre.

'What beats me is why they give these places such high falutin' names.' Drew had said during one particular conversation. 'You'd think that it was a luxury apartment in the leafy groves of an exclusive collection of villas. Perhaps the architects, or council officials think that naming these awful places like they do will have all of the residents aspiring to better things. Mind you, I think that Scott and his mother would like to try. I don't know if it's the few spoiling it for the many or vice versa but Scott fell in with the wrong crowd and ended up in trouble once too often.'

'What were Scott's crimes?' asked Beth.

'He got caught creating impromptu works of urban art on buildings that weren't officially available for an artistic overhaul.' said Drew.

'I know it's bad and it can look a mess - but at least it wasn't drugs or a violent crime.' said Beth.

'Actually Scott's art is really good. It's in a particular urban style but it's tasteful - you'd like it, Beth. He's got a Twenty First Century take on William Morris - not that Scott knows who William Morris was. Actually, he does know now, thanks to his time at the gallery. You can tell that he absolutely loves being there. He's so eager to learn it's quite humbling. The masterpieces that we take for granted and barely give a second glance he gapes at in wide-eyed wonder. It almost feels wrong to tear him away to get his chores done. '

'How lovely to hear a story with such a happy ending. Don't you wish it could always work out like that! Does he live on his own?'

'He lives with his mum. I think she's had her hands full with him for some years. It's the same old story there, I fear. His dad isn't on the scene. I don't know if he left or if he died. Scott was too strong willed and hot headed to heed his mother's pleas when he started mixing in the wrong circles. Hopefully that's all in the past now.'

'She must be thrilled to see him finally come to his senses.'

'Scott brought his mum to meet everybody at the gallery the other day and the dear lady practically wept as she wrung my hands to thank me for "taking him on." I don't think she believed me when I said that I genuinely liked the lad and I was pleased to find a new friend in him.'

Such friendship was evident now as Drew and Scott sat sharing tea and biscuits.

'These biscuits are delicious, Mrs Williams. Did you make them?' asked Scott.

'Who on earth is Mrs Williams?' asked Drew. 'It's Beth to you, young man - and yes, she did make them. Hand them over, they're my favourite.'

'I realise that this may seem like an obvious question, but what on earth are you doing to the shed wall?' asked Beth. Scott looked startled and Beth was surprised to realise that he was actually afraid that he was in trouble again. She hastily tempered her comment to reassure him. 'Of course, I can see that you and Drew were busy creating priceless art, but what are you painting? And why on the shed wall?'

Drew came to Scott's rescue and explained. 'Over these last weeks Scott and I have been consulting each other as fellow artists. Not only is he an invaluable help to me when I'm cataloguing the Constable collection for storage but he's also had many valid and helpful insights into my own artwork.' Scott's colour rose as a blush blossomed from the collar of his shirt and set his cheeks on fire. 'I've seen some photographs of Scott's own branch of art but a screen-shot hardly does them justice. Now that the shed is clear I thought that it was the perfect canvas for him to show me what he can really do. He's been extremely patient with my initial efforts. An aerosol is much trickier than a paint brush. It's harder than it looks!'

'Do we need to increase the home insurance policy to cover the shed now?' asked Beth.

'I don't think so, just yet. I'm not quite a Banksy - but I can hope!' said Scott.

The conversation turned to the work they shared at the gallery and of the minor gripes and politics that inevitably simmered in the background.

'I wish Theodore would stop peering over my shoulder.' said Scott. 'I don't feel like I can go anywhere without him breathing down my neck! He never used to be like this. Doesn't he trust me any more? I thought he did, but now it feels like I'm back to square one.'

'You mustn't take it to heart - it's nothing personal.' said Drew. 'He's like that with us all just at the moment. You haven't changed and neither has Theodore. It's just that work has progressed and we're now dealing with a new section in the gallery. It's Constable that's the problem - you should blame him! It's an absolute passion that Theo has nursed and fed for years. He's spent the majority of his working life building up connections to buy or exhibit Constable. This collection is the fruit of his life's work and we're packing it away while the building work is carried out. He can't bear it being shut away and yet, at the same time, he can't bear the thought of anything getting damaged by the builders. He's having a hard time of it trusting any of us. If he could he'd wrap every single sketch himself only that won't get the job done in time.'

'That reminds me. How's the preparation for your talk for the WI coming along? It's nearly upon us and I know you always leave things until the last minute.' asked Beth. 'I was hoping to get a sneak preview.'

'It's almost ready I'll have you know! But we both know that's only because my little helper here is constantly nagging me to get on with it.' said Drew. 'Scott was going to ask you if his mum could visit your group as a guest for the talk. Would that be OK?'

'Of course! That'd be lovely, your mum would be most welcome. I'm glad that you've got Drew in hand otherwise he'd be organising slides into the small hours of the morning on the day of the meeting. Do I get a sneak peek?' said Beth.

'I don't think that I want to spoil it for you. You'll find it too boring at the meeting if I show you all of the slides beforehand and I've not decided on some of the final slides yet. Scott's helping me to choose the images and to time the talk - there's so much that I want to include but I know that I'm restricted to about forty-five minutes. I will say that I am, of course, including lots of Constable and I've a special addition that was suggested to me by

Diederick which will suit a group of ladies.' said Drew.

'Who is Diederick? I've not heard you mention that name before.' said Beth.

'Diederick van der Molen, or Rick for convenience, is on a secondment from Amsterdam to the Manchester City Art Gallery. We've recently spent a good deal of time debating the various merits of our respective nations' artistic heritage.' said Drew.

'Drew showed me some pictures on the internet. I don't care what Rick says, I think that Dutch portraiture from the Seventeenth Century is downright ugly.' said Scott.

'I couldn't agree more but it doesn't stop Rick from trying to convert me. Suffice to say that I won't be including much from that genre in my talk. However, I am willing to acknowledge the attraction of some of the floral still life paintings and I thought it would be particularly appropriate for you lovely ladies. Scott agrees that they fit into the schedule nicely.' said Drew.

'I'm sure that green-fingered Kirsty and Hyacinth will enjoy that especially - and Nicola too, being a florist. No doubt the rest of us will appreciate it on a less informed level. Kirsty and Hyacinth can impress us by giving all of the flowers their official Latin names and Nicola can give us a RHS winner's opinion of the composition.' said Beth. 'I suppose that I'll let you keep your little secrets and wait for the meeting. In the meantime would you prefer to turn your attention to the more mundane matter of properly filling your stomachs?'

Both Drew and Scott heartily agreed that, although they didn't realise it until now, they were both utterly ravenous after their artistic exertion. Scott said he'd call his mum to prevent her worrying if he was later home than he'd originally said.

'Yes, please call her.' said Beth. 'Tell your mum that I look forward to meeting her at the WI next week.'

Beth set to scrambling some eggs. The hens were in full production mode and there were plenty. In a last minute burst of inspiration she vamped them up a little by shredding the remnants of a packet of Tortilla wraps into the frying pan and then added some finely sliced green peppers and some chilli flakes. The vivid yellow yolks from the freshly laid eggs and the green of the peppers made an appealing combination.

'Wow! Those eggs are bright. What have you done to them?' said Scott.

Beth laughed. 'I haven't done anything. This is what fresh, free range eggs should look like. I fetched most of your supper from the hen house only this afternoon. They make supermarket eggs look very pale in comparison, don't they?'

'Now that Summer is almost here we'll be eating eggs until they come out of our ears. Enjoy them while they're a novelty, you'll soon get tired of them.' said Drew.

'Are you in the gallery tomorrow?' asked Scott.

'Yes, if you're free I could do with a hand moving some of the larger Constable frames and we'll photograph the last few images for my talk while we're at it. If you want to join me for lunch I'm going to the Manchester Art Gallery to photograph the Dutch works as the last bits of reference. I'll treat you to lunch there if you can make it. The soup is delicious.' said Drew. As an afterthought he dutifully added, 'Though not as tasty as your leek and potato soup, Beth.'

Everybody helped to clear the dishes into the dishwasher once the meal was finished, which didn't take long. Drew then suggested that it was time to get Scott home as they'd all got an early start in the morning.

'It was lovely to meet you, Scott.' said Beth. 'I look forward to seeing your mum at the WI meeting. Will you be coming along too?'

'If I can, I'd like to see the presentation in order. I've only seen mismatched bits and bobs. But am I allowed? I mean, it is the *Women's* Institute after all.' said Scott.

'As you're in the capacity of Technical Assistant I'm sure that will validate your admittance. It'd be a shame for you to miss out. Let me assure you that the cakes alone will make the trip entirely worthwhile. Natalie is on the rota and her cakes are particularly special - she's a regular WI trophy winner.' said Beth.

The gents said their goodbyes and left. Savouring an hour to herself Beth, put her pyjamas on and settled into a chair with her signature milky drink of hot chocolate, malt extract and vanilla. Noodle, the aged Bichon, nestled into her lap and the two were gently falling asleep when Drew returned home.

Chapter Two

Theodore Hunter hovered nervously over the shoulders of anyone and everyone as they carefully stowed away precious works of art into containers, to be placed into storage while the scheduled refurbishment work was carried out in the Whitworth Art Gallery. Each worker was wearing cotton gloves as they wrapped the artistic outpourings of greats such as Constable, Turner and Ford Madox Brown in buffered, acid free tissue paper. The three percent calcium carbonate buffering was to protect these national treasures from acid migration by acting as a filter to neutralise any acid in the atmosphere. Each piece was also protected by a sheet of silica to absorb any moisture and offset any changes in humidity. Only then was each item wrapped in a polythene foam and stowed away in a packing case. The gallery's archives had the aura of the sanctum sanctorum and nobody had said a word for some time. The only noise had been the rustling of paper and Theo's laboured breathing as he scurried between the workers in turn.

'Oh for goodness sake Theo, go and get some lunch! You're making us all jumpy. You can trust us to take care here. Otherwise feel free to do all the work yourself. As it is you're no help at all, in fact you're a positive hindrance.' said Drew.

Theo threw his arms up in the air and, incoherently muttering to himself, he blustered out of the door. As he blundered away he collided with a figure attempting to enter and join them. Looking slightly perplexed, a tall, thin-framed man with a shockingly large, hooked nose came through the doorway. As he stepped into the archive he straightened his dark blue, double breasted jacket which perfectly matched the sharply creased trousers. With the carriage of a naval officer he realigned his bright red tie and scanned the room for a familiar face. Glancing across the room his eyes passed over the other silent figures until they rested upon Drew.

'Rick, how nice to see you. You chose your moment well. Let me introduce you to my colleagues.' said Drew. 'Sally, this is Diederick van der Molen. He's from a gallery in Amsterdam and is spending some time at the Manchester Art Gallery. Rick, meet Sally Bickerton. Sally is Assistant Curator here. I'm not entirely sure that you two will get along, one of Sally's areas of responsibility here is the Constable collection.'

The two shook hands as Rick attempted to dispel Drew's gloomy introduction. With a broad grin that revealed long and slightly crooked teeth, Rick said, 'Drew likes to tease me because I do not share his depth of love for the work of some of your English painters. I do not tease him about his lack of appreciation of my national artistic heritage. We seek to educate each other.'

'Indeed we do.' said Drew. 'Now let me introduce you to Scott Malkin, our budding protégé. Scott is on placement here and he's become invaluable to us - to me in particular.'

'Hello Scott. I'm pleased to meet you. What did I just stumble into? Wasn't that Theodore Hunter who just stormed past me?' asked Rick.

'Yes, it was. He's making all of our lives an absolute misery. He's so on edge that he's making us all nervy. He's so worried that something will get damaged but he's making it worse and none of us can work properly. I make so many mistakes when he's hovering over me and I can't concentrate because of his constant fidgeting. I can understand his concern and it's quite natural, but he's got to get a handle on it. He's got to let us do our job.' said Sally.

'I don't know about anybody else but I've had enough of being cooped up in here for one morning. I was going to bring Scott over to MAG to photograph some paintings with me later this afternoon but I've had enough for now and I think it's time that I educate this young man in the delights of the delicious soup that's served there. Who'd like to join us?' said Drew.

Sally shook her head. 'I'd better go and calm Theo's ruffled feathers. I made a packed lunch for today so I guess I'd better eat it after going to the bother of preparing it.'

'I'll walk back with you if you're finished here. It's obvious that now isn't a good time for a tour - you can show me around another time. I've yet to experience British soup, I'll join you if I may and find out what I've been missing.' said Rick.

Over lunch the many facets of British and Dutch painting were covered at length. For the most part Scott just sat and listened, although it may have been that he was intently busy consuming soup and vast quantities of bread, but the expression on his face showed that he was horrified that there existed on this planet at least one person who couldn't fully appreciate the merits of John Constable.

'You've trained your young apprentice well, Drew. I can see that he disapproves of me already. Let me reassure you, young man, that my mind is open and I am willing to be taught to really love your Constable. Indeed, I already appreciate the value of many of your artists. However, you must allow me to reserve the right for my own nation's artists to take first place in my heart. It is only right and fitting, don't you think?' said Rick.

'Well, now you've confused him. He's not used to curators and critics being so fair or generous in their opinions.' said Drew.

'I suppose that it's all a matter of cultural heritage but I much prefer the unstaged simplicity of paintings like The Hay Wain over some of the portraits I saw in the Dutch collection. I saw a painting of a small child all trussed up in lace, draped with gold chains and other paraphernalia. It all looked so phoney.' said Scott.

'I think I know the picture that you're referring to.' said Rick. 'It's by Jan Albertz Rotius. The chain indicates that the figure is a boy - all young children wore dresses then. The lace and the gold rattle were to display the family's wealth and, if you remember, there was an obedient dog and grapes also, which represent obedience and education.'

'That's just my point. It's showing off.' said Scott.

'Yes, compare the naval scenes by Ludolph Backuysen to By the Battle of Trafalgar by Turner. Turner depicts the ravages of war in conjunction with the might of the seas pitted against frail humanity. Backuysen uses his art as a form of propaganda to parade the pomp of the nation.' said Drew

'You are right in that we always promote our naval heritage. Our glory has ever been in the sea. Even so, you do us an injustice, my friends. Not only are the artists that you compare separated by hundreds of miles but they are also divided by hundreds of years. Putting that to one side I could show you the rural landscapes of Isack van Ostade or Jan van der Heyden which capture rural tranquility beautifully.' said Rick.

'Well said. In fact, I'll be heading over to that section to take some snaps to pad out the last bits of my talk.' said Drew.

'What talk is this? I didn't know that you gave presentations.' said Rick.

'You could hardly call this a presentation, I'm afraid. My wife is part of the Women's Institute and the group that meets in our village. She asked me to give a talk explaining something of what we do at the Whitworth and art history in general. I'd like to feature some of the paintings here too, to complement my slide show. I think that the ladies would particularly enjoy some of the floral still life paintings by van Os.' said Drew.

'Drew's wife, Beth, did ask Sally but she was busy that night. I do wonder if it wasn't just an excuse.' said Scott.

'I'm glad you stepped in then, Drew. It wouldn't do to disappoint the ladies.' said Rick. 'It's a shame that Sally couldn't join us for lunch, but I suppose she must grease the wheels to keep the workplace happy.'

'I've a hunch that there's more to it than office politics. I suspect that their shared passion has spilled over past the confines of the Old Masters. I think they take more than their work home together these days.' said Drew. 'It's fair enough. They're thrown together often enough so it's inevitable, really. I only hope it stays that way. If their relationship gets rocky the museum is a small place to host a cold war.' said Drew.

'I can't believe they think that nobody has noticed.' said Scott. 'The receptionist is really put out. I think she nursed hopes for herself, but she knows she's dashed now. All the women get silly when Theo's around. I can't imagine what they see in him.'

'He's definitely got a certain something about him and he's got dashing good looks. He's got a good brain too. I just hope that Sally can keep him calm while all this building work is going on.' said Drew. 'It's not my problem anymore today. I'm going to get these photos taken and then I'm going home. Have you got time to come with me, Scott, or do you need to get back?'

'I'm not rushing back, I'll give Theo time to calm down. He's more tetchy than usual when I'm around. If he complains I'll tell him that I'm widening my experience and need to keep learning from whoever I can. I'll listen very carefully to whatever Rick has to say and I'll write an essay on it if I have to. Anything to keep out of Theo's way for a bit.'

'That's the spirit.' said Rick. 'But it's a long time since I marked an essay so we'll keep it verbal if that's OK with you. By the way, I've no idea what I've just eaten but it was really delicious. I'm learning that there's more to your cuisine that roast potatoes.'

As the three of them walked through the museum Drew kept his camera poised and Rick maintained a steady flow of informative commentary. Drew just hoped that he'd be able to remember some of these insights into the life and work of selected luminary Dutch painters.

'Just hang on a mo, you two. I've got to limit content and watch my timings, but I can't really give a talk to the WI and not include this lovely floral art. It seems to me that van Os is of primary importance so just give me a minute to photograph these.' said Drew.

'I don't know why, but these paintings remind me of gypsy caravans and canal boats.' said Scott.

'That's a very pertinent observation.' said Rick. 'The colours used here are very bold. It's all about contrast and form. I also think that the ageing effect of the varnish contributes to the patina that strikes you.'

'Even this really dark canvas gives the same impression. I do like them though.' said Scott.

'You see, we learn.' said Rick smiling. 'The van Huysum demonstrates a particularly effective use of bold, contrasting colours. The dark canvas accentuates the bright fruit and flowers. They look luscious, don't they? It's a very effective still life.'

'I'll photograph that one too, though how I'll decide which ones to use I don't know. I only have a time frame of about forty-five minutes and that will soon go. I'm going to have to have a photo cull before today is done.' said Drew as he turned to leave the artwork.

'Theo is in such a temper. I daren't go back.' said Scott.

'Yes. I'm glad I'm going home. The building work is proving too much of a strain on him. Hopefully he'll relax when all the art is safely stowed away. Sally will have worked her magic on him by the time you get back though, so you'll be OK Scott, don't you worry.' said Drew. 'Rick, we'll look over the Constables another day if you don't mind.'

Rick nodded his agreement and escorted his new friends back to the museum's entrance.

Chapter Three

In the reception area of the Whitworth tension was obviously bubbling very close to the surface of Theo's superficial pleasantries. His usual charm was coming to the fore as he ostensibly welcomed a motley group of dishevelled teenagers who were loitering in studied languid poses, hoodies drawn over their heads. Earlier that morning Drew had decided that the photograph he'd taken of a Constable cloud watercolour study was too blurred for his presentation at the WI that night and he'd hurried to the gallery to take another shot. Scott had arrested Drew's attention as soon as he'd entered the building and was now giving him desperately pleading glances. Unsure of what he'd just walked into Drew got straight to the heart of the matter.

'I thought that the gallery was closed to the public whilst the building work is ongoing. Have I missed a party?'

'Drew, let me introduce you to some of Scott's chums.' said Theo. He pronounced the word "chums" with a special tinge of disdain only perceptible to those who knew him well. All that the gang would have heard was Theo's boyish charm. 'Let me see if I can remember the names of these gents. If I get stuck then I know that Scott will help me out.' Scott flinched at the mention of his name, it was as though he'd been physically struck. Everybody knew that Theo held Scott responsible for this unwelcome intrusion and that he'd pay for it later one way or another. 'It seems that Scott has been enthusing about the work that we do here. So much so that his good friends couldn't keep themselves away any longer. Finn here has decided to take all of his friends' education in hand and has enforced an art history tour on us and his pals. He's quite insistent that they need to learn some culture.' Here Theo glanced at the group's obvious ring leader. 'Leighton and Brad have consented to be subjected to the curriculum.' He introduced each gangly, greasy haired youth in turn, proving that his flair for retaining names and faces hadn't yet left him.

Drew said "Hello" and shook each hand in turn. The gesture was obviously unfamiliar to the lads and proceedings took on the aspect of a pantomime. 'I'm on a flying visit to re-photograph a Constable.' he explained.

'Excellent.' said Theo. 'You can begin the show by telling these eager chaps a bit about Constable. It's a pity they can't come to your little talk tonight, though maybe it really isn't their scene.' At this point he roared with laughter. The thought of these delinquents sitting in on a WI talk about art history was an hilarious incongruity and was just suited to Theo's abstract sense of humour. It was bizarre that they were in the gallery at all.

'Come on then.' said Drew. 'I've got a few minutes, let's go and have a look.' He strode off along the corridor leaving Finn and his crew to shuffle along behind. Once Scott had recovered his senses he scurried to catch Drew up.

'What am I going to do? Theo's going to kill me now for sure. But it isn't my fault at all!' Scott looked utterly desperate. 'I hardly talk to Finn at all these days and even then it's only when I absolutely have to. I've sold out as far as they're all concerned. If Finn says I'm "out" then the others wouldn't dare talk to me at all and Finn has made it perfectly clear that I'm no longer one of them. Finn's up to something - I know it!'

'Well, there's nothing we can do about it now. Just play along and I'm sure it'll be fine, they'll soon go away. Theo can handle it for as much as he blusters.' said Drew.

'Something smells very bad about all of this, it's not right. I don't like this at all.'

Finn and his entourage were catching up which put an end to their discussion. Once inside the archives Finn had been taking an overtly lively interest in absolutely everything, even in the bare corridors and scaffolding but the others just shuffled along with their heads down and their hands in their pockets. They were obviously there under sufferance. The requirement was for them simply to be there in body only, their minds were free to be elsewhere. They were protesting their disinterest by making full use of what rights of absenteeism were available to them as far as they were able and weren't even pretending to be remotely interested. Nevertheless, Drew told them of the conservation work that was going on and explained how the art was stored. He described the importance of artists such as Constable and Turner in the canon of British art history and showed them some of the pieces which he was stowing away for safety. As he photographed the cloud study he had particularly come for he talked about the magical combination of scientific accuracy and artistic expression that the sketch combined.

Finn became animated and exclaimed loudly at everything he saw and heard which was disconcerting to everybody else in the room, even his chosen companions. Drew was now certain that Finn's enthusiasm was intended to provoke Scott and insult his new found passion and change of lifestyle. He could only presume that the others were in attendance to reinforce the insult by imposing and looming over Scott's shoulder to show him that he wasn't free of them yet. Poor Scott, he was in for a bumpy ride whichever way he looked at things. Drew escorted the informal tour back to reception. He quietly arranged transport for Scott and his mum so as to be ready for the WI meeting that evening and ran over Scott's responsibilities as assistant. After that there was nothing more that he could do so he bade his farewells and left Scott to his fate.

The bow of burning gold had been brought, the arrows of desire were spent and the final chords of the piano were dwindling in England's green and pleasant land. More specifically the echoes of the WI's signature song were dying away in Mossleigh village hall as Beth closed the lid on the piano and took her seat ready for the President to welcome the visiting speaker. Mrs Malkin, or Mary as Beth had been instructed to call her, gave Scott an encouraging smile as he took up residence next to the laptop to oversee the slideshow for the talk.

'Good evening ladies.' Drew began. 'It's so lovely to be able to share with you my enduring passion for art history. I know that many of you have been collared by me in the past as you've popped in to visit Beth. Tonight I have you all cornered. I've got a captive audience and I'm looking forward to making the most of it.'

Amid the general chuckles of laughter the entrance door opened and Beth's twin brother, Benedict James, popped his head into the room. Beth turned to see the latecomer and scurried to greet him with a hug. Waving protocol aside she ushered him to a chair next to her and Mary.

'Lexi has gone away for a couple of days so I thought I'd come and surprise you.' he whispered as they walked to their seats. 'I totally forgot about tonight's meeting until I arrived to an empty house. I hope I'm OK gate crashing. I'd like to hear Drew's talk.'

Beth dispelled his concerns and they turned their attention to Drew. The lights were already dimmed for the slideshow, which had masked their interruption. Drew was warming to his subject.

'Constable came from a wealthy family. His father was a corn merchant which enabled him to pursue his desire to paint. Nevertheless, he didn't get off to a successful start in his career. Landscapes were what inspired Constable but were frowned upon by the establishment. He did garner success and acclaim in France where he was showered with praise and bestowed with accolade, which necessarily brought with it prospects for commission. Such success was not well received by Constable who particularly hated the French. The end of the Napoleonic wars had brought with it mass unemployment and famine which was exacerbated by the introduction of Parliamentary corn laws which imposed restrictions and hefty taxes on grain. This then created a massive downturn in trade and profit for the Constable family business and John blamed the French for such misfortune. Nevertheless, he did eventually gain a half hearted and much belated acceptance into the Royal Academy. Nobody today can doubt his contribution to our artistic heritage.'

Drew gave a nod to Scott to change the slide from a portrait of Constable to the watercolour study of clouds. 'The Nineteenth Century was a time of renewed interest in art and science. There was a zeal for exploration and discovery. Constable combined this zeal for learning and knowledge with a new expressionist form of art. On the one hand many of his nature studies are wondrously free and expressionistic. However, he added to this naturalistic manner an insistence on scientific veracity. This sky study of a cirrus cloud formation is testament to his continuing fascination with clouds and meteorology. His studies and paintings attest to his insistence that natural lighting and elements of the weather were always correctly partnered with the appropriate cloud configuration. In fact, he said of his own work that he couldn't envisage any form of landscape painting where the sky was not the key note. This particular sketch is dated 1822.

'Throughout his career Constable's cloudscapes were frequently stormy or rain filled. When you consider that the Nineteenth Century was also a period frenzied with psychoanalysis one can't help but wonder whether his brooding skies vented his mood as he faced hostility and rejection from the artistic establishment. I'll let you decide.

'Constable applied this same scientifically focussed study to all aspects of nature. This next slide - thank you, Scott - shows a study of tree trunks, dated 1821. It epitomises the artist's use of naturalistic colouring. It also explains to a degree why he was faced with such rebuttal from the Royal Academy. The abstract angle is ahead of its time and Constable's expressionistic style was too avante-garde for the old school members that controlled admittance into the association. Constable was consumed by the desire to faithfully represent the everyday aspects of life, especially country life and particularly the Suffolk countryside that he grew up in. This is in stark contrast to his contemporary, Turner. Turner had an eye for the dramatic and would even reposition buildings and rocks to suit his purpose and give the work a more exaggerated Romantic aspect.'

After a further nod to Scott, Drew continued. 'This landscape, dated 1812, seems to be merely a backdrop for the skyscape and prominent double rainbow. Constable shared a preoccupation with rainbows and wrote in a letter of the debt he owed to the influence that Rubens had on his own work. As an aside I must confess to you that I'm enjoying an ongoing debate with a Dutch colleague, arguing the merits of our respective nation's artistic heritage. Of course, I hold the corner for Constable in our discussions. I haven't yet dared to admit the debt that Constable owes to Seventeenth Century Dutch painters, not only in the aspects of stylistic influence but also the everyday subject matter they portrayed.

Once I admit that to him I know that I'll never hear the end of it.

'Today we take Constable for granted. Probably his most well known painting is The Hay Wain. It is reproduced so prolifically now that we could easily become sick of it.' Scott recognised his cue and produced the next slide. 'My mother in law had place mats with this scene on them and I heartily disliked them for years, until I grew to appreciate the painting itself outside of the setting of roast beef. In so many ways this scene is central to Constable's art. The family mills were near to Flatford and Dedham and the scene painted here in 1821 is based in Suffolk, near Flatford on the river Stour. It is a setting that the artist continued to draw inspiration from, despite the flat and seemingly uninspiring landscape. It's interesting to note here that the bulk of Dutch landscapes are necessarily flat and initially uninteresting too. Constable wrote that such scenery in his childhood had made him the artist he was and expressed gratitude for the fact.

'These next slides show some of the works of Henderick Martenz Sorgh. It is immediately apparent that paintings such as these could have been influential to the young Constable centuries later. The subjects for the paintings are commonplace and uninspiring outside of the artist's brush. Here we have a fishmonger of all things, in fact many of these paintings revolve around the sale of fish. It seems that the Dutch finding glory in the sea continues from the naval and extends into the domestic arena. Imagine Harry, from Mossleigh butchers, finding himself the focal point of half a dozen paintings.

'To finish, I thought it appropriate to include these final slides of still life paintings by the Dutch artist Jan van Os. The paintings of flowers and fruit are from the late seventeen hundreds. I've heard it said recently, by my kind assistant here, that the style is easily likened to our canal barge art.'

After the last few slides were spent Drew rounded off his talk. 'I'd like to thank you for allowing me to indulge in my pet topic. I sincerely hope that I haven't outstayed my welcome. In my defence I must point out that my talk tonight is a fraction of the length it would have been had it been my boss at the Whitworth talking to you. I will also add that Scott has been filming my little presentation and, when I'm feeling generous, I will show it to my Dutch colleague and let him have his moment of glory.

'If you have any questions please don't hesitate to ask, but don't let me keep you from the delicious cake that I know is waiting.'

Beth stood to give the vote of thanks on behalf of the group. 'I've been kept away from tonight's subject and I've eagerly looked forward to hearing all about it after so much cloak and dagger suspense. It's been good for me to have a thorough grounding in one sitting on this subject tonight, rather than bits and bobs over dinner. I've really enjoyed it - I'm sure that we all have. I would also particularly like to thank Scott for his continued help and patience with Drew, not just tonight but over the last few weeks. I know that without Scott's gentle reminders matters would have been left until the last minute and it would have been much more stressful at home. As it was, Drew was still taking photographs this morning. So, thank you Scott, I'm very grateful.'

A tide of applause and cake soon enveloped Drew and he was kept busy chatting and answering questions until home time came around. Mary, Scott's mother, had secured a lift home from a new found friend and recurring visits to Mossleigh WI seemed highly likely. Scott had opted to return home with Drew, Beth and Benedict so that he could tell Drew about his afternoon with Finn and Theo. The poor lad looked like he needed to get a lot off his chest. As tomorrow was the weekend Drew had suggested that Scott stay overnight with them. Benedict's addition to the plan didn't imply any change and so they all headed home via a fish and chip shop in a neighbouring village.

'This scene would make for a contemporary Mortenz Sorgh, there's plenty of fish about.' said Benji. 'Do you think that his sombre palette would make much of the green of these mushy peas?'

'Not at the rate Scott is eating them.' said Beth. 'He'd be painting an empty plate.'

'So what happened at the gallery after I left?' asked Drew.

Scott groaned and covered his face with his hands. 'Oh Drew, it was awful. I thought Theo had it in for me but now I know it. It'd have been better if I'd never started at the Whitworth. I knew it was too good to be true.' said Scott.

'Rubbish!' said Drew. 'You fit right in and you're an absolute godsend. Don't be so negative. Theo can be a bit theatrical at times but you learn to take no notice of his eccentricities.' said Drew.

'You don't understand.' said Scott. 'If you'd seen him you'd know just what I mean. I can't imagine why Finn decided to turn up today. He thinks I've become a snob since I started at the Gallery and he'll hardly even look at me, let alone talk to me or come and see me. I was glad he was finally beginning to leave me alone. He must have been concocting a plan to make me suffer and turned up today to rub my nose in it and show me he's still the boss. You should have seen the look on everybody's face when he barged in with the others at his side. He thinks he's some kind of mobster with his trusty side kicks. Theo was determined to make the most of it. He really called Finn's bluff by giving him the most exhausting tour you could imagine and all the time he knew that he was making me squirm for every long minute of it! I'm sorry enough for what I did in my "bad days" but nothing is ever going to be enough to convince Theo.'

'I'm sure that's not the case at all.' said Benji. 'When the courts applied for your Community Service to take place Theo had every opportunity to reject you and you'd have never known about it.'

'Benji's quite right. I suspect that Theo forgot who his audience was and just got carried away. You know what he's like when he gets started. I wasn't joking at the WI, if they thought I rambled on a bit they should try listening to Theo. Constable is his life's passion and the gallery itself comes a very close second.' said Drew.

'I wish you'd been there. I've never seen anything like it. It was like a game of poker. When Finn turned up he opened the pot but Theo raised him, knowing he had the upper hand - and he won hands down. He told them in depth about the renovation of the building and his plans for the future, having them trekking all over the gallery as he talked. He showed them what art works were available to view and then he capped it all off by taking them to see the Constable pieces again. He made me join in and follow them around, just to see me suffer. Brad kept giving me the dirtiest looks imaginable, blaming me for giving him the most boring morning he'd ever had.' said Scott.

Drew actually laughed but stopped when he realised that Scott was genuinely upset. 'Oh, let Theo play his games. There's no malice intended I'm sure. If he does have a problem it's that he is quite selfish and never stops to consider how others might feel. He'd not stop to think about how his little joke would affect you. You really need to lose this chip on your shoulder and enjoy being part of the team, for good or bad. The very fact that Theo didn't stop to think about your feelings means he's treating you as he would any one of us should be enough to reassure you. Theo is self centred it's true, but he isn't malicious or cruel. You're ''one of us'' so you'll have to take the rough with the smooth I'm afraid.'

'There's only one solution here, I think.' said Benji. 'Drew, you'll have to crack open that bottle of Talisker you've been saving. A single malt whisky is the only way to solve this problem.' Benji clapped Scott around the shoulders and guided him, gently but firmly, into the lounge and the drinks cabinet. Drew followed willingly and by the time Beth had loaded the dishwasher and popped in to say good night the atmosphere was relaxed and congenial. She kissed Drew, hugged her brother and ruffled Scott's hair as she made her way to the stairs. Drew joined Beth a good way down the bottle later.

It was obvious that Drew had been asleep for some time, judging by his bleary eyes and lack of initial focus, when the telephone woke them with a start. His attention was quickly captured and his features took on a grave aspect. Of course, it had to be bad news at this time of night. Beth switched on the lamp and scrutinised Drew's brief responses to the conversation in an attempt to discern who the caller could be. As soon as the call was terminated Beth launched her inquisition.

'Who was that, Drew? Whatever is going on?'

'It seems that Scott was wiser than we gave him credit for. He had every right to worry about the invasion at the gallery yesterday. It was Theo calling. There's been a break in at the gallery. We'll get all the details tomorrow but Scott and I have to be at the Whitworth first thing this morning for questioning. It's either that or we go to the police station.'

Chapter Four

Sally had shown great presence of mind by ordering in a selection of speciality coffees and she had the foresight to order a few ambiguous extras for any unexpected visitors. It was a testament to the skill and tact she employed every day as assistant to Theo. Such pre-emptive thinking went a long way in keeping the museum running smoothly. As such it wasn't a problem when Benedict tagged along with Drew and Scott that morning and he was happy to claim an Americano that was surplus to requirements. Recognising the Inspector who was conducting the preliminary interviews he strode forward to greet his colleague.

'Good morning Baskeyfield. What better than a trip to the art gallery to start your weekend? How lovely for you.'

'Hello. I didn't expect to find you here, it's not often you're in the City these days. I would have expected Chief Inspector Monroe as it's more in his line of work, but not at this early stage.'

'Quite right. I'm not here in any official capacity but seem to find myself caught up in the middle of things. I thought I'd stick around and see what's going on but don't let me get in the way - I'm just here for the coffee. This coffee really is excellent, by the way. I do love a strong blend. Thank you to whoever.'

Sally gave a nod of appreciation for the thanks.

Baskeyfield turned to the gallery staff that had congregated. 'Please allow me to introduce myself. I'm Inspector Baskeyfield and I'll be your point of contact, or at least for the time being. This is a colleague of mine, Detective Chief Inspector Benedict James. I'm not entirely sure how he came to be with us this morning but I can assure you all that it's a bonus for him to be around. DCI James has a knack for getting to the bottom of things. We're lucky to have him, if only for a very short time. He used to be a regular visitor to the Manchester Met. and he has quite a reputation - all good, of course.' DCI James waved away the accolade. Once the formalities had been observed Baskeyfield struck at the heart of the matter. 'During the small hours of this morning, at just before four o'clock, there was a forced entry here at the gallery. Mr Hunter joined the police as soon as we could enter the building and made an initial search of the premises. Not much could be achieved whilst the fire service was making sure that the structure was safe. The police were also searching the building and a glazier has been hard at work. The security services have kept a close watch during all these proceedings. At this moment we are unclear what, if anything, was stolen and so I need everybody to carefully check their own areas of responsibility so that we can be absolutely certain if anything is missing.' At this point everybody began asking questions and voicing their concerns all at once. Baskeyfield raised his hand to request silence. 'Of course I'll do everything I can to answer your questions, I'm sure that there is a lot you want to know, but we must consider our priorities and then deal with matters in an orderly fashion. The most vital point just now is to ascertain if anything has been damaged or stolen. Please would you go and check your archives and report back here as soon as possible. Before you go, could I please remind everyone to wear their usual cotton gloves. In this instance it's not the care of artwork that concerns me, it's to prevent contaminating a crime scene. Try to make as little disturbance as you can as you look through your store. After that I'll be happy to answer your questions.'

All of the staff hurried to the task leaving DCI James and DI Baskeyfield to catch up on what had brought each of them to the museum that morning.

'It's a pleasant surprise to find you here, Sir. This is all a bit above my head, the art world isn't really for me I'm afraid. I'm more at home with stolen goods from the High Street. I can gather the facts but after that I can't begin to guess what to do next.' said Baskeyfield.

'Nonsense.' said James. 'You're just the man for the job and this is the break, if you'll pardon the pun, that you need. Believe it or not, I'm here because I gate crashed my sister's Women's Institute meeting and then stayed over for the sake of an excellent single malt. Nevertheless, if I can be of help don't hesitate to ask. I'm agog to find out what went on here, but I'll spare you from having to keep repeating yourself and wait for the others to return. I can hear it with them. However, I do have an inkling as I heard Scott bemoaning his lot to Drew over the aforementioned single malt. It seems he knew that trouble was bound to follow after a visit from his old gang and we wouldn't have it.'

'The moot point here is, exactly how wise is he?' said Baskeyfield. 'You say he was with you last night?'

'Yes. He stayed at my sister's house after playing assistant for Drew in the art history presentation he gave at the WI. We stayed up late chatting and he slept in the room next to me. He was there when Drew got the telephone call from Theo early this morning. I don't see how he could have gone anywhere without our knowledge. I know we'd had a drink, but we weren't addled.'

'That's got to be the best alibi that I've ever heard of, it's almost too good. I'm not sure that it clears him overall though. In fact there's a cloud hanging over everybody here until this thing is cleared up and I've absolutely no idea of how to go about achieving that at this present moment.'

Any further conversation was prevented by the return of the staff who, by degrees, came to report their findings. Drew and Scott were the last to return and their taut expressions didn't bode well.

'It's the cirrus cloud study that I photographed yesterday morning. It's missing.' said Drew.

'I knew it'd be bound to be a Constable.' said Theo. 'After you'd photographed the sketch it was easily to hand, everything else had been re-packed away. Those no good chums of Scott's just couldn't resist, could they? To them it's no different than nicking a packet of cigs over the counter. What I want to know though is just how much of this is down to chance, hey?' This last remark was hurled at Scott. 'Did you put in some overtime last night?'

'He was with us all last night Theo. It couldn't have been Scott, not that he'd consider doing such a thing.' said Drew.

'Well let's face it, it's irrelevant where he was. He told them all they needed to know and that's enough.' said Theo.

DI Baskeyfield decided that enough was enough and intervened. 'Now, now! Steady on, let's not be rash. We'll get to the bottom of this, don't you worry. What can you tell me about the missing piece, Mr Hunter? Was it valuable?'

'Valuable? It was priceless! It represents the artistic tension between the pioneering of Romantic Impressionism and the accuracy of scientific study. It's the epitome of Constable and marks the beginning of a new era in art history. It's a jewel in the crown of British painting. Good grief man, of course it's valuable!'

Baskeyfield stood stock still in stunned silence as he attempted to process Theo's outburst until Drew came to his rescue.

'That's not quite what the Inspector was asking Theo, though you're correct in every detail of course. Inspector Baskeyfield's enquiries must run on more fiscal channels I'm afraid.' Turning his attention to Inspector Baskeyfield he said, 'The stolen picture is a watercolour sketch on paper. It's four inches by seven inches and, although it's not likely to fetch millions of pounds, I guess it would be worth a significant number of thousands. It's not something you could easily sell and it would be highly suspect if it were sold through the usual channels. If word got round it would be far too hot to handle in established circles.'

'Can I please interrupt?' asked Sally. 'I keep waiting for a convenient pause but I don't think I'm going to get one, so I'll have to butt in. How on earth did the thief, or thieves get in? We have cameras and security systems. You can't just walk in and help yourself.'

'That is a very interesting question.' said Baskeyfield, unable to refrain from taking just a little professional pleasure at the ingenuity of the break in. 'The perpetrators made use of some of the scaffolding from the ongoing renovation. They lowered themselves down through a skylight which they broke, using a rope to gain access. A small fire had been gradually smouldering in the security office which meant that, according to protocol, once the fire was discovered and the smoke alarms activated, the security guards had to leave the building. We have only one brief glimpse of the thief before all of the cameras were quickly deactivated - for a very short time - and he (or she to be fair) had free access. Only a little time elapsed before the fire services were on the scene and security could patrol the building - but it was long enough for what needed to be done. The means of access was quickly found owing to the alertness of the security guard who commented on the rope discarded on the floor. It could have been easily explained away as being discarded by the building contractors but the guard insists that he would have noticed it earlier on his rounds. He always tidies up bits and bobs as he goes along, attributing it as a throw back from his army days.

42

Don't be blaming him for leaving the building and following procedure, he did a first rate job last night and got us ahead of the game from the start. We could have thought it was just a fire and missed the slight glimpse on the cameras for quite some time. However, thanks to his perceptiveness we're already on the look out for this Finn character as our first port of call and the Art Theft Registry are on the alert, even though we weren't sure what was or wasn't missing. They're already on stand-by as a matter of course. I'd say your security guard has earned himself a pint, and probably needs one after the tense night he's just had.'

'I hope you've cuffed that scum, Finn. Scott will know where he is if you haven't got him yet. In fact you might as well grab this one here now and save yourself a chase later.' said Theo. 'It's all the same in the long run.'

Scott looked as if he didn't know whether to run and hide or to just break down and cry where he stood. Drew put his arm around the lad and gave his shoulders a squeeze as a token of solidarity.

'You know that I can't do that, Mr Hunter. It's no good just throwing blame around. However, let me assure you that we are searching for, and will find Finn. We'll also be talking to everybody here. If anybody has any advice or information to offer it will be treated with sensitivity.' said Baskeyfield.

Scott knew that this was aimed particularly at him and decided to make the show-down here and now in public, attack reputedly being the best form of defence. 'It may well be that Finn is at the heart of this, I wouldn't put it past him. I know that it's all my fault.'

'Ha! What did I tell you? He even admits it himself.' said Theo.

'That's not what I mean though. I know what you think, Theo, and I'm really sorry for the trouble I've caused you. I'm so grateful to have been part of the gallery and this isn't what I'd want to repay you with. It's my fault that Finn came here yesterday, but I didn't know that he was coming and it's not what I wanted. Ever since I've been here I've totally cut all connection with the old gang. I love it here and I've started a new life.' At this point tears welled up in Scott's eyes but he mastered himself and continued. 'Finn couldn't stand it because he knew that he wasn't in charge of me any more. My ignoring him made his blood boil. I have to keep dodging Leighton and Brad on the stairways because I know that Finn has told them to teach me a lesson. It's been hell. When I saw him at the museum yesterday I knew that he'd got fed up of me avoiding them all and had come to get his revenge another way. If it was Finn he'll have done all of this to get me into as much trouble as possible. He's making me suffer for selling out on the gang. What I don't understand is why he bothered to steal anything, not that he'd be above that. What I mean is, it's just not his style.'

'What do you mean, Scott?' asked DCI James. 'What specifically is Finn's style?'

'It'd be more like Finn to break in and trash the place. The fire would be like him, but he wouldn't let it smoulder slowly. He'd rather see flames licking the walls while causing as much wanton damage as

44

possible before he had to get out. I can't think why he'd steal any artwork, he might destroy some for kicks. He doesn't even know who Constable is, or didn't - and even now he's learned a bit about him he wouldn't care. If he has stolen it he wouldn't have a clue about its value and wouldn't know what to do with it once he'd got it. Knowing Finn, he'd sling it into the first litter bin he came to, or scrunch it up and throw it in the road.'

Theo dropped to his knees and groaned. The thought of a precious oil sketch discarded as rubbish was too much for him. 'Any old tramp could have it now, or it could be chewed up on Oxford Road. It doesn't bear thinking about.'

'That's very interesting, Scott. Thank you.' said Baskeyfield. 'We'll certainly think on what you've just said. I think that's enough for now. If you can make sure that you give your statements and contact details to the Sergeant who'll be along any moment now, then I think you can all go home. If you can please specify where you were last night along with any other information which you think might be helpful. I suspect that I'll be in touch with you again very soon. If you get tired of me popping up and asking seemingly arbitrary questions you'll have to just be patient, it can't be helped. What matters is that we find and catch the culprit.' Here Baskeyfield gave Theo a warning look. 'In the mean time you need to remember that everyone is innocent until proven otherwise, so please leave the detective work to me and my colleagues. I know it's a stressful time for you all but you must try and go about your usual work.'

As Drew stood waiting his turn to make a statement he quietly chatted with his brother in law. 'What can I do, Benji? I'm sure that Scott isn't involved in any way but I can see that it looks bad for him. Can you help? Please, if you can help in any way I'd be eternally grateful. I feel implicated myself. I was the last person to handle that sketch and it's only my say so that I did indeed put it back. Scott could vouch for me but I don't think that would count for much as things stand. Of course, if I was going to steal the sketch I needn't have gone into the charade of a break-in. Even so, I don't like this at all.'

'I wondered when the possibility that you're a suspect would dawn on you. I'm a little awkwardly placed here, knowing you as I do, but a little careful wrangling should clear my way through - and you know how good at that I am. I'll certainly do my very best to get involved, Drew. To begin with, I can at least keep tabs on what's afoot and keep you posted. In the mean time I think you'd better take care of that young man. His poor mother could probably do with some reassurance too. I don't know, but it might be best if he stays with you for a while - lay low as it were. See what you think. Take him home and try and console his mother. She's bound to know by now, word will have got around the flats - you know how fast gossip spreads. She'll be out of her mind with worry.'

Drew pumped Benji's hand energetically in token of his gratitude and, as soon as Baskeyfield had got what was needed he took Scott to his car to drive him home.

'Do you think you'd better stay with us for a while, Scott?' asked Drew.

'That's really kind of you Drew, but no thank you. I'm better off at home.'

'Are you quite sure? I think you've kept your problems to yourself for long enough. I didn't know that you were in danger of a beating all this time. I can't believe you never told me.'

'What could I say, Drew? That's life at Cherry Hill, you get used to it. Don't forget that I was that "bad guy" not so very long ago and I haven't forgotten how to look after myself. I could have fought it out with Brad and Leighton ages ago but I was trying to leave all that behind me. I thought that dodging and ignoring them was a better way. I should have dealt with them once and for all, then we wouldn't be in this mess now. It's too late now, though.'

'Why don't you stay with us then?'

'I'm not leaving my mum alone while they're crowing. I don't think they've sunk to bullying old ladies yet but I'm not giving them the chance. Mum will be so frightened she won't dare leave the flat without me. If I'm there they'll at least crow a bit quieter, especially if Finn is hiding away. Anyway, I won't let them run me out of my own home. I don't think that Finn quite understands what he's got himself into. He thinks he's brave but he's mostly stupid. He may not have realised it yet but he's stepped way out of his league and he won't have a clue what's coming to him. He's way past ASBOs now! He won't know until it hits him, stupid fool.'

'You know your own mind best. However, you must promise to call me if you have any concerns, any time - day or night. And remember, Beth's brother is doing his best to help both of us, so we're in good hands.'

Baskeyfield was gathering together his notes and preparing to leave. 'I think I've done as much as I can here. I'm going back to the station to see if I can gather some uniforms to scour the streets nearby, though I don't hold out much hope of finding anything. If it's mingled in with McDonald's wrappers in some rubbish bin then I suspect that's the last of the epitome of British art history, or whatever it is. I'll muster together as much manpower as I can but I haven't enough to go on to warrant a full scale search across the streets of Manchester. If it's tossed in some skip then it's unlikely we'll find it, you know that.'

'Do you really think that it was this Finn character, or someone from Scott's old gang?' asked James.

'They have to be our prime suspects and I'm afraid that your brother in law's protégé is next on the list. Of course, you know that we can't rule out a myriad of other possibilities until we've gone over every detail, but you have to admit that it's a coincidence following yesterday's performance here. We both know that coincidences rarely happen in crime, though. It's usually the most obvious solution, isn't it? That's why the Met can afford to send a lower pay grade like me. There isn't much thinking likely in this case. The "who-dunnit" isn't really the teaser here. The "where-is-it" is a different ball game altogether. No doubt it'll surface if there's money involved.'

'I'm sure you've got better things to be doing with your weekend, so I'll leave you to organise the search for the artwork and the ruffian and then, no doubt, you can move on to happier things. I'm afraid that you may not be quite rid of me though. I'm going to do my best to intrude on this case if I can. Is that OK with you?'

'I couldn't be happier at the prospect, although I'm not sure how long I'll be kept on this case. It's not my usual department but we're so stretched for manpower that I'm the best they'd got today. I'd be grateful for any help. But for today, if it's all the same to you, I'd like to get home as soon as I can. It's my wife's birthday and I'd promised to take her out tonight - unless you have other ideas?' The inflection at the end of Baskeyfield's sentence showed an attempt at keenness but he couldn't quite hide his hope for the rest of the day off.

'I hope you've got something special planned. It won't do to upset your wife.'

'I had booked tickets for a pre-show meal and then we were going to see *Wicked*.'

'Well, it's still your show Baskeyfield. Don't change your plans on my account. I can't see that there's too much to do yet, unless you want to start chasing miscreants yourself.'

'Certainly not. Those days are long gone, thank goodness!'

'Well I'll leave you to wine and dine your wife and I'll see what I can square with our bosses. If you're that stretched at the Met then I might even see if I can draft a Sergeant I know into the mix. If there's anything to report before Monday I'll be in touch but keep your phone on silent tonight - anything can wait a few hours. I'll put myself as the contact for now and then we'll renegotiate the work load at the start of next week.'

Stuttering his thanks Baskeyfield headed back to the station. DCI James decided to return to his own home instead of his sister's. He'd booked the weekend off to be with his wife but she'd been called away by a medical emergency with her mother and was staying away for a few days to care for her. A quiet house and time to process his thoughts was just what he needed. He'd clarify his thinking and then plan his strategy for the coming Monday. As he drove he activated hands free and made a quick call to Baskeyfield's station redirecting relevant calls to himself for the weekend and then he'd get sanction from their superiors one way or another on Monday morning. As he drove questions and theories were already queuing up in his mind. A strong coffee, pen and paper would soon solve that problem.

Chapter Five

As DCI James entered the office of Superintendent Fox he saw two more men that he didn't recognise, sitting at their ease, awaiting his arrival.

'Good morning James, nice to see you again.' said Fox. 'Let me introduce you to DCI Monroe from the Metropolitan Art and Antique squad and Chief Inspector Argyle of our Cultural Heritage division.' James shook hands and exchanged the usual brief salutations. 'Take a seat. I've ordered some coffee so let's get our heads together and see how we can sort this mess out. This isn't your usual area of expertise, is it James?'

'I'm not entirely certain what my area of expertise is but I can assure you that this is by no means a speciality of mine. Nevertheless, it's an area that I know something about through personal interest and domestic connections. That's why I'm here at all to be honest.'

'You're referring to your brother in law?' asked Fox.

'Yes, and also my twin sister who is also knowledgeable in the arts generally. I was attending a presentation, given by my brother in law, that she organised. The talk featured the stolen artwork the night that the robbery took place. Also, I know the gallery staff quite well through my family connections.'

'You could say that you're well placed and already "on the ground" as it were? Alternatively it could also be construed that you're a little bit too close and personal. What do you think, Monroe?' said Fox.

'It could work either way. You know DCI James best.' said Monroe. Turning to James he said, 'Ordinarily this would be straight onto my desk but my hands are full enough just now. We've had a tip-off that a Turner that was stolen from a travelling exhibition at the Manchester Art Gallery years ago has finally resurfaced. It's a big piece and the estimated value has hiked since its infamous disappearance. I've been waiting a long time for this moment and I can't afford to let the trail go cold now. It might be my only chance.'

'British art, especially the Old Masters, is suddenly in vogue and previous catalogue prices have gone through the roof since Brexit.' said Argyle. 'Who would have thought that politics could so affect the sale of art, both above and below the counter?'

'How was the Turner stolen? I don't remember hearing of any theft there.' asked James.

'It was stolen years ago but nobody knows who and really nobody even knows when the theft occurred. It had to be an inside job.' said Monroe. 'Consider how much art is quietly tucked away in storage. Galleries can only exhibit so much at any given point and rotate what artefacts they have. Some pieces don't see the light of day for years and years, although the National Art Register online has done a lot to alter this more recently. The Turner must have been surreptitiously slipped out, in plain sight as it were, and nobody would have been any the wiser. Believe it or not but I've heard of priceless treasures being casually popped into a postal tube and put through the office franking machine to get them away. The Turner was only noted as missing when rumours of its sale travelled through the grapevine. Imagine their surprise when the curators went deep into their archives to find that the painting really wasn't there. We kept it as quiet as we could so that we wouldn't frighten off any potential sales.'

'That's what Drew said when he realised that suspicion would naturally fall on him. He said he needn't bother with pyrotechnics if he wanted to steal anything, he could just quietly stash something away and record it as still being in storage. He said that it could be months or years until a piece was missed.' said James.

'We've just been discussing this point.' said Fox. 'However, there's no way that this Finn character would have attempted art theft, or pulled it off so successfully if somebody in the know wasn't steering him.'

'In that case, it could be absolutely anybody, either inside or outside of the museum.' said James.

'Exactly, which is why we're considering drafting you in. Serendipity had you waiting in the wings. Monroe here has the scent of a different chase in his nostrils and, although I'm the cultural expert, I'm no sleuth. If you think you've a taste for this then you can count on me for advice.' said Argyle.

'You could have Baskeyfield for some of the time but this isn't really his forte and he's desperately needed on a different case entirely.' said Fox. 'I'm led to believe that you might be able to grab a Sergeant to save you some leg work. Is this correct?'

James inwardly thrilled at the thought of working with Sgt Maddox from Mossleigh once again. 'I think that I can safely say that Maddox would be willing to help us out. It'd be a change from drinking tea with old ladies. He's a capable lad when given the chance. I'll need to check with Superintendent Holloway that I can be relieved of my other duties first. He may have other plans for me.'

'Don't worry on that score.' said Fox. 'I've cleared it with Holloway myself. It'd be polite for you to speak to him, but it's all officially sorted. Just make sure that you keep everybody that needs to know "in the know." Especially make sure that you keep Monroe here up to date as it's his case really. His network spreads far and wide.'

'Certainly, Sir. No man is an island, I know. You needn't worry on that score.' said James.

'I'm trusting you to ensure that the personal element doesn't prevent you from being objective - everybody is under scrutiny here, do you hear? Baskeyfield will be keeping tabs on that, under my orders, so don't make his life difficult.' said Fox.

'That's fair enough. I'm sure that Drew will withstand scrutiny, so I won't stint.' said James.

'Excellent. Well then, gents, lets get to it.' said Fox.

As James walked along the corridor Monroe caught up and walked apace with him.

'Just a word of caution, Chief Inspector, if you don't mind the advice.' said Monroe. DCI James stopped walking to give Monroe his full attention. 'I imagine that you're accustomed to getting your man and I sincerely hope that you do in this case too. However, I must tell you that in my world only about fifteen percent of stolen art is ever recovered and even then it doesn't necessarily follow that the perpetrator is found. You have to learn to be patient and even let things be, otherwise you'd go mad. That's why I can't let the chance of getting this Turner slip by, it's a rare opportunity. I've been after this piece for years and years. I'm just saying don't go all out or you'll simply die trying. Do your best of course, but don't get stressed and give yourself a coronary.'

'How encouraging. But I take your point, thank you.'

'Oh! I forgot to mention, I've spoken to the team that collate the stolen arts register and they're on the lookout for the specific item now. If anyone tries to sell it through our known channels - which are many and not all above board - then you'll be the first to hear about it, or at least the second if I get there first!' Monroe laughed and strode away with the thrill of the chase in his heart as he picked up the scent of the missing Turner.

Beth and Drew were about their usual weekday routine, which invariably involved numerous shared tea breaks. They'd established a pattern during their early years together, based around the vending machine at art college - which soon extended to tea and cake eaten around their respective timetables (and also, if they'd admit it, during a few scheduled lectures that they'd forgotten to attend). Life carried on now in much the same way, after a couple of chaotic decades and three children later. During the week Drew worked in his studio, when not at the Whitworth. His work varied from various commissions to convert architectural schematics into artist's impressions of the finished building, complete with potted plants and imaginary landscapes, through to corporate boardroom artwork. Beth pottered about the house attending to the domestic sphere, marked music theory exam papers and taught piano most evenings. All of this could be interrupted at any moment by either of their boys who chose to come home uninvited, or more often by their daughter Emma and their granddaughter Primrose. In such cases Drew would exchange his watercolours, oils and drawing board for pencil crayons and the kitchen table with Primrose, who at six years old demanded such attention and innumerable colours. Even without these pleasant unscheduled interruptions their routine was regularly interspersed with tea breaks which were signalled at will by the ring of a service bell. Beth had launched the institution when the children were small and she grew tired of yelling over the house that dinner was ready. As the children's understanding matured the system of ringing became more sophisticated; the first ring meant that dinner was almost ready, the second ring meant that dinner was served. If there was a third ring it was more urgent and frantic, meaning that dinner was now going cold and you'd have to hurry before your meal was in the dustbin. Nobody ever dared push for a fourth ring. That same old bell served a similar purpose still, the only real change was that it was now rung less repeatedly and with less violent tones - it also now reported that the kettle had boiled and the tea was brewed.

Not surprisingly, since the robbery at the gallery, Beth and Drew had found it difficult to focus on their usual duties and the bell had been working overtime as they talked over recent events and the implications for themselves and those they knew. Beth was in the process of repeating the ritual yet again when her brother strode into the kitchen and greeted her with his usual bear hug. Any physical similarities that they had once shared when they were young were now forgotten. Beth was much daintier than her twin brother. Benedict was heavy set with big bones and solid proportions at a towering six foot two inches tall. Beth's hair was pale brown whereas Benedict's was dark brown, almost black, albeit now peppered with a distinguished grey. Beth had hazel coloured eyes but Benedict's were a deep brown which could have seemed sorrowful were it not for the crow's feet at the edge of his eyes which belied an inclination to laugh. They had however retained a sensitivity to each other's mood and their thinking invariably followed similar lines. They also shared in continuing a family heritage for logical reasoning and problem solving. Joint research had revealed that their maternal grandmother had been involved in the code deciphering team at Bletchley Park and her personal speciality of de-cloaking misdemeanour was also a trait that her grandchildren continued to credit.

'Benji, I'm so pleased to see you. It's so awful and we just can't concentrate on anything properly. We simply can't think of anything other than the robbery. Drew will be through any second, I've rung the bell for tea, then you can tell us all about it.' said Beth. As predicted Drew had quickly responded to the summons of the bell and they gathered around the kitchen table.

'What's the state of play, Benji?' asked Drew. 'Is it certain that Finn is the culprit?'

'Nothing is certain at all just now. Don't you worry though, we'll get to the bottom of this - and I do quite literally mean we.' said Benedict. In response to their enquiring glances he explained. 'Thanks to a shortfall in manpower I'm on secondment to the Met's Antiques and Art Squad. I can also commandeer our dear friend Maddox from your own humble constabulary. We're back in business!'

'Oh, that's brilliant! I've felt so helpless not being able to do anything, but if we can help you in any way you know we will.' said Beth.

'That's exactly what I was banking on you saying. I'm afraid that Drew will have to come under the microscope, just like everybody else, but as soon as that's cleared up we can crack on unshackled.' said Benedict.

'Oh, don't mind me.' said Drew. 'You can get the interrogation lights out and turn them onto full beam as far as I'm concerned. It's young Scott that I'm worried about. I'm not concerned about his actual innocence, that's a given as far as I'm concerned, but proving it won't be so easy.'

'Proving guilt where it's appropriate won't be easy either and I don't want the lad to have a cloud of doubt hanging over him just because we can't point the finger at the real villain. Something like that could totally ruin his chances, no matter how much we say he's innocent unless proven otherwise. The bad news is that, according to the experts, the clear up rate for crime in the art world is less than good, but I won't sit back and accept that. I'm hoping that we can do better. Between us we'll have all angles covered. I've got the official clout and you've got inside knowledge.' said Benedict.

'Do you think it was Finn who broke in and stole the Constable?' asked Beth.

'We're presuming so for now and it's highly likely to be the case. Even so, can't ignore other possibilities. We can't know for sure until he's found and brought in for questioning. The one quick glimpse, which is only for a fraction of a second before the system shuts down, shows a figure of Finn's height and stature but his head is covered by a hoodie and his face is concealed behind a mask of sorts, probably a stereotypical balaclava. It's most probably him, but we can't be totally certain yet. In my experience there is never a mysterious Mr X. It's usually the prime suspect and it's usually somebody that you know.'

'I do agree with Scott that it just doesn't make sense for Finn to move into high art crime. His main idea would be to make life difficult for Scott, which doesn't suggest stealing one particular piece of art.' said Drew.

'We don't know that the piece was particularly chosen or if it was just chance that dictated what was taken. We can't know that until we speak to Finn. He's gone to ground for the time being, which does bolster the theory that he's our man. He'll have to surface sooner or later, then we'll have him. What's going on at the gallery, Drew?' said Benedict.

'I'm not there every day but I gather that Theo has told everyone to stay away for a few days. The forensic team are just finishing up and the builders get back to work tomorrow but he's told everybody to take the rest of the week off saying he'll call us if he needs anything. Theo reckons that we all need to just calm down for a bit and let the dust settle.' said Drew.

'Very sound advice.'

'Do you think so? I think it's a ruse because Theo is in a huge temper and can't stand the thought of seeing Scott there. He can't tell Scott to stay away and let us carry on as normal so this is the next best thing.' said Drew.

'Well, if it's his own feathers that need to settle, the advice is still good. After that he'll have to get over it and let us do our job. Life has to carry on and he must abide by the law too. He's first on my list for tomorrow. I'll have a quiet word with him to remind him of the fact.' said Benedict.

Beth glanced at the clock and mentioned that she needed to prepare for her evening's pupils. 'You will keep us informed, won't you? I understand the whole confidentiality thing but we'll help as much as we can.'

'I'm counting on it, Beth. Meanwhile I'm going to head on over to Mossleigh station to see if I can purloin Maddox. I wonder if he fancies himself as an art sleuth?' said Benedict.

'I know that he fancies himself as your sidekick. If you don't rescue him all he has to look forward to is policing Mossleigh Village Flower Festival and our Annual Croquet Competition.' said Beth.

'Poor lad. If I'd known that I'd have gone there first to give him a ray of hope. I'll march over to his rescue this very moment.' said Benedict.

Chapter Six

Situated on the outskirts of Mossleigh village next to the police station was The Badger's Den, or simply "The Badger" to the locals. It was famed for its speciality local ales, its picturesque thatched roof and its one glorious Michelin star. Beth nursed her pint of Cheshire Set. She didn't see the point in going to the bar twice and knew categorically that a mere half pint wouldn't see her through the night. She listened intently to the conversations buzzing around her until the meeting was brought to order. The date for the launch of the Flower Festival was almost upon them and, as previous Britain in Bloom winners, there was a lot at stake and a meeting had been arranged to finalise details. In the capacity of proprietor of the village florist shop and also as a RHS exhibition winner, Nicola Farrington was the obvious choice as Chairman. Nicola kept the title of Chairman even though she was most definitely female, as she held a severe abhorrence of the title Chairperson, maintaining that the title sounded far too impersonal. The committee agreed with her view that Chairwoman sounds much too similar to "char woman" which wasn't the same thing at all, and so she let the title of Chairman roll over from the previous occupant undisturbed.

Nicola stood to open the meeting. 'First of all I'd like you to raise your glasses to toast Kirsty and Hyacinth. We've spent far too much time together this last week or two and we've worked through the night on numerous occasions.' Everybody cheered and took this as a good excuse to down a good portion of the drinks in their hands. 'And now you can finish your drinks by toasting yourselves, because we now hand on the baton to you all here, and anybody else you can requisition. We need everything ready and in place at the beginning of next week.' More cheering and drinking hammered the point home. Once order of sorts had resumed Nicola continued. 'Can we confirm that Millwoods are booked for the dates to install the fixtures and fittings?'

'Conrad spoke to them yesterday.' said Hyacinth. 'He uses them for all of his business and architectural work and he assures me that they are reliable and punctual. He spoke to them about the festival so I'm sure they'll have it sorted. He also asked me to remind you that you're to send the invoices to him. He insists that it's his contribution.' A round of applause and further quaffing in the guise of a toast registered the group's thanks.

'It's such a relief not having to put every wall plug and screw in place ourselves this year. We are so grateful to Conrad for his generosity. It also takes away the burden of worry about health and safety scrutiny off our shoulders. We don't want the responsibility of "death by Dahlias" on our conscience because of a wobbly hanging bracket. I'd offer to send him a bouquet but it seems a little tactless in these circumstances and it won't properly convey our gratitude. Does anybody have any suggestions for a gift?' said Nicola.

'There's more than one sort of bouquet you know, Nicola.' said Drew. 'I'll send him one of my extra special bottles of single malt whisky. He's had his eye on my bottle of Scapa for a while now.'

'That sounds more like it. Thank you. If you give a receipt to the Treasurer we'll reimburse you.' said Nicola. Drew waved away the suggestion and the meeting continued. 'The site for each arrangement has been allocated on a map that Terry has sketched out for us and each sponsor has a plaque waiting to be mounted next to the display they have sponsored. Natalie, did you say that Terry would be available to direct the workers if any queries arise?'

Not realising that she was about to be called upon Natalie was intent on her signature "Gin and It." Even at choir concerts she took a flask of Gin and Italian Vermouth, insisting that it was good for her vocal chords. A thumbs up did the job of clarifying that this indeed was the case. On this particular night Natalie's hair had just changed from a vibrant purple hue to a shade of deep burgundy. She must have been well into her seventies but her kaleidoscope hair colour and her indomitable spirit made it impossible to guess at. Nothing seemed to quench her. When her husband,Terry, was struck by a sudden seizure whilst performing his own roof repairs, which rendered him partially paralysed, she just seemed to shoulder it and carry on. Terry was invaluable to the Floral Committee as he was available at any time and was meticulous in his planning and paperwork. Although Natalie was named as the Treasurer she freely admitted that it was Terry that kept it all ship-shape. The question of availability could have been addressed to Terry himself but he was currently unavailable as he was engaged in taking a list of drinks to be renewed to the bar.

'All that remains is to make sure that the rota for watering everything is ready and those involved get a copy.' said Nicola. Kirsty handed out watering timetables and that concluded the first round of business along with the first round of drinks. 'The only other significant item on the agenda is the croquet competition, so I'll hand over to Mae for this next item.'

'The Croquet Crown has been part of the WI calendar for many years so, as the Mossleigh WI President, it falls to me to stand here. I'm afraid that the credit isn't mine at all, however, as the whole of Mossleigh WI are intrinsically involved in the preparation and planning. No doubt, in time honoured WI tradition everything will run smoothly I'm sure. There'll be tea and cakes a-plenty as we'll get lots of visitors to the village for the Flower Festival and we hope that they'll linger by the green and enjoy the game and some refreshments. The game is open to members and non members alike. There are a few slots available for any last minute competitors. Does anybody have any names to add?' said Mae.

'Theo and Sally have expressed an interest. I can't think that they've changed their minds so if you can squeeze them in they'll be thrilled, I'm sure.' said Drew.

'Darcy will be acting as referee so we can be sure of fair play. But, do remember that it's purely for fun so don't lets get too serious.' said Mae.

'It's bound to be serious if Darcy is involved. She terrifies me.' said Henrietta.

Mae laughed. 'Oh, don't be alarmed. She's really lovely, it's just her no nonsense brusque American manner that takes a bit of getting used to. It comes in quite handy when she's judging cake competitions or overseeing how many cheques need countersigning. She's an amazing WI Treasurer.'

'What happens about the croquet competition if it rains?' asked Emma. Emma was Beth and Drew's daughter and she was currently enjoying a night out after leaving Primrose and her husband Nathaniel together for the evening. She and Henrietta had struck up a friendship soon after Henrietta had moved to Mossleigh. Henrietta's son, Toby, was of a similar age to Primrose which was a good place for the friendship to begin. Since then Hetty had joined the WI and her ongoing friendly understanding with Sgt Robert Maddox meant that Toby was now being cared for by Bobby's mum for the evening. Henrietta knew that it would be difficult to tell which of the two would have had the best time. She'd hear all about it from Toby in the morning but no doubt pastry and baking would be involved somewhere. The smile on Mrs Maddox's face reassured her that babysitting really wasn't an imposition. Mrs Maddox had been a widow for many years and had time and love to spare. It was a joy for Hetty and Toby to get a share of it, life hadn't been particularly joyful for Hetty until recently.

'We'll keep playing.' answered Mae. 'I know it's pleasant in the sunshine but in years gone by we've played wearing wellies with a few trusty assistants following us around with brollies. It was quite fun, actually. If you live in Britain you have to be prepared to enjoy yourself whatever the weather. Even if we tried to reschedule there'd be no guarantee of the weather for the next time and the ground would just get muddier. So long as we keep the cakes and sandwiches dry and there's a hot cup of tea available, we'll be fine.'

More surreptitious toasting affirmed the sentiment and the official meeting broke up. Very few of the committee were ready to leave, which was due in part to the small but sumptuous buffet that Edward Gibson, Chef in residence and son of the landlord presented with his compliments to the Floral Committee. Further explanation could readily be found in the lure of the fine ales made available by Edward's father, Arthur.

Emma and Henrietta settled into comfortable conversation.

'Mum tells me that Bobby might be working with Uncle Benji again.' said Emma.

'He is and he is so thrilled. They got it all sorted earlier this week and are going to the gallery tomorrow to talk to the curator and his assistant. Bobby thinks he's hit the big time now. The way he talks you'd think he'll be going up against the Mafia.' said Hetty.

'I think it might be worse than that. He's got my dad as a suspect.' said Emma.

'Surely not! Bobby won't like that.' said Hetty.

'My dad is as likely as anybody else, or at least as far as the eyes of the law are concerned. They can't leave him out of the investigation so he'll have to get used to the idea.'

They turned to speak to Drew on the matter to find that he was embroiled in a debate on the merits and defects of Garden Croquet as opposed to Association Croquet. Deciding that now was a good time time to leave, Henrietta said her good byes.

'I think I'd better get back so that Mrs Maddox can go home. She said that I needn't rush but it's late enough.'

'I'll walk with you.' said Emma. 'Nat is supposed to be at the dairy first thing so he'll have gone to bed early. I'd like to see him off so I'd better get some sleep too.'

Beth hugged the girls and said goodbye but Drew was still arguing the merits of Garden Croquet. The girls left utterly assured that it was the only sensible option, the alternative Association Croquet taking a ridiculous amount of time and accounting for a considerable amount of tomfoolery into the bargain.

Chapter Seven

'It seems that you and I are back in business.' DCI James shook hands with Sergeant Maddox in the foyer of Mossleigh police station. 'Honour demands that we need to set the record straight and solve this case. I won't accept the fifteen percent success rate stance. They haven't met us yet! Let's go and plan our attack. There's not much room here and the facilities aren't very convivial. Let's walk over to Beth's and requisition her kitchen table. We'll get a better cup of tea there and some cake if we're lucky. It'll also save me having to say everything twice as Beth and Drew will want to know our every move.'

'I'm really thankful for you including me, Sir.' said Maddox. 'You know I'll do my very best but I am concerned that I'm out of my depth. I'm not very cultured, I'm afraid,'

'Neither am I, but don't tell anybody I told you that. There are plenty of arty experts for us to tap in to. Ask them and then just nod as if you knew it all already. It works for me.'

Maddox laughed. 'I'm not sure I should be bluffing my way through an art theft, but don't say I didn't warn you. I'm not convinced I even know what questions to ask but I'll do what I can. If I keep my mouth shut I should escape discovery.'

'That's the very best kind of copper; mouth shut and ears open. We'll make a formidable team, with our unofficial Special Constables. Drew will be an invaluable ally getting behind the artistic façade and Beth has an uncanny knack of getting inside people's lives. We'll get to the bottom of this between us. I'm only sorry I couldn't claim you earlier. Does this mean that you're now excused duty for the Flower Festival and the highly contentious WI Croquet Crown?'

'I may have to cover the odd shift, but I'm happy to say that I'm off the hook for the most part. Once again, thank you!'

James laughed as they turned the corner into Beth's driveway and after a token knock at the back door let himself into the kitchen. To announce his arrival he vigorously activated the silver service bell. He then put the kettle on to boil in acknowledgement of the summons that he'd just made. Very quickly the sounds of the piano in the music room died away and the sound of brushes being cleaned began. Cups of tea and coffee sat waiting ready for the commencement of the ad-hoc burglary squad.

'I've relocated my office for the morning, Beth. You serve better cakes than Winsford canteen and Mossleigh station doesn't even have a vending machine. What have you got in? I need a sugar rush to kick start my thinking. We've got some sleuthing to do and at this very moment I haven't a clue where to begin.' said Benedict.

'What would you say if I told you that I don't have any cake?' said Beth.

'I wouldn't believe you. I'd start searching without bothering for a warrant and I may consider arresting you for obstructing the course of my enquiries.' said Benedict. He substantiated the claim by pulling a cake tin from the dresser.' Ah, what do we have here? Hidden in plain sight, eh? Always the most effective method.'

Beth rolled her eyes and fetched plates and forks to serve the remainder of the Victoria sponge that her brother was brandishing. 'What's the plan, Benji? Where do we start?'

'I think that Maddox and I need to go back to the very beginning. Baskeyfield did a good enough job with his preliminary enquiries but I need to get a feel for this myself. It'll be very annoying for you all at the gallery I know, but it can't be helped. I'm going to go back to the gallery and interview everybody all over again. I can chat to Drew any time and I'll leave Scott off my list for now as I heard everything he had to say right here after the WI meeting. Maddox, I think I'd like you to go and talk to Finn's gang. Don't go in uniform but put your jeans and a tee shirt on so that you don't seem too official. I expect that, once you've introduced yourself as police, they'll instantly clam up but you're bound to fare better than if I go. Ask them about their morning at the museum and see if you can squeeze a hint about where Finn might be hiding. It's a long shot but we've got to try.' said Benedict.

'OK, Sir. I'll go straight away. I'll see what I can get out of them but I suspect it won't be much.'

'It might be an idea if you could pop in on Scott and Mrs Malkin, if you're going that way.' said Drew. 'I'm concerned about the pair of them.'

'That's a good point Drew. Yes, do your Community Officer duty too. Scott can look after himself I'm sure but I know you're good with old ladies - Mossleigh has given you some valuable people skills. Let Mrs Malkin experience the full force of your charming personality.' said Benedict.

'I'll also go and see Monroe. I'll ask him if there's any news of the sketch surfacing onto the market place. I'm presuming that the motto "follow the money" is just as applicable for a work of art as a jewellery theft. Cash is usually the key to solving the problem.' said Benedict.

'What can I do?' asked Beth.

'For now just keep us in tea and cake. There isn't much that any of us can do at present, but things will warm up as we get going, don't you worry. Drew, you just need to stay especially alert when you get back to the gallery. Keep your eyes and ears open for anything just a little out of kilter, anything out of the ordinary no matter how inconsequential it might seem.' said Benedict. 'We'll see what the end of the week brings and then we'll have another chat amongst ourselves.' Nods of agreement called the meeting to a close and the group then gave Beth's delicious cake the attention that it deserved.

'I am truly sorry to be going over all of this again, Miss Bickerton.' said DCI James. It must be so very tedious for you that I'm disturbing your work again for the same old rigmarole.'

'You must do your job, of course.' said Sally. 'Do you want to stay here or shall we go and get a coffee? I'd appreciate a breath of fresh air and a change of scenery.'

'Let's go to the place where you got those take-out drinks from. The coffee was delicious.'

As they walked Sally chatted about the people at the gallery and the work that they did there. 'We're usually such a happy team. It's so sad that it's been knocked. Things are settling down gradually though, thank goodness. Theo is more like his usual self. He did take the security guard out for that pint as suggested - well, quite a few pints from what I can gather! I think Brian was so relieved to know that Theo didn't hold him responsible. It was a very stressful night for him. I'm sure he's been through worse in his army days but he does take the theft personally.'

'It's good to hear that morale is on the mend. What about relations between Theo and Scott?

'Theo called in at Scott's home to apologise for his initial reaction. He took some flowers for Mrs Malkin, too. I'm sure that Scott is glad of the apology but it'll take some time for mutual trust to build. It's a step in the right direction though, and it shows that the intent is right.'

The coffees had been served and they found a quiet corner where they could chat. This was the cue to begin the official interview.

'If you would please cast your mind back to that Friday. I know all about Finn and his pals turning up but was there anything else in the course of the morning that was a little out of the ordinary? Even if it seems totally irrelevant please don't refrain from mentioning it. Any little thing at all.'

Sally sipped her coffee as she brought that day back into her mind. Although there was no flash of recognition she recounted her thoughts to DCI James. 'The builders were coming and going as usual. I couldn't say if there were any new men that day, you'd have to speak to Millwoods. They are overseeing the building work here, maybe they subcontract parts out to various other workmen?'

'What a small world. Millwoods are overseeing my sister's village Flower Festival too.'

'That's certainly a variety of work. Nevertheless, I suppose bricks are bricks whatever you do with them.'

'True enough, unlike art!'

'No piece of art is the same and everybody reacts differently to each piece. Everybody's personal tastes are so distinctive and firmly held ... Oh! That's a point.' exclaimed Sally. 'I've just remembered that Rick came to the gallery not long after Drew left. He came to see Drew but had just missed him.'

'Who is Rick?' asked James. As usual, the technique of making the interview feel informal and relaxed, with chit-chat about inconsequential side topics, had worked its magic and potentially relevant information had floated to the surface unbidden. Very often it worked out that the harder somebody tried to be helpful the less that they could actually think of anything useful to add. The displacement activity of drinking coffee, the relaxed atmosphere of the coffee shop and the pleasant chit-chat about builders and flower festivals meant that Sally's imagination wasn't forced. This was much more conducive.

'Rick is a visiting curator from Amsterdam. He's spending time at the Manchester Art Gallery. He's struck up something of a friendship with Drew and they're currently attempting to convert each other's tastes.'

'I've heard Drew mention him, although not by name. Drew said that he was trying to convert a colleague to the merits of Constable during his talk for the WI. Weren't you asked to give the talk first?'

Sally blushed and at least had the grace not to hide her guilty expression. 'I said that I was busy that night, but I wasn't. I couldn't face the thought of a bunch of old women and I didn't really know quite what it was they expected from me so I bottled out. Drew seemed happy enough to pick it up so I left it at that. I had arranged to be with Theo but he didn't hang around at my house for long and left to do some work. He can't rest until everything's safely packed away.'

'I need to warn you to be careful how you refer to my sister. She's a member of the WI and wouldn't thank you for referring to her as an old woman. Nevertheless, I can quite understand your misconception of the ladies but that was the WI of the old school, and not necessarily any the worse for that. Did you know that the Isle of Man WI groups provide tea and cakes for the motorbike fans during the TT races? The Glastonbury WI does the same during the rock festivals. They dress up with vintage hairdos and bright lipstick. Can you imagine how much cake they get through? It's all homemade, too. They insist that they won't run out though - in true WI fashion. Actually, I read an article in a police bulletin referring to the WI as this country's largest criminal organisation.' Sally actually choked with laughter at this comment. 'I'm serious! All the berries that they pick - tons and tons of the stuff - are picked from public spaces and then sold. That's illegal.

Nevertheless, I don't think Downing Street or Her Majesty are considering pressing charges. This country owes a debt to their industry with the preserves as it saved our nation from starvation during the war. A government initiative couldn't have done it, but each village - in fact each individual in her own kitchen - taking the initiative not to allow anything to go to waste kept this country on its feet. We'll let them keep on with the blackberries.'

'I wish I'd gone now. I feel positively dull in comparison.'

'It is true, or at Mossleigh at any rate, that there are some old women but they bake a mighty sponge cake. You did miss out there. My sister told me that at the last committee meeting a member arrived and, standing in the doorway, made a grand announcement exclaiming in all seriousness, "Breaking news on the sponge front!" The ground breaking announcement was that sponge cooked in a fan assisted oven required a higher fat content than traditional ovens in order for the sponge to rise well. Everybody fell about laughing but I can vouch for the fact because the Victoria sponge I ate earlier was out of this world.'

Sally laughed out loud. 'I didn't think I'd be interrogated about sponge and jam today. I'm afraid that I only know about art and a little bit about textiles. What a small world view I have.'

'I do apologise. I forget my position so easily. Surely cake is the priority in all of our lives? However, please tell me about Rick's visit to the gallery and I'll try and put cake out of my mind for a short while.'

'There's nothing much to it. Rick came to find Drew because he'd promised to show Rick the Constable paintings they'd been debating. He's tried to see them before but they've never managed it yet. Theo heard what Rick had come for and took him down to the archives with Finn and his cronies. He stayed for about twenty minutes and then left.'

'That's really helpful, thank you. Gradually the picture unfolds (if you'll pardon the expression) and eventually we'll see everything that we need to. The Manchester Art Gallery isn't far from here, is it? I'll walk over there now and try and speak to Rick myself. Before I go can you tell me when the security guard from that night is next on duty?'

'I think that Brian is on nights again. If so he'll be in at six o'clock.'

'That should work in nicely. If you could you let him know that I'll be along shortly please, I'd be grateful. Thank you.'

'Of course. I hope that I've been vaguely useful.'

'You've been a great help. All these little bits and pieces will eventually form a complete whole. I've made it a personal mission to get to the heart of this case, so don't you worry. In the mean time, don't forget to increase the quantity of margarine or butter in your sponge cakes. You won't regret it!'

'As if I ever switch the oven on, but thank you for thinking that I might - I think.'

On entering the gallery DCI James could easily identify Rick. Although he wore a conventional blue suit there was a distinctive non-British quality to the way he carried his outfit. The tailoring was definitely not English. It struck DCI James that he'd never realised until this moment that national heritage could be conveyed in couture but it was an obvious truth. James introduced himself at first as Drew's brother in law.

'How lovely to meet Drew's family. He has been such a good friend to me. He is a good man. It's so sad to hear about the misfortune he is suffering at the Whitworth.'

'Indeed it is. In fact that's what brings me here today. I'm a police detective and it's fallen to me to investigate the theft.'

'How marvellous that you can help Drew so. How can I assist you?'

'I understand that you called in at the Whitworth and joined Theo in escorting some young men about the premises. Can you tell me about that?'

'You are correct. I've been trying to meet Drew at the Whitworth as he has offered to show me the Constables they have there. Each time I've tried it hasn't been convenient and so Mr Hunter allowed me to join him as he showed the other young men.'

'Were the youngsters very attentive? Did they seem particularly interested in what Mr Hunter had to show them?' asked James. ' I ask as it's unusual that they were there at all. I understand that the gallery is closed to the public at present.'

'That's right, but I believe that these friends of Scott and Mr Hunter is always so keen to share his knowledge and passion. One of the group was very interested in the art. He was keen to hear about anything and everything in the gallery but the others seemed very bored as far as I could tell. I couldn't understand why they were there at all if it was so dull to them. I think that Finn, if I remember his name correctly, was very much the boss of the group and was demanding that they at least try and learn something. I invited them to the gallery here too. Not that they needed my invite as we are open to the public as usual. Anybody can walk in here during regular opening hours.'

'And how did they respond to your invitation?'

'Finn seemed pleased to be asked and was very excited to come. I was surprised when they did come later that day all the same.'

'They came here that day as well?'

'Oh yes, they came straight after their time at the Whitworth. I don't know why they bothered though. Even Finn didn't pretend to be interested once he was here. Not one of them could be bothered to raise their eyes to look at anything that I tried to show them. It all seemed too much effort and after about ten minutes they made some feeble excuse about having to get home for their dinner. It was only the merest show of politeness. In fact, it was very rude of them. I very much doubt that they go home for their dinner very often at all.'

'I suspect you're right about that. How very strange. Have you seen any of those boys since?'

'No, I haven't. I don't expect to either. They weren't remotely interested, so why would they come back?'

'Why indeed?' James thanked Rick for his time and took his contact details for future reference.

'I intend to return home to Amsterdam at the end of the month. I'm sure that there is nothing more that I can tell you but I'll make sure you get my card for the gallery back home before I leave.'

'That's very thoughtful of you. Thank you.' James wasn't sure how any of this helped further his search for the thief but he knew that he was now embarking on a trail marked out by breadcrumbs, few and infrequent to begin with, but they would eventually lead him to the solution. For now all that he could do was collect information crumb by crumb. The next crumb, Brian, was waiting for him at the Whitworth.

Brian handed James a mug of tea. If the rigid posture, muscle bound physique, crew style haircut and immaculately polished shoes didn't mark Brian out as ex-military, then the bright orange NAAFI tea removed any lingering doubt. DCI James particularly disliked the taste of tea but knew better than to get off to a bad start by refusing the hospitality. He accepted the brew and pulled up a chair.

'It's a bit cosy in here, isn't it?' said James. The tiny office space hadn't been designed to accommodate two such men.

'We'd have to get along if we spent much time in here together.' said Brian. 'Still, compared to the belly of a tank there's room to spare in this place.'

James gave a minute nod as the final piece of the puzzle slotted nicely into place - ground forces. Brian was all that James expected and decided that with such a man it would be better to get straight to the point. 'I gather you had quite a time of it the other Friday. What can you tell me about that night? We need to catch whoever did this. What can you suggest?'

'I'll tell you everything that I can, Sir. What help it'll be I can't guarantee but for what it's worth I'll do my best.'

'Excellent. Let me decide what is or isn't important, just tell me everything as you remember it.'

'I knew you'd be wanting to talk to me sometime soon and I wanted to be ready. I've taken all of the security camera discs home from that day and that night, and also a couple of days before. Of course you can take them and look for yourself but I thought I'd save you the bother. I've watched every minute myself. I haven't fast forwarded or skipped anything and there really is nothing there to see. The usual builders come and go and the general staff go about their business. I can vouch for all of the gallery staff easily enough and I know most of the builders by sight from my day shifts. There are a couple of unfamiliar faces among the builders but they just go about their work without a hint of any funny business. Nobody is remotely concerned with the skylight that was used to gain entry into the building and none of the builders pays any attention to the archives. The only time anything fishy occurs on that Friday morning is when those good-for-nothings in hoodies barge in and I'm sure that you know all about them.'

'What a saint you are! I'm grateful for your efforts here and I know that my Sergeant will consider himself eternally in your debt for sparing him the task of trawling through the security footage. You must have had a dreadfully dull few days.'

'It can't be shirked though, can it? Somebody has to do it and it might as well be me. At least I know who should or shouldn't be about. You can get your Sergeant to look, but he won't know who is in the right place or if anybody looks out of place.'

'If it's all the same to you I'll spare him the duty. I wish there were more like you.' James took a sip of his tea as a token of his appreciation, if only Brian knew the sacrifice of the gesture.

'What galls me is that if I was the type of security guard that sat on his backside watching cameras all shift then this wouldn't have happened. I came to work at my usual time - I work from six till six either side of the clock, four shifts on then four shifts off and rotating days and nights each time. I checked into the security office to relieve the day time guard and everything was fine. He had nothing to report and had probably spent all shift reading the paper, there's not much you can be doing in the day while the gallery is closed. There's no point watching the builders' every move and the gallery staff know their own business best. There was no sign of a fire then. After that I make it a point to avoid any sort of routine or pattern. The only consistent thing is that I'm rarely in the office. I can get the images from the cameras redirected to my tablet and I look at them as I patrol the building. I would normally go back to the office for a drink and my supper but while the gallery is closed I've tended to picnic in the gallery. It's not a very big space in here as you say and, if I'm honest, it can sometimes bring back old memories. I don't really suffer with PTSD but I'm a bit more prone to claustrophobia now than I might have been before my army days. The main thing is that I can hear better out here, sound really travels in the gallery at night as it's open plan. I didn't see or hear a thing before the fire alarm went off. How that happened I can't explain because there's nothing on the footage to show who or what might have caused the fire. I can vouch for everybody in the building that show up on the CCTV until those lads turned up, but they left soon enough it seems. I know that everything's a bit haywire with all this maintenance work but the staff never seem to have homes to go to, they're so dedicated to their work. That's why it's so upsetting, to them it's their life that's been stolen. They live for this place.'

'You've been extremely helpful, Brian. Thank you. Please would you keep hold of those discs for me and also get me some copies made, just for my own reference? Also, would you note down the next few shift patterns for the other guard for me?' Asked James. Brian set about the task straight away and then handed the list to James. Putting his mug down to take the paper James said, 'Would you look at that! I got so engrossed in all that you've been telling me that I've let my tea go cold. My apologies.'

Chapter Eight

The start of the next day saw DCI James and Sgt Maddox sitting in DCI Monroe's office. The meeting didn't really justify that everybody attend but James figured that there was always something new for Maddox to learn and now that he had taken the young Sergeant under his wing James was determined to give him as much opportunity for Continual Professional Development as possible. This was the official line of reasoning but the real motivation behind the gesture was that James liked Maddox and thought that he would enjoy it.

'I can see why you advise patience as a key virtue in the world of art crime.' said James. 'I've spent most of my days recently chasing my own tail. Nevertheless I'm to keep you informed, so here we are. I'd also like to pick your brains to get some idea about art thefts in general. I don't suppose that there's anything unique about this particular case so maybe generalisation can help me out a bit. I'm hoping there might be a template of sorts. I've no previous case histories to guide me.'

'What are your current lines of enquiry?' asked Monroe.

'I've spoken to the gallery staff again and also a visiting colleague from MAG who had popped over to the Whitworth at an opportune moment. I've spoken to the night security guard, to whom you owe a massive debt of gratitude, Maddox. He's saved you from having to watch hours and days worth of CCTV footage. There's nothing of note from these interviews that I can gather at this point, although a couple of details are starting to niggle at the back of my mind - just a bit of an itch that I can't quite reach at the moment. Other than that I've arranged to speak to a fire officer to get some information about the fire. I need to know how long before it may have started and I'm hoping that will give me another angle of investigation. What about you, Maddox? How did Brad and Leighton like your visit?' said James.

'I can't pretend that they were overly happy to see me.' said Maddox. 'They're pretty miffed with Finn though, that much was blatantly obvious. I think that this made them more vocal than they'd have been ordinarily. They feel that they've had their noses pushed out and they're not at all happy about it.'

'How interesting. Do go on.' said James.

'They don't doubt that Finn is the culprit and didn't bother to hide it. They didn't specifically say so but they have no reason to think otherwise. What annoys them is that Finn used them to recce the gallery and then went on to play his own game and leave them out of it entirely. Their loyalty has been sorely abused and now they're angry. He hasn't confided in them at all and it smarts. I believed them when they said they knew nothing about the break in. They didn't even know why they had to go to the gallery in the first place but once news of the theft got round they put two and two together and felt mightily ill used. They've not seen Finn at all since that morning and have no idea where he is now. They've checked all his usual haunts because they're after his blood. Of course, they didn't tell me where those hideouts are specifically but I'm quite sure that he isn't there. The one thing that they were adamant about was that they wanted a go at Finn before we get to him, after that we're welcome to him.' said Maddox.

'Dear, oh dear. A falling out amongst thieves, or would-be thieves. I'm sure they'd have joined in given the chance.' said James. 'I don't suppose that it's unusual in your field, is it, Monroe?'

'Tiresomely predictable, I'm afraid.' said Monroe.

'I've been trying to imagine what type of a thief, or mastermind behind the thief, it is that we might be looking for. Is there any rule of thumb or stereotype to guide me? Because it was just one specific piece that was taken, despite being surrounded by countless other treasures, does that tell us anything about who wants it stolen?' asked James.

Monroe shook his head. 'I'm afraid that the movies have done a lot to misrepresent the world of art theft. We're led to believe that an eccentric connoisseur has singled out this one piece that he simply must have. We're led to believe that it will be taken to a remote castle and kept secret for his pleasure only. I imagine that you're picturing laser beams and sewers as a means of access - all so that one artistic recluse can bask in the glory of owning this one picture and henceforth require nothing further from this life.'

James laughed at the stereotype but admitted that this was guiding his thinking.

'Surely it has to be an art lover of some sort that wants this piece. Why steal it if this isn't so?' said Maddox.

'The media has glamourised what is in fact a very sordid and cruel criminality. In all my years in the department I have never, ever known this popularised ideal to be true. For the most part pictures are chosen simply because they've been featured either in a brochure or on TV and then used as collateral, like a down payment until ready cash is available to complete the balance.' said Monroe.

'You're saying that a thief will see a painting in the press and think, "Oh, that's valuable, I'll take that one" and then use it as a deposit for some dirty deed?' said James.

'That's precisely what I'm saying. I've known a Van Gogh to be featured on a gallery brochure and the next thing you know it's been nicked. The thief walked past walls and walls of equally valuable and more accessible art to make a bee line for the featured painting. They'd probably never even heard of Van Gogh before it was featured in the literature and they went specifically for that piece, probably because they had no knowledge of the value of any of the other works. It happens more than you'd guess.' said Monroe.

'How depressing. Maybe the galleries shouldn't promote these things.' said Maddox.

'Surely that's the very point of their existence. They must promote their exhibitions. Arts funding requires that the public benefits from having these works on show; it's to make art accessible to all. If not you may as well keep the Whitworth closed and keep all of the art shut away in packing cases down in the Welsh mines for safe keeping - like they did during the war. Art demands to be seen, otherwise it's futile. That's why the National Art Register is such an amazing resource, it now makes works accessible, via the internet, which ordinarily wouldn't see the light of day for years. ' said Monroe.

'You think that it's highly likely that Finn stole the Constable and purely because it was brought to his attention - simple as that. Is it really that simple?' said James.

'In my experience, yes. But proving it is the hard part. It's usually the impossible part, I'm afraid.' said Monroe.

'But what on earth would a small-fry like Finn need a down payment for?' asked Maddox.

'The motivation isn't always the same. I'm quite sure he'll have taken the sketch purely because it was there, with no further thought. What he'll do with it now is another story. It's quite feasible that he just took it to show Scott who's boss, a display of power if you like, and it's probably discarded somewhere - maybe lost for ever.' said Monroe.

'It won't be because he's an art buff, that's for sure.' said Maddox.

'What other stereotypes of art thief are there? There must be more than one general type.' said James.

'Although I've never, ever known art to be stolen intrinsically for its own sake there are motives other than money. The Mafia are major players in the world of antique trafficking and art crime. Often it's as a cash alternative but at times it's a status symbol.

The Nazis stole art to steal away heritage and culture as a means to promote their own power and to procure status. There are thieves who steal art so as to bolt on a semblance of culture and sophistication. The fact that they know nothing about the art doesn't deter them from parading it and bragging about their acquisition. It's like an attempt to buy into a higher class, albeit in a criminal social structure.' said Monroe.

'Scott said that he'd been having trouble with the gang. When I popped in to see how Scott and his mum were he told me of the trouble Finn had been causing on the estate, goading him to fight and generally throwing his weight around. He reckons it'd have been easier if he'd just knocked him out and had done with it but Mrs Malkin didn't seem to approve of that method. Of course it's all gone quiet now. Do you think Finn was actually jealous of Scott, now he's moving in so called high society?' said Maddox.

'It's true to form that this would be a crook's way of foisting himself into artistic circles, or he might see it this way. It's a bizarre sort of one-upmanship, "You work in a gallery but I have my own," sort of idea.' said Monroe. 'Most art thefts are conducted by career criminals. They start small and climb the ranks, armed robbery and art theft go hand in hand. As the value of the item increases so does the violence. It's a squalid world. Your security guard should consider himself lucky, if he'd got in the way it could've got very nasty.'

'All of this puts me directly back to square one. Any ideas I might have had are no good at all, it seems. If it's unlikely for the sketch to have been stolen specifically I'm not sure where to look next. We'll just keep putting one foot in front of the other and see where it takes us.' said James.

'If you can follow the money then you're in with a chance once the sketch surfaces on the black market. English Old Masters are in vogue at the auctions. Although the unofficial markets won't reach the sale price that the catalogue listings might they do follow the pattern, albeit a peg or so lower on the scale. If the Constable doesn't come up for sale then you've little chance of catching either it or the culprit. Nevertheless, we'll keep our eyes and ears open whilst hoping for the best.' said Monroe.

'Thank you for your time. I'll keep you informed, even if there isn't much to report.' said James. Walking back to the car he chatted to Maddox. 'That wasn't the most encouraging meeting I've been in, but it was interesting. I'm pleased with what you tell me about your chat with Finn's cronies. Their falling out could really work in our favour if we play our cards right. I'm pleased with that result at least. Nevertheless, I've had enough of this for today. I've got a mountain of paperwork waiting in my office, I think I'll attack that this afternoon. Filing and form filling always clears my head. Would you be a good chap and speak to the fire officer for me?'

'I'd be happy to. What do you want to know?'

'Try and get your head around the science of how a fire starts and burns. How long can a fire smoulder before it'd set off the alarms? If we can figure that out it will give us another angle to find who's at the bottom of this, or at least a time frame of when the mischief started. Does Finn's expertise run to setting controlled fires? I'd have had him down as a quick flash and fast burn type - more showy that way and less skilled, I imagine.'

'That's a good plan. It'll give us a time frame to scour the security footage for, rather than being faced with days and days of CCTV with no clue what we're looking for.'

'I need to clear away the stains of the seedy underworld.' said James as they drove back to Mossleigh. 'I'll drop you off and then pop in to see Beth before I head back. In the meantime tell me all about your lovely Hetty. I can say "your" Hetty now, can't I? Don't be shy and tell me all the details. There's nothing like the story of young love to give me hope in humanity again.'

Maddox blushed profusely, but the twinkle in his eye suggested a willingness to talk and the journey passed quickly in the glow of romance recounted.

Chapter Nine

The sun was bright and the unblemished blue sky boded well for a dry Saturday. A succession of dry weather had kept the volunteers of the watering rota busy but it meant that the ground was perfectly dry and conditions were optimum for the Annual WI Croquet Crown that day. The Green was a pasture directly off the High Street which bisected the village into two halves. Directly opposite was a small row of shops which served the community of Mossleigh and the long stretch of grass was backed by a small lake before houses once again filled up the geography of the village. Even at this early hour there was plenty of activity as people went about the necessary preparations. Mae, the WI President had set her husband Richard the task of marking out the courts. Just then the hoops looked set for a game more appropriate to Alice in Wonderland but the layout was gradually taking on a more conventional aspect as Terry shouted and gesticulated to redirect Richard before he hammered the hoops home.

In the planning and preparation stage a whole evening had been spent in The Badger finalising tournament timetables and deciding upon the rules of play. Association Croquet was out of the question. The court would be too large for the space available on The Green, the game would last too long for the number of competitors and, if truth be told, the rules of play were far too complicated for all but the most dedicated players. The first plan had been to play Golf Croquet, this being the simplest form of the game. Even beginners could take part if they chose as it really is just a matter of taking turns at hitting a ball with a mallet through a series of hoops. This was quickly shoved out of court, in every sense of the word, as too simplistic and quite boring for the more seasoned players. Croquet has acquired a reputation for encouraging a spirit of vicious competition over the centuries and Mossleigh contestants were no exception. After much discussion, and many of Arthur's famed pints, Garden Croquet was agreed upon. This followed the Lawn or Court setting which is within a rectangle that can vary in size. If contestants played doubles and each game consisted of only one turn through the six hoops each leg of the tournament could be over within an hour. The earlier matches would be over much quicker until the competitors became more evenly matched. As it was, the size of the court meant that they would be able to host two games consecutively so that competitors wouldn't have to wait too long between matches. Garden Croquet allows more scope for a good game between well practised players as bonus strikes can be earned although no penalties are given if the ball is struck off the court, leaving not too much of a handicap for the novice players. Natalie also had the excellent idea of setting up a few hoops away from the competition courts so that those not in the tournament could enjoy a knock-about and join in the fun. Kirsty had completed the arrangements by offering some of her white science lab coats left over from her university days, so that the referees could look the part. A referee isn't a strict requirement for a croquet match but as the Croquet Crown trophy was at stake it seemed a wise precaution to have a couple of unbiased individuals on hand. Terry had offered his expertise and, although his body wasn't as capable since his stroke, his knowledge and expertise was undiminished and invaluable. Darcy was to preside over the second court as, although she still kept on referring to Hoops as Wickets and was more accustomed to the American nine hoops game, she was a seasoned player. She was to defer to Terry for advice on any dispute or discrepancy but the committee were hoping that a pervading atmosphere of generous sportsmanship would prevail.

Sgt Maddox had been called upon to fulfil his civic duty and be present in his official capacity that day. He wasn't required to be on duty until later but he was already wandering about The Green in his uniform, albeit with his jacket off for the time being. His boss, Chief Inspector Buckley was also hovering around the sidelines. No doubt her elevated rank excluded her from such menial duties but as she was competing in the games and vying for the Croquet Crown there was no keeping her away. Likewise DCI Benedict James was also visible on the scene. The saxophone case slung over his shoulder suggested that he was also off duty.

Beth let go of Drew's hand and ran to greet her twin brother. 'Benji, you made it! Are Lexi and the girls coming too?'

Benedict hugged Beth and shook Drew's hand. 'Lexi says she'll be over later if she can. I think the girls will be with her too - as moral support I suspect. They hate my squeaking, as they unkindly refer to my musical attempts.'

'I'm so glad that you and Jonti have laid aside your musical snobbery and have joined forces.' said Beth.

'It's as Jonti often says, when you're playing in the middle of a busy field nobody is listening anyway.' said Benedict.

Beth's son, Jonti, was a trombonist with the BBC Philharmonic and his Uncle played first clarinet in the Police Band which led to much light hearted jesting. Today however they had called a truce and were to play together. Jonti had called together some chums from his Brass Band competition days, when scores in Blackpool Winter Gardens would make or break his weekend. He tried to revisit his roots whenever Mossleigh had a "bit of a do." He insisted that it was good for his pride but Beth wondered if it was more to do with the excellent ales at The Badger, which often came with the landlord's compliments to the star who had come back home. Today, along with his Uncle, Jonti and his associates made up an ad hoc swing band and were embracing the trend for all things vintage by performing a Glen Miller tribute set. They were to set up their music stands next to the tea tent as per Jonti's instructions. He'd insisted that this was to maintain the vintage theme and would guarantee them an audience but Beth knew her son better. Ever since he was a small boy Jonti had possessed the knack of befriending old ladies in possession of a tea pot. Nowadays this had progressed to older men in possession of a pint tap, but as The Badger didn't open until midday he was falling back into his old ways.

'Who's competing in the Croquet Crown this year? Will it be stiff competition or is it already in the bag?' asked Jonti.

'I can't remember who's in the earlier stages but I can take a guess who'll be in the quarters or the semis - unless a wild card surprises us and climbs through the ranks.' said Beth.

'Such as?'

'Natalie, CI Buckley, Mae and your dad are hot favourites. Natalie has an unofficial book open on them if you're wanting to put money on it.'

'I'm shocked at the seedy underworld in this little village. It seems so unassuming at first glance.'

'I wouldn't be too shocked. There's a limit on how much you can bet. I think Natalie has said a fiver.'

'I'd better go and put my five pounds on dad then - don't let me down, will you?'

Drew waved away the gesture. 'You can't be sure, anything could happen. As for wild cards, Theo and Sally are completely unknown and Gareth Foster can be pretty handy with a mallet, or so I've heard.'

'Are you competing, mum?' asked Jonti.

'No.' replied Beth. 'I'd like to have played with your dad but I'm not good enough and I don't want to spoil his chances. He's paired up with Richard today.'

Benedict walked over and joined in the conversation. 'The village looks truly amazing, Beth. I hope you win the Britain in Bloom award. Mossleigh deserves it! Every basket and hanger looks perfect.'

'Thank you Benji.' said Beth. 'Everyone has worked so hard. I hope that we at least get Runner Up or Highly Commended. Morning and night people are on a rota to dead-head and water all the pots and baskets. It's never ending in this dry weather. I'm glad it's made a good show though, the village is already busy with visitors. I think that Arthur will be busy at The Badger, Eileen in her tea rooms and there'll still be plenty of visitors requiring refreshment in our WI tea and cakes tent. Speaking of which, I said I'd help to get things ready so I'd better be off.' Beth walked over to the bunting-bedecked gazebo where Natalie, Emma and Hetty were already busy.

Drew and Benedict stayed chatting.

'I've asked Rick to come over. It's quintessentially British in Mossleigh today, with the Croquet Crown and the floral displays. He really should see it. This is English rural life at its best, a bit cliché maybe but none the worse for that.' said Drew.

'It's a good job that the tournament is scheduled for early summer or he'd have missed his chance.' said Benedict. 'When does he fly back home?'

'Oh, there's no rush. He's with us for the foreseeable future I should say. He's got the chance of taking up a research post at MAG and I think he's accepted it. I know that he intends to and I presume that the formalities have been processed.'

'He must have changed his mind then. I spoke to Rick the other day, just for some background on the Constable case, and he said that he'd be sure to leave me a forwarding address as he was planning to go home very soon.'

'Did he? How strange!' said Drew. 'I hope the grant didn't fall through, he'll be so disappointed. I know he likes it in England and he has a special affection for MAG, so he'll be sad to leave. Did you know that he stayed here many years ago as a young student? Apparently he was on a student exchange programme when he was working on his Master's dissertation.'

'I didn't know that. It's a small world, isn't it?'

Benedict seemed to ponder on this last bit of information and was mulling over several implications which it may or may not hold. That was the trouble with his job, nothing could stay as innocent as it seemed and it bred an inherent distrust. However, his face cleared as he recognised Jonti waving as he approached from the opposite end of the field. That is, he presumed that it was Jonti. What he saw was a group of figures, all carrying musical instruments of varying sizes. One of the group was waving heartily and although his eyesight wasn't as sharp as it used to be it had to be Jonti gesticulating wildly. He waved back enthusiastically and relished the introduction to Jonti's fellow musicians. He was looking forward to spending the day with his nephew and knew by stereotype that his brass playing friends would be notoriously easy to get along with, especially when a bar featured in the equation. Although his more mature years meant that his distance vision was diminished, the benefit of such maturity meant that his advanced career easily allowed him the ability to pay for more than his fair share at The Badger. To a group of jobbing musicians this would make him an exceptionally welcome member to their group and would encourage them not to mind his encumbered musical ability. He'd already organised with Arthur to set up a tab to his account and had also requested some of Edward's choice bar meals to be thrown into the mix. He figured that he could absorb the shock and considered it a fair price to be admitted into such distinguished musical society. Saying goodbye to Drew he marched off to join his nephew and new friends with an unusual jauntiness in his step.

The sequence and projected times for the games had been posted but most of the contestants had gathered for the opening of the tournament. Darcy and Mae stood behind a table on which stood the coveted trophy. A miniature silver croquet mallet rested at an oblique angle and a silver crown was fixed as though hanging on the edge of the handle. Along the plinth were rows of the names of the contestants who had won and subsequently handed on each year. The lineage of victors stretched back over many years. At either side of the main trophy were two silver plated miniatures of the trophy which could be retained permanently. At either end of the long table rested two magnificent bouquets supplied by Nicola Farrington, proprietor of the village Florist shop. Not being content with a degree in Floristry, Nicola was a newly fledged RHS winner and her increasing level of skill and creativity was evident in the sumptuous displays which would also be given to the winning couple. Ringing the silver service bell, loaned from Beth's hallway, Mae officially opened the tournament. The two referees, in almost white lab coats, led the first four couples to their courts. Terry leaned on Natalie's arm as he crossed the grass to the court. A seat in the centre of the taped court edge meant that he could sit comfortably all day and keep a sharp eye on proceedings. Darcy had been provided with a similar convenience but it was doubtful that she would make much use of the provision. Even at this early stage she was stalking the players up and down the court, which was particularly off-putting for the novices who were chalked up to play these opening games. Although these early games were entertaining, with mallets striking haphazardly and red or yellow balls veering off indiscriminately, they weren't particularly captivating and visitors began to wander around the other amusements available. Emma took her daughter through the paces on the knock-about court while her husband, Nathaniel, sat making a daisy chain to crown her as victor regardless of hoops missed and mallets manhandled. The WI refreshment tent did a roaring trade. Cake and sandwich plates magically restocked thanks to the previous week of busy baking from the WI members. A few craft stalls gave a pleasant diversion and filled charity tins with notes and coins. Many of the items were rare finds of old school skill and were going for a song in aid of a good cause. The newly formed swing band were obviously "In The Mood" judging by the gusto of the performance and the extravagant ad lib. sections, and the open trombone case was steadily filling with a regular flow of notes and pennies as a testament to the visitors' relish of their performance. All proceeds were to be donated to the WI's chosen charities.

The afternoon wore on and volunteers changed shifts. Beth handed over the tea pot to another pair of willing hands and hurried to the croquet courts to be in time to see Drew and Richard win the toss to break. Drew chose to play yellow. They were playing against Theo and Sally who had proved to be deceptively good players having hidden their light under a bushel until it was time to shine. This was the semi-final and they'd got to this stage with relative ease. The band had stopped playing so that Jonti and Benedict could join the spectators. Even Sgt Maddox was neglecting his duty and was standing with Hetty, Nathaniel and Emma to watch. The game passed without much comment until a groan broke the tense silence as Drew made a push instead of making a clean shot. He raised his hand to confess and acknowledge the fact before the referee made comment. Theo took up his advantage and pegged out his first ball. Determined not to let his team mate down Drew redoubled his efforts and won a bonus stroke for a roquet. Balls inevitably veered off court to be returned one length of the mallet into the boundary and balls played out of turn were returned to the status quo ante as before the mishap. The noise from the spectators rose and fell, from murmurs of approval to groans of disappointment as the tide for victory rose and fell. It was a closely matched game and took some time to conclude. The concurrent match had finished a while ago and whoever won this game would face Nicola's fiancé, Gareth, and CI Buckley in the final. It was down to the last hoop when Drew and Richard's doom was set. Unfortunately, nobody but Beth and Benedict noticed that Theo's winning stroke was a disqualifying double tap. The crowd was less than silent by this point and the duplicate noise went unheard but Beth and Benedict saw the repeated action which gave extra impetus for Theo's ball to peg out first. A roar of applause overtook the competitors and Drew and Richard gave hearty congratulations to Sally and Theo. Neither Terry nor Darcy, who had joined in watching since the other court had concluded, had seen the misdemeanour and there was nothing that the witnesses could do but nurse their disgust.

As they watched the final match Beth recounted that final stroke to Drew who just shrugged his shoulders as there could be no redress. Justice was served in a fashion as CI Buckley and Gareth were on top form and Sally and Theo knew that they were out of their depth. Theo tried a change of strategy by playing a series of scatter shots. It was to be presumed that the thinking behind this tactic was that, if they couldn't place their own balls well enough to compete, they could at least scatter their opponents balls to a less dangerous position. However, such a negative state of play is rarely productive and the winning couple were too ahead of the game and too adept to be thwarted. Drew reassured Beth that the double tap was irrelevant as they would have lost in the final anyway. CI Buckley had achieved what she'd come for and Gareth was thrilled to be on the winning team. The Chief Inspector happily accepted the complimentary bouquet but Gareth didn't think that Nicola would want her own flowers back and so presented them to Darcy with gratitude for her role as referee.

As Beth and her family walked back to the house they discussed the highs and lows of the day.

'I'm sorry that Rick didn't come today. He's missed a rare opportunity to see Britain at its best.' said Drew.

'Yes, it's a shame. I'm sad that Matt couldn't come either. I know he wanted to hear Benji play his sax.' said Beth.

Matt was Beth and Drew's youngest son. He'd been abroad on business but had hoped to attend the festivities as soon as he got off the plane. On entering the lounge they encountered his long figure stretched out, fast asleep on the sofa. Jet lag had obviously got the better of him. This state of affairs wasn't to Primrose's satisfaction though and, ecstatic at finding that Uncle Matt had come to visit, she pounced on him with shrieks of delight soon rearranging matters to suit her liking.

Chapter Ten

Benedict had decided to go home and catch up with the wife and daughters he'd inadvertently continued to miss throughout the day at the Croquet Crown. He suspected that they'd purposefully avoided his "squeaking." However, Primrose couldn't bear that all of her Uncles should abandon her at such short notice and so Matt had been persuaded to attempt to counter his jet lag on Emma's sofa later that night. Jonti had opted for a real bed in his old room and everyone had agreed to meet back at Beth's for lunch the next day. There was a surfeit of sandwich and cake left from the WI refreshment tent and Beth was sure that they wouldn't go to waste if she bought a supply back home. However, after a day of dainty nibbles on the Saturday Beth felt sure that everyone would appreciate something a bit more heartening. Although it made for a strange Sunday lunch Beth took the WI resolution to reduce food waste seriously and was determined to make use of the surplus stock whilst there were plenty of willing mouths to feed. As a supplement she bubbled up a large pan of leek and potato soup bolstered with courgettes and sweet potatoes and then made a couple of quick treacle puddings in the microwave to fill any unsatisfied corners. The jumbled menu suited the family party atmosphere and people happily dunked ham sandwiches into the soup as they chatted. Whether there was space or not everybody managed at least one helping of treacle sponge and custard.

'I'm disappointed that Rick didn't show up.' said Drew. ' I was hoping he could have stayed over and spent some time with us. I'd like to get to know him better, he's a very clever man although he doesn't blow his own trumpet.'

'Unlike me!' said Jonti.

'In oh so many ways.' said Matt, fulfilling the obligatory brotherly banter quota.

'I've heard that, not only is he the head Curator of his museum but he is also Director of a board that has oversight over several prestigious museums throughout Holland. He has a wealth of knowledge which crosses over many cultures and he gives lectures all over the world. I do wonder if all this learning restricts his heart and soul a little when it comes to art.' said Drew.

'Brace yourselves, here comes the Constable debate again!' said Emma.

'I'm just saying that knowledge isn't everything.' said Drew, realising that his audience wasn't in a sober enough mood for a serious art discussion. He changed his tack to suit the homely atmosphere. 'He is learning to appreciate our cuisine though and he's missed out on your mum's legendary soup.'

'In that case I'm glad he's not here now, otherwise it'd mean less for us.' said Jonti who had eaten considerably more than his fair share already.

The shrill tones of the telephone ringing made Beth jump to her feet but Drew stopped her with a gesture as she was penned in by diners who had pushed back their chairs to stretch their legs. As Drew had a clear path he went to take the call.

Conversation dwindled as people strained to understand the increasingly ambiguous one-sided conversation. Drew returned to the table and all eyes were expectantly raised in enquiry waiting for curiosity to be satisfied.

'That was Benji. He reckons he's not destined to sit down to a family Sunday lunch more than once a month. They've found Finn. He's not dead, but he's only just alive.' said Drew.

'Where was he found?' asked Beth.

'I gather he was found behind the Whitworth. It sounds like he's been knocked about a fair bit and then left for dead in one of the Museum's trade refuse skips. Benji is taking Forbes to the hospital now to have a look at the lad to see what can be learned from his various bumps and bruises until he can speak for himself, presuming that he'll ever be able to. I'm not sure that's a certainty from the way Benji spoke.' said Drew.

'I thought I'd heard you say that Forbes was a forensic pathologist.' said Nathaniel. 'Isn't he supposed to wait until they're dead? Hopefully his services won't be required at all if the poor chap pulls through.'

'You're quite right, Forbes is a pathologist, but he's a unique specimen. He's an unlikely mixture of "geeky nerd" and "dashing wanna-be detective." In safe company he's quite willing to read between the lines and make a prognosis off the record.' said Beth. 'I knew Benji was sure that Finn would turn up eventually but I don't think he expected it in such a manner as this.'

'He's going to the hospital now but he says he'll drop by later tonight to let us know how he gets on. Maddox is meeting him at the hospital and he says he'll come back with him unless something else crops up later.'

Emma brought matters back to a more palatable subject by explaining that Primrose needed to go home for a bath and early bedtime as tomorrow was a school day, term not quite being over. So as to squeeze in as much uncle therapy as possible Matt and Jonti were to go back to Lilac Cottage and partake of milk and biscuits once Primrose was washed and in her pyjamas. The question of who was to have the honour of reading her a bed time story was yet to be decided. How she would choose between her dad, who was her usual favourite, and either of her uncles would have to be seriously considered while Emma was washing her hair.

After clearing away the dishes into the dishwasher the evening was left free to Beth and Drew. Once the statutory cups of tea were shared Beth decided to go and play piano while Drew and Noodle, the aged Bichon, settled to snooze together on the sofa. Noodle was very old and spent most of his time asleep regardless of external events but he cherished the opportunity of a slumber buddy and snored away with a deeper contentment curled into Drew's chest, their noses almost touching as they both slept.

Beth wanted to think things through but was desperately short of material facts to contemplate. No doubt more factors to fit into the equation would appear as time progressed but as yet there wasn't anything to occupy her mind. She filled the void with a technically demanding Mozart Sonata. The Sonata in F was a piece that she'd played many years ago at college when she'd first met Drew. Her piano teacher's promptings were still doing their job in the pencil markings on the score she had played all those years ago. The technical complexities of trying to remember the notes whilst figuring out the irregular rhythms of treble and bass combined to occupy her mind while the simplistic beauty of the melody soothed her soul. She could remember, as if it were only yesterday, chatting over a mug of coffee in her teacher's music room. They'd discussed the lyrical qualities which Mozart's music always boasted. Although played on the piano, parts of the slow second movement at first suggest an oboe solo but then transform into an operatic aria. At that time Beth was studying "Le Nozze di Figaro" and she was convinced that the middle section of the movement reminded her of the Countess's plaintive aria. They were so convinced of the allusion that the opening lines of the libretto, "Dove sono i bei momenti" was scribbled over the treble clef melody line. It was a long time since she'd played this sonata properly, in fact she wondered if she had ever given it her proper attention - being mostly consumed by thoughts of Drew at that time. Now seemed as good a time as any to give it the proper concentration it deserved. Given the romantic nature of the aria she'd likened the piece to, there was a decided irony in her neglect of the music all those years ago, her mind being absorbed in a romance of her own. "Where are all those beautiful moments of sweetness and pleasure?"

was now getting the full works in its imagined application to Mozart's Sonata in F, Adagio K332. Some hours later Beth returned to find Drew and Noodle still sleeping and was grateful that in her life, unlike the Countess, those "beautiful moments of sweetness and pleasure" still remained. She kissed Drew gently to wake him and went to put the kettle on. Seeing Benji pull into the driveway she reached for another mug and also the tin of cupcakes still lingering from the previous day..

Once suitably stocked with refreshments the three sat and chatted over recent events.

'Well that was a bit of a shock, wasn't it?' asked Beth. 'I know you expected Finn to resurface sometime but I don't think you expected to find him in a rubbish heap, did you?'

'We all expected to find the Constable in the bin, but not the culprit!' said Benedict.

'He wasn't exactly in the bin though, was he?' said Drew.

'In actual fact we think he was, to begin with.' said Benedict. 'I took Forbes to the hospital to have a good look over the lad and he thinks that he may have actually been thrown into the bin. The signs hint that the attacker strangled the foolish creature and then, presuming him to be dead, quite literally dumped him. Fortunately for Finn this wasn't quite the case and in a brief moment of consciousness he managed to climb out before he fully succumbed to his injuries. Fortune really did smile on the lad because the bin was quite full, giving him plenty of refuse to clamber up and climb out. It's doubtful he'd have had the energy to haul himself out of an empty one as those trade bins are deep. The bruising around his throat and the decided stink emanating from him would seem to support such a theory.'

'The poor thing. He must have been terrified!' said Beth. 'It sounds like he's a regular scoundrel himself but nobody deserves that.'

'Whatever he's been through he's out of it now. He's totally unconscious and looks to remain that way for some time. The doctor has sedated him quite heavily, even though he was already unconscious. Apparently they do that to give the brain time to settle and heal after being starved of oxygen and getting a rattling. They've scanned him but there's too much swelling to see much of any potential damage to his brain. Once the sedation wears off, if he wakes up, then they can decide what they're dealing with. He's got plenty of bruising showing on his head and upper body. Forbes gave him a thorough examination but there's no knowing if this occurred before or after he was strangled. Because it was only to within an inch of his life there's no time of death or stages of lividity to establish a sequence of events. It could be that all the other bruises are a result of being flung into a metal rubbish bin. It'd be heavy work tossing him high enough to go into one of those big bins.' said Benedict.

'It was good of Forbes to go the extra mile and examine a live body.' said Drew.

'I said as much to him myself when I thanked him for his prognosis. Forbes reassured me that the poor creature was more dead than alive and so it wasn't too far outside his comfort zone. He's a good chap and, although it takes some time for him to admit it, he likes a bit of action outside of the lab. He thinks it impresses the ladies, not that his natural charm and twinkling eyes aren't enough to win them over in the first place.' said Benedict.

'So where does this leave us? What's your next line of enquiry?' asked Beth.

'I'm afraid that Finn's unhappy escapade doesn't give us any new leads as yet. There's no point in Forbes doing the whole forensic thing as the rubbish in the bin will have contaminated any fibres there might have been and he'll be covered in traces of all sorts of stuff. We just have to hope that he comes round and is cognitive so as to be able to give us a sufficient explanation of events, from that very first day at the museum up to this present crisis. No doubt he'd have been secretive in the normal run of events, but hopefully this will have scared some sense into him - if he gets the chance to learn his lesson. In the meantime I'd like to speak to Drew's friend Rick, but as yet nobody has been able to get hold of him.' said Benedict.

'Why do you want to speak to Rick?' asked Drew.

'I can't quite put my finger on it. There are a few things that just don't add up, like his sudden decision to leave the country. There are also a few vague elements that seem to be adding up rather too nicely, I fancy, but I may be getting ahead of myself here. It's just a good old fashioned hunch I need to lay to rest. The fact that nobody can get hold of him gives me even more cause for concern.'

'You can't seriously think that Rick is responsible for the Constable theft? Surely he wouldn't go around starting fires and leaping through glass rooftops?' said Drew.

'No, of course Rick hasn't turned cat burglar or arsonist. I'm quite certain that Finn has those deeds on his conscience. But why shouldn't I consider that Rick is behind it? He's as good a candidate as any.' said Benedict.

'Don't forget you're still under the microscope, Drew. It could be anyone at all.' said Beth.

'So it could. I'd forgotten that I'm technically still under suspicion.' said Drew.

'Indeed you are.' said Benedict. 'However, I wouldn't lose too much sleep over it as you're only under the spotlight as much as the next man, and the glare on you is diminishing as each new day fades away.' said Benedict.

'With regard to Rick, just bear in mind that it is Sunday. He could be anywhere. He's got a wide network of friends and he's notorious for not taking his mobile with him. He could be anywhere in England and having a jolly day with a clear conscience.' said Drew.

'Of course he could, but it's my job to prepare for the worst, I'm afraid. I've set up an all ports alert in case he has the inclination to make a dash for it and I've the paperwork in motion for a search warrant to gain entry into his flat and have a very earnest look around.' said Benedict.

'Oh dear. That does sound serious.' said Beth. 'There's more to this than you're letting on, Benji. Never mind, you keep your secret if you must.'

'It's not quite as sinister as you're making out, Beth.' said Benedict. 'I've only set things in motion,

I'm not making it a priority yet. I can't request a fully fledged raid based on a mere hunch. I'm not keeping secrets - you know me better than that. I've just got a feeling that our Dutch friend might tie in with a very old case that a colleague of mine is working on. It's nothing more than overlapping circles of coincidence and I won't besmirch your friend by gossiping until I've solid facts to go on.' said Benedict.

'You're on about the old Turner theft from years ago, aren't you? You're like a TV sleuth!' said Drew.

'How on earth do you know about that?' asked Benedict.

'Oh, come on, Benji. You know that artistic circles are the worst gossips out!' said Drew.

'What Turner theft?' asked Beth. 'Don't you dare leave me in the dark! You'll have to tell me now, if Drew knows as much about it anyway. Even if you are wrong you'll have to explain yourself fully now, it's only fair.' pleaded Beth.

Benedict sighed and fortified himself with more cake before giving Beth all of the background of the case that DCI Monroe was working on. 'Monroe said the trail was suddenly warming up after years of waiting. Once I'd learned that Rick had been at MAG as a student it didn't take much imagination to join the dots. I don't know the specifics of the case but the timing fits perfectly. It may just be a series of coincidences but we all know that's rarely the case. The point is that we won't know until I've managed to find Rick so that he at least has the chance to exonerate himself. Meanwhile Finn is fighting for his life.'

'You can't think that Rick is responsible for Finn's injuries. Would he resort to violence and murder? I just can't imagine it!' said Drew.

'Who knows what a person is really capable of when pushed? Although I have to admit that I struggle to imagine Rick beating up a fit young lad and then heaving him into a rubbish bin. Nevertheless, I've seen stranger things.' said Benedict.

'He doesn't look physically strong enough.' said Drew.

'It's quite shocking what a frail body can do when the adrenalin is pumping and the red mist rises. I wouldn't rule him out purely from that perspective.' said Benedict.

'There's no point in sitting here and guessing.' said Beth. 'You're wasting your energy on "ifs" and "maybes". You'll just have to wait and see.'

'You're quite right, Beth.' said Benedict. 'I've already lost my Sunday afternoon and I'm not going to lose my evening too. I want to see Maddox again in the morning so I was hoping that I could stay here tonight and speak to him in person instead of driving back tonight and discussing matters over the phone. Is that OK with you, Beth?'

'Of course it is. You know you don't need to ask. So how are you gentlemen going to finish your evening?' said Beth.

'I was wondering if you both fancied a stroll over to The Badger? The beer in the city pales in comparison with Arthur's ales. His cellar is excellently managed and I like to give credit where it's due. In this case the only true compliment is to walk over and buy a pint.' said Benedict.

'You two can go and you can drink my pint for me.' said Beth. 'I'm tired after a long day yesterday and not much rest today. I'll take over your shift on the sofa with Noodle.'

Drew was already reaching for his shoes and they were soon walking in the cool evening across The Green, laughing at how seriously the Croquet Crown was taken only one day earlier. The Badger was already bustling and the two new additions were greeted with a hearty welcome as they walked into the bar. Bobby Maddox looked a little flustered when Benedict entered, torn between wanting to please his temporary boss but not wanting to leave the pleasant company of Henrietta. A quick shake of the head reassured Maddox as Benedict shook his hand and was introduced to Henrietta.

'Don't worry. We're both off duty tonight.' said Benedict. 'I'm hanging around here tonight so that we can have a meeting first thing tomorrow. How about breakfast at Beth's?'

Business being suitably arranged Benedict said goodbye and went in search of Drew who had got absorbed in conversation at the bar. It transpired that Matt and Jonti hadn't yet made it back to the city and had lured Nathaniel away for an hour or two despite an early start at the dairy in the morning. Jonti made moves to buy a round, insisting that he owed his uncle at least one drink after his generosity the previous day. Benedict was inclined to agree. He'd thought that he was prepared for the total but he was shocked nevertheless at the musicians' aptitude to accommodate free beer. Drew overruled the decision and insisted on buying everyone a drink as it was an opportunity to celebrate all the male members of the family finding themselves together for a time. When he returned with a tray of drinks Jonti and Benedict were already embroiled in debating the various merits and failings of brass band, swing band and wind orchestra. Benedict had so enjoyed his day playing sax with his nephew's band that he was energetically agreeing with everything Jonti said. Unusual as this was, it wasn't a conversation destined to thrill the rest of the party. Drew caught Nathaniel's eye and, with his usual straightforward bluntness, Nathaniel told Jonti to shut up so that folks could talk about topics that people actually care about. The group laughed and occupied their mouths to better purpose by drinking their beer.

Chapter Eleven

DCI James and Sgt Maddox made an early start to their day. The enthusiastically early meeting was due in part to their desire to make some tangible progress on the case, but was probably largely due to the pile of bacon and egg muffins that Beth laid on for breakfast. Long ago Beth's mother had taught her the simple truth that the way to a man's heart was through his stomach. Drew had revised this maxim to suggest that for Beth food bought her information. Beth simply acknowledged that in life there are many absolutes: Wealth procures power whilst food secured secrets. She often said that waiters would make the best intelligence sources insisting that they must be privy to all sorts of secrets on every level, from small domestic intrigue through to high flying business and politics. There was nothing underhand in Beth's motives and the arrangement suited everyone. Benedict could be comfortable and well fed while Beth could be kept in the loop. As twins they'd always worked together and it was natural to share the workload and thinking now. This morning was no exception and, as Drew pottered about cleaning brushes and packing for a morning at the Whitworth, Beth ironed a pile of shirts while Benedict and Maddox ate a hearty breakfast and exchanged news and information gathered over the weekend.

'I met with the Fire Officer as you asked.' began Maddox. 'I meant to tell you about it yesterday but it got pushed aside once Finn was found.'

'Was it a worthwhile meeting? Can it help us?' asked James.

'I'll leave that for you to decide. It was as much as I could do to pare down the scientific jargon to something that I could understand. I made notes of everything he told me so I could read those out or I can give the gist as I understood things first. Which would you prefer?'

'Just give me the gist and we'll refer back to your notes to get into the science afterwards as and when is necessary.'

'I think I'll need my notes a bit, but I'll paraphrase. The Fire Officer said that the most relevant information regarding the fire that set the alarms off is that sparks and hot spots can linger for a long time - like a really long time.' Maddox began.

'That sounds vague. How long is really long?' asked James.

'Apparently it could easily be overnight. He gave an example of so called primitive societies that can bank down fires to keep embers smouldering overnight, or even so as to be portable in nests of moss. Apparently it's all down to something called the fire triangle. Three things combined cause fire; heat, oxygen and fuel. If a spark is insulated to keep its heat but oxygen is restricted it can stay dangerous for hours. The heat source is too weak to ignite flames, which makes it difficult to detect, but it's easily initiated and easily unleashed. It's one of the most significant causes of residential fires - your typical cigarette dropped down the sofa. A smouldering fire can spread slowly and silently for hours until it hits the critical combination of the three elements and then it erupts.'

'Thankfully that didn't happen at the gallery. At least the alarm went off before the place went up in flames. Vague as this is I do believe that this information is extremely helpful. Go on. What else did he say?'

'The main difference between smouldering and flaming combustion is that a flame occurs in the gas phase whereas smouldering occurs on the surface of whatever is fuelling it. Also, the temperature and heat of a smouldering fire is much lower. It grows slowly, about ten times slower than a flaming combustion. Often the first cause of damage is the toxic gas, such as carbon dioxide. It's gases such as this that eventually accumulate and are then finally ignited into a flaming fire.'

'In a nutshell, the fire could have been started days ago, although probably only a few hours previously. Is that right?' asked James. 'I presume that either a lot of skill or a lot of luck would have been needed for it to smoulder for a long time. What do they say was the source, or the fuel for the fire and what triggered the alarms?'

'The source of the fire was found under the floor boards at the back of the security suite. A light bundle of mattress foam and cotton sheeting had a central cloth that was gradually smouldering through the layers of graduating thickness. The museum has a CO fire detector as well as a standard smoke detector. The CO detector is the most sensitive and would have been more likely to activate the alarm. Alternatively a CO detector isn't so sensitive to plumes of smoke but in conjunction all bases are covered.'

'This tells us that the mastermind was quite calculating and very clever. It's likely that they're the thoughtful type and particularly wanted dear Brian out of the way.' said James.

'It also says that they didn't want flames licking the walls of the Whitworth or damage to any of the stock.' said Beth.

'You're quite right, Beth.' said James. 'It really does seem to point to a connoisseur, regardless of how strenuously Monroe keeps telling me that it won't be.'

'Or it tells us that somebody was either very lucky in not creating unwanted damage or very unlucky in mucking it up and not getting the pyrotechnics they'd hoped for. They might have wanted a show and it didn't pull off. Maybe they wanted more time and confusion but didn't manage it - maybe they had to get out quick before they'd got everything they wanted.' said Maddox.

'An excellent point.' agreed James. 'However, I'm inclined to view the concoction in the security suite as something that was carefully prepared after being tried and tested.'

Drew was washing his brushes in the kitchen sink whilst listening to the conversation and sensing the noose tighten around his absent friend's neck. 'I know it looks bad for Rick,' he said. 'I just can't imagine him giving way to such elaborate schemes. It really could be that they just botched the job but at least succeeded in getting Brian out of the way just long enough to do the job, or at least part of it.'

'Thank you, Drew, for dampening the flames of our enthusiasm. I really thought we were getting somewhere, but as you and Maddox say - anything is possible at this stage, more's the pity.' said James.

'I suppose that at least one of us should get some real work done. I'm off to the museum.' Drew spoke to Beth to arrange their domestic schedule for the afternoon. 'If you can wait until I get back we can have a late lunch together before you start teaching.' He kissed her and said goodbye.

Drew was just grabbing his portfolio and bag when Benedict's mobile rang. After a few seconds of listening Benedict waved at Drew, gesticulating for him to stop and wait. After issuing a few short commands to the caller and asserting that he would leave immediately he ended the call. Whatever the call was about it was obviously bad news. First in everybody's mind was the fate of poor Finn.

'I'm afraid I've got some bad news Drew, you'd better come back into the kitchen and put your things down.' James said. Although Drew would have been sad to hear that Finn had succumbed to his injuries he was surprised at Benedict's solicitude as he took his bag and portfolio and guided him to a chair. After a brief pause Benedict relayed the news of the phone call. 'That was the Met. Sally rang the station not too long ago. I'm afraid that your friend, Rick, can now explain his absence. Sally found him dead at the Whitworth this morning. He wasn't found straight away as he was in the archives. I am sorry Drew, I know that you liked him and had become quite friendly. I'm so sorry.'

'What on earth was he doing down in the archives? How long had he been there?' asked Drew. All sorts of questions came tumbling into his mind. Then, after seeing Benedict's expression, Drew realised that he hadn't yet heard the full story. He looked at his brother in law and steeled himself for what was to come. 'How did he die, Benji? Did he suffer?'

'I really am very sorry to have to tell you this, Drew. It's not nice, I'm afraid. He was strangled.'

'Oh, how awful!' Drew sat with his head in his hands as he imagined his friend's last tortured moments.

Forbes is on his way and Maddox and I will be meeting him there. I presume that you'll want to come with us?' Benedict phrased this as a question but he knew that Drew would want to face the situation head on.

Drew nodded his agreement and his face took on a resolute expression as he prepared to face some ugly scenes. Understanding the quiet strength of his gentle brother in law Benedict recognised Drew's determination to right these wrongs. It was a way to cope with such bitter truth.

'We will get to the bottom of this, Drew. Whatever it takes we'll find whoever did this.' said Benedict.

Beth knew that Drew needed to chase this one on his own in order to find peace and so she stayed home so as to be ready with food and comfort when he returned. Some might laugh but such practicality was tried and tested over the ages. Food was indeed the way to many hearts and Drew's heart would need some extra care and consideration. Let folks laugh, Beth knew how to care for those she loved.

On arrival at the gallery a sepulchral silence reigned, broken only by Sally's gradually subsiding sobs. Theo was administering the time honoured remedy of tea which was gradually working its wonders after her shock from finding Rick in such grisly circumstances.

Seeing Benedict, Brian made a hasty beeline to clear his reputation. "I can't believe this has happened, sir. Not on my watch again! I don't know what more I can do, whatever I do the fiend works around me!'

'Nobody holds you responsible, I'm sure.' reassured Benedict. 'Your conscientious approach is never in doubt. Just tell me what happened.'

'I'm on days this week. I did the usual handover at 6am and there was nothing to report. After the fiasco of the break-in I was determined not to get caught out and so I stayed in the security lodge watching the monitors like a hawk. You know I don't like being cooped up in here for too long, so when I couldn't stand it anymore I walked into the foyer to stretch my legs a bit. I kept flicking through the screens on my tablet and there was absolutely nothing to see. I kept a special eye on that glass roof - I know it's been repaired but once bitten, twice shy and all that. The cameras are also heat and motion sensitive but nothing set the alarms off.' said Brian.

'Well, there wouldn't be either of those elements, would there? Neither were available to the poor man.' said Benedict. 'It's not your fault that you didn't detect anything, how would you guess something like that?'

'Ordinarily I'd have patrolled around but that got me into trouble last time. I just can't win! If I'd stuck to my usual routine I'd have found him.' said Brian.

'And he'd still have been dead.' said Benedict.

'I know that, but I just feel so foolish. A dead body and I didn't know. What kind of a security guard is that?'

'Don't be so hard on yourself. Go and make yourself a brew and I'll come back to you after I've been downstairs. We'll put our heads together then and see what we can come up with.'

Pacified by James's reassurance Brian went back to his security suite and followed Benedict's instructions to the letter, NAFFI tea calming him as Earl Grey had calmed Sally. Drew smiled in appreciation of what he'd heard in the exchange. Benedict had calmed the distraught guard and yet still made him feel a valued part of the team. Realigning his thoughts to prepare for the spectacle below Benedict squared his shoulders and, taking Maddox and Drew with him, headed down to the archives.

After passing the PC on guard they stood on the threshold of the archives, surveying the tragic scene. Where Drew and Rick had amicably chatted, taunting each other's artistic preferences Rick now lay next to an overturned chair with arms and legs outstretched. Drew knew that it had to be Rick as Benedict had told him so. The particularly dapper clothes, now uncharacteristically disarranged and the long limbs supported the theory but the face bore no resemblance to the one that Drew had hoped, one day, to call friend. The once consistently composed face was now grotesquely contorted and dried blood covered the bottom and sides of his face. Drew turned away and stepped into the corridor to gather his wits. Forbes raised his head from scrutinising the corpse to see figures in the doorway and waved them in. He shrugged his shoulders to indicate that their caution not to contaminate the scene was unnecessary.

'There's nothing here to spoil. The place is as clean as a whistle. I've taken a few dust and fibre samples for form's sake but I can't think there's anything new to find. What you see is what you get here, I'm afraid. You don't need me for this case, you can see it all for yourself - it's as plain as day.' said Forbes.

Benedict let Maddox pass through first and then guided Drew into the room, keeping an eye on both, being fully aware that this was their first taste of gruesome death.

'Come on in, Drew.' said Benedict. 'I think it's important that you hear what Forbes has to say for yourself.'

Picking up the discarded chair he motioned for Drew to sit down but both Maddox and Drew manfully opted to stay standing.

Sensing that he had an audience Forbes explained the scene before them. 'There are no mysteries to unfold.' he began. 'The ligature marks around the throat suggest the obvious and the bleeding from the nose and ears confirm this. If the windpipe is only partially closed then such bleeding is likely to occur. I hardly need to go deeper to confirm my theory. The deep cut will be the fatal one and will have probably even severed the trachea. That will have done the damage as much as strangulation. He wouldn't have suffered for long - a minute at most.'

Benedict blessed Forbes for his tact in referring to the disturbing procedures required for post mortem examination as "go deeper." This term barely touched the reality of just how deep his examination could go. Acknowledging Benedict's gratified nod Forbes continued.

'There are a few ligature marks but the deepest measures 1.2mm and coincides with this wire that's so readily available nearby. You don't have to be a member of the Fine Art Trade Guild to know that this is industry standard.' said Forbes.

At this point Drew managed to find his voice. 'It's part of the gallery's old hanging system. It's a strong stainless steel that is wound and finished so as not to fray. It works in conjunction with a track and hanging system. We've stopped using this and now use invisible fixings.'

'There are no fingerprints, except the victim's. You can see the cuts on his fingertips where he grappled initially. The struggle would have been mercifully brief before his consciousness faded and his hands would have clenched in reflex.' said Forbes.

'It was too much to hope that the murderer's fingerprints would be left to save us the time and trouble ourselves.' said Maddox.

'There are plenty of cotton gloves to hand here, if you'll pardon the pun. I can take them for testing if you like, but it's doubtful that any of these were the particular pair that could have been used - they're all spotlessly clean. There may be DNA or sweat to help us but we'll have to eliminate the staff here first and that will take some time to process. It's highly unlikely that any of these gloves will show traces of the wire. Why would they leave them behind? ' said Forbes.

'We'll leave no stone unturned.' said Benedict. 'You'd better get on with it. In the mean time we'll revert to some old fashioned police techniques and time honoured detective thinking. Can you get the gent tidied up a bit and moved when you're sure there's nothing else to see, Forbes? Drew, you'd better join the queue and give Forbes and his pals the key to your soul - it'll only take a couple of swabs. Maddox and I will see what more our dear Brian can give us. Hopefully it won't be his awful tea.'

Sally had recovered her composure and seeing the efficacy of a good coffee the last time disaster had struck in the museum she'd repeated the gesture. DCI James returned to the atrium to be greeted with a freshly ground coffee which meant that, when he walked into the security lodge, he could legitimately wave away Brian's offer of a brew.

'Let's get down to business.' James began. 'Brian, you and I need to figure out how this fiend keeps slipping between our fingers. Nobody can be this lucky and somebody obviously thinks they've been mighty clever, but they'll have slipped up somewhere. You need to help me find out where.'

'I wish I could, sir. I really can't see how, but I won't stop trying.' said Brian. 'I'm taking this personally now. I can't have bad business like this happening under my nose.'

Scott had been visiting Finn at the hospital all morning and as soon as he entered the gallery he could tell that something was very wrong. Drew's pale and worried face convinced him that all was not well and he rushed over to his friend.

'Whatever's wrong, Drew?' You look like you've seen a ghost.' said Scott.

'I've seen a blighted and departed spirit, that's for sure.' said Drew. He then recounted the morning's unhappy discovery.

'Drew, that's awful! I'm so sorry. He seemed like a lovely bloke.' said Scott. The horror of what he'd just heard slowly sank in and Scott dropped onto a nearby chair as his legs became wobbly with the shock.

'I thought he was a lovely gentleman, but now I'm not so sure. Nobody is who I thought they were, or that's how it's beginning to feel.' said Drew.

'Well I'm just plain old Scott, you can be sure of that.' Scott regained his composure and stood to grasp Drew's hand to affirm the statement.

'That's reassuring.' smiled Drew. 'I gather that you've been to see Finn this morning. I thought he was still unconscious, did he know you were there?'

'No, he's completely out of it. But the nurses say that it's good if somebody talks to him, it might help bring him back. That PC on guard isn't going to chat to him, is he? So that just leaves me.'

'What about his family?' asked Drew.

Scott laughed. 'You're joking! His mum won't trouble herself to move away from the TV and her ciggies, and she's the only family that he knows of. His dad might still exist somewhere and he might even have a brother or sister, but if they do exist nobody knows of them. Brad and Leighton haven't the gumption to sit with an unconscious body and they won't go near the place because of the police guard even if they felt inclined to see Finn. They're still sulking anyway and he can rot for all they care.'

'Poor kid. He really is short of friends when he most needs them. It's good of you to go, especially as it's his fault that you've got all this trouble.'

'We may have followed different paths more recently but, in his own way, Finn was good to me when my dad died. I know he got me into all sorts of trouble but he helped me in the only way he knew how. He included me into his circle and kept watch over me. The stupid idiot never did know when to stop and he's really out of his depth now. But I won't forget the friend he was to me, not if I'm all he's got left.'

'If he does recover I hope he takes this second chance and puts it to good use. Maybe it'll be a new start and the opportunity to turn over a new leaf?'

'We can only hope he gets the chance.'

Sgt Maddox interrupted their conversation and asked if Scott would come with him and allow Forbes to take some swabs so that his DNA could be eliminated from the enquiry. The dreadful reality that he was actually now also in a murder enquiry hit Scott with full force and he was suddenly very afraid.

'You can't honestly think that I'd murder anyone? Oh, Lord. I'm the one with a criminal record - you're bound to think it was me! I wasn't even here, I've been at the hospital all morning.' Scott would have continued to babble if Drew hadn't come to his rescue.

'It's alright, our DNA will be all over the place here and they just need to match our DNA so that they can then ignore it.' Drew said. 'We've all done it, Scott. It's a shock, I know, but you're in safe hands. Maddox and James will sort it all out in the end - just remember that.'

Maddox put a caring, but guiding arm around Scott's shoulders to take him over to the corner where Forbes had set up his temporary forensic surgery.

'Just give Forbes here what he needs and then grab yourself a coffee.' said Maddox. 'You'd better leave the drink until after, otherwise "café arabica" might become the prime suspect. Mind you, that stuff is criminal. Take my advice and have a decent cup of tea.'

Chapter Twelve

Beth was in holiday mood and the bright sunshine of the day added to the brightness that Beth felt. Although it was still only morning she was already selecting clothes and jewellery for later that night. Her usual evening pupils had been reallocated to other slots and she intended to spend the whole day preparing for the long awaited dinner party. The full extent of her preparations actually amounted to weeks, if not months. They'd begun with an entire weekend in her pyjamas cutting and sewing the meticulously designed and crafted outfit. The construction process had now come full circle as she sat once again in her pyjamas stitching on a last minute addition of some handmade lace tatting to the neckline of the dress she'd made. It was a bargain find at a WI craft show and was the exact shade of vintage cream to coordinate with the colours of the dress and jacket she'd been so carefully working on. She insisted that she stay in pyjamas when dressmaking so as to be comfortable when crawling around for cutting and pinning, and also for ease of access when trying and fitting the garment. Drew knew that the reason was most likely to be that her thoughts were far too consumed with the project in hand to give thought to choosing commonplace, everyday wear. Admittedly, in this instance she was still in her night clothes because she was relishing a day off in the middle of the school term and had no intention of dressing until the time came to don the long planned outfit she'd been labouring over for so many weeks.

It was Conrad's birthday and his wife, Hyacinth, was hosting what was bound to be a spectacular dinner party. It was a select guest list with only six people dining. Theo and Sally would be joining Beth and Drew in dining with Conrad and Hyacinth. Hyacinth was pulling out all the stops and was bringing a professional chef into her kitchen. For as long as Beth had been designing and making her outfit she had been meeting regularly with Hyacinth to discuss menus and table decorations. The firm that Hyacinth had hired would have dealt with all of these considerations but Hyacinth had particularly wanted to attend to these matters herself. Because the staple matter of food was provided for she could have free rein in the details of staging the table. Conrad was being indulgently generous, as he usually was with his wife. He adored Hyacinth and did his best to spoil her, which wasn't difficult as she was easy to please. In this particular instance he insisted that he wanted everything to be a complete surprise and wanted Hyacinth to arrange matters entirely to her own taste saying that he'd be sure to like it if that was the bargain. His only stipulation was that she should spare no expense and must forward all invoices to his secretary so that he had no inkling of what was afoot. Conrad had suggested the option of enlarging the guest list but Hyacinth thought that quality was better than quantity, in both menu and guests alike, so only their closest friends were invited.

Beth was jolted from her quiet reverie as she stitched by the sharp tones of the telephone. Drew brought the receiver to her explaining that it was Hyacinth who wished to speak to her.

'Hello Beth.' said Hyacinth. 'There's a bit of a hiccup in proceedings tonight. The two waitresses that were due to attend tonight have been involved in a car accident. It's not serious, only minor injuries were sustained. However, they can't really be expected to work tonight. The chef says that all his regular staff are engaged elsewhere. He says that, at worst, he can approach an agency but this could take time and it's also a bit precarious as he can't personally vouch for who they might send. He wondered if we could suggest a couple of willing candidates. He can easily explain what they need to do, the most important things are that they are nicely presented, are pleasant and can follow simple instructions. I immediately thought of Hetty and Emma. Would Emma be willing and able to help, do you think?'

'I'm sure she'd be willing if she isn't too busy. Obviously I can't offer to look after Primrose for her so it depends upon if she's free and if Nat can look after Primrose. I'll call her straight away and ask. Have you spoken to Hetty yet?'

'Yes, I have. She's quite keen if Emma is able to help. She said she'd quite enjoy a chance to try something different. I explained that of course I'd pay the going rate and I understand that the chef will give them a meal. He said that there's nothing worse than serving delicious food when you're ravenously hungry and can't try what you're serving. He makes sure they get a taste in-between serving.'

'I'm sure that Emma would love to join in, especially if it involves a nice dinner and an evening with Hetty, even if she does have to look after us and clear up all of our dishes. I'll try her now and get back to you straight away. Don't worry, I'm sure we'll sort something out between us: You shall go to the ball!'

Hyacinth laughed and hung up so that Beth could call Emma. Of course Emma was keen to join in with the plan and Nat was happy to stay home with Primrose. The scurry was then on to find a uniform. Thankfully Beth didn't have to quickly sew up a black pencil skirt as Emma remembered her old youth orchestra uniform and a bow tie of Drew's finished the outfit. Hetty cobbled together a pair of black trousers (regulation funeral outfit) with a white shirt of Bobby's. The hunt was on for a second bow tie but if one couldn't be found it was a small concession which the chef said he'd overlook in this particular case providing Hyacinth didn't mind and no photographs of the incomplete uniform were posted and linked to his website - he did have standards to maintain after all.

It was typical of Conrad to celebrate his birthday by making sure that everybody else had a good time. He'd made sure that transport was provided so that his friends could enjoy his fine wines with a clear conscience. Although this merely meant that the local taxi firm would be doing the rounds, Hyacinth had maintained the tenor of the evening by stipulating on the invites that carriages would be at 7pm and 12 midnight. Beth and Drew were ready and waiting when the horn outside sounded promptly at seven o'clock.

With a glass of exquisite white wine and canapés of tiger prawns and guacamole or mushroom and white wine bruschetta, Beth stood in the vast lounge chatting merrily to Hyacinth and Sally.

'I hadn't realised that our circles overlapped. I didn't know that you two knew each other.' said Beth.

'We've known each other for some time, on the fringes as it were.' explained Hyacinth. 'Conrad has been on the Committee of the Whitworth for years and there's talk of him taking on the Chair. However, it's this business of the theft that's really thrown us together, isn't it, Sally?'

'I don't know what Theo would have done without Conrad. He's always been a vital part of the team but he's been an absolute life saver recently. I bet he's utterly sick and tired of Theo calling him up at all hours to ask his opinion on this or that, and his marvellous business manner has smoothed things with the police amazingly.' explained Sally. 'I don't think Theo would have coped if it weren't for Conrad's calm efficiency.'

'It's a small world, isn't it? Of course, it's obvious that Conrad has artistic tendencies.' said Beth whilst looking around her to add weight to her statement. The bespoke furniture, ornamental sculptures and paintings on the walls gave testament to this fact. 'But I didn't know that it went further than that.'

'Years ago, when I first met Conrad, he did a second degree in Art History at Manchester University. Over these later years he's completed a Masters with Edinburgh University, distance learning of course.' said Hyacinth.

'Goodness! Your husband is a man of hidden talents. Is he contemplating a career change?' said Beth.

'Oh, no.' replied Hyacinth. 'He always insists that this is for his own personal satisfaction. Conrad says that there's no money to be made in the art world, unless you're buying and selling great works, but he thinks that to do that is to sully beauty by reducing it to commerce. It's just a hobby to him, but one that he sincerely loves. Of course, you know of his spell in prison.' Hyacinth blushed a little here, but gathering her courage she pressed on. 'It was while he was inside that he really got back into seriously studying art history. He was bored, once the prison accounts were done, and he had no desire to while away his days reading trashy novels. He decided to put the time to the best use that he could and got his nose buried in text books to fill the time.'

'And we're reaping the benefits!' exulted Sally. 'Theo is always saying how grateful he is for Conrad's input. We could never pay him for all he gives, his discernment mixed with his sound business sense gives immeasurable help and yet he seems to think he should thank us for letting him join in.'

'Well I certainly thank you.' said Hyacinth. 'You give him plenty to keep his brain occupied and provide us with something more pleasant to talk about instead of business - and you keep him out of mischief.'

'The conversation can't have been particularly pleasant recently, not since the theft and the awful murder.' said Beth.

Any further discussion was curtailed as Henrietta entered the room. She rang a small silver hand bell and announced that it was time to be seated. Her manner was reserved and quite proper to the occasion but the twinkle in her eye and the smirk that was breaking out around the edges of her mouth suggested that she was thoroughly enjoying acting the part.

As the party walked into the dining room Beth sneaked the opportunity to hastily whisper to Hetty. 'You managed to get hold of a bow tie! Where did you find one?'

'It was Bobby's dad's.' Hetty replied. 'Bobby remembered a box of bits and bobs that his mum kept in the spare room and found it buried in that. It was left over from a police charity function decades ago. It's a bit big but his mum stitched me into it to make it fit. Goodness knows how I'll get out of it later.'

There was no doubt that Hyacinth had enjoyed preparing for tonight and her eye for detail was evident everywhere. The table was laid with silver cutlery atop a black table cloth and each setting was laid around a purple silk place mat. The backs of the dining chairs were covered with a shimmering purple chiffon scarf elegantly finished in a bow at the back. A sprig of lavender was the finishing touch to each napkin. Beth had noticed that the canapé trays were decorated with various flower heads and now saw a striking arrangement lying low and long down the centre of the table. Guessing it to be Hyacinth's work she complimented her friend on the beauty of the centrepiece.

'I chose to make the arrangement as I wanted to be sure we'd see each other as we dine. There's nothing worse than trying to hold a conversation over dinner through a jungle in the middle of the table.' explained Hyacinth.

Overhearing the topic of their conversation Conrad joined in. 'The point here is that we all actually want to chat together. I did however once go to a business dinner where the host admitted to me that he particularly placed guests opposite him with a large floral centrepiece between them because he positively detested them and wished to avoid any sort of exchange. He said it worked a treat and he'd recommend the trick to anybody.'

'We're honoured that you designed a low arrangement then, Hyacinth.' said Drew. 'But if I'm ever placed by a tall bunch of flowers I know I'll develop an inferiority complex now you've told me that.'

The first course was brought through by Hetty and Emma. They had been carefully tutored to properly serve each dish. It had been explained that "serve from the left, remove from the right" was an urban myth.

'Food is only served from the left if it is to be removed from a platter.' the chef explained. 'The thinking behind this is that it presumes the server and recipient are right handed.'

It was with gratitude that Henrietta stood at Drew's right and placed his crab stuffed avocado without too much awkwardness. Being left handed the concept of left side serving would have been tricky. As it was the blue borage floral decoration to the starter dish stayed artfully in place.

Hyacinth's influence could be seen in every course and flowers figured greatly in the menu, both as ingredients and as garnish. A main course of lamb shank and lavender with minted new potatoes, decorated with purple chive heads continued the theme. Lemon tart, decorated with lemon balm leaves and tiny white lemon balm blossoms stayed with the floral theme and the cheese and biscuit boards were lavishly scattered with edible blossoms. Even the radishes were sculpted into tiny mice which ostensibly nibbled roses and marigold heads.

The conversation inevitably turned to the museum and, as nobody seemed to mind talking shop, the topic of the missing Constable was covered once again.

'I have to admit that I'm sick to the heart because of it all.' said Theo. 'It makes a mockery of my life's work. I love the art for its own sake, of course, but I also love its place as a marker in our social history. To me it represents a bastion of who we are and where we come from. But now that somebody has died - maybe even two will die, if Scott's chum doesn't pull through. Well, is it really worth it? A human life is worth more than some paint on a piece of paper when all's said and done. And just think about this,' said Theo, warming to his theme. 'We're surrounded by works of art every day and they attract no special notice. That's a crime in itself, and I'm guilty of overlooking it for all these years.'

'I do take your point, Theo.' said Drew. 'It's inevitable that you should be unsettled by what's taken place, but it's also inevitable that an accepted canon is formed. It's the same with music and literature. Some works attain renown whereas others, maybe even those with more merit, pass by unnoticed.'

'It's a shame that this trouble has jaded your enthusiasm By all means enjoy and appreciate the everyday wonders, but don't discard your love of the established greats.' said Sally. 'Constable waited his whole life for such recognition, don't deny it now!'

'Don't you think we get weighed down with concentrating on the "everyday" art from centuries ago and stand the chance of missing the beauty that is freely around us today? It's ludicrous when you think about it. Here we are, the six of us; Conrad, Sally and I get kudos and acclaim for hoarding and eulogising work that's not of our own making whereas Hyacinth, Beth and Drew create beauty everyday as a matter of course. Hyacinth designs gardens and floral sculptures that would shame Capability Brown, Drew paints with skill and creativity every day of the week and Beth quietly stitches small miracles just because of the outpouring of her heart.' said Theo.

'Steady on, Theo!' exclaimed Hyacinth. 'You exaggerate simply to make your point stick.'

'Nonsense. Look at the table and the dishes we've had tonight - beautiful! And have you seen

Beth's embroideries? They're so intricate and beautiful. In fact, I mean to go further. I want to buy one, Beth. How much would you accept so that I could have one for myself?" asked Theo.

'I'm not sure that I could charge you anything, if I thought you were at all serious.' said Beth. 'They take me so long to sew I really couldn't put a price on them, and then I would hardly charge my friends. Do be serious, Theo.'

'Don't you see? It's not fair for you to keep them all to yourself. Beauty should be shared. At least I can walk in Hyacinth's garden and see what she has done, and enjoy it. The museum is still closed or I'd demand you hold an exhibition. As it is you really should let your friends benefit from sharing in what you make. Drew tells me that you've just finished a small Celtic design and are waiting to get it framed. What size is it , Beth? I want to buy it.' Theo demanded.

'I hardly know if you're joking. It's a little smaller than A4, landscape. But, if you're quite serious I'll make a gift of it to you. You may be disappointed when you see it.' said Beth.

Hyacinth could see that her friend was acutely embarrassed at suddenly finding herself in the spotlight and stepped in to dissipate the attention. 'Theo is hardly without accomplishment, despite what he'd have us believe.' she said. 'We'll move back into the lounge for coffee and some inevitably delicious hand made truffles. While we relax Theo can repay our hospitality by playing the piano for us. Since our son, Quentin, emigrated to America the piano doesn't get nearly enough attention and my feeble attempts are an insult to such an instrument. If we're talking about the necessity of sharing one's gifts then it's your turn to be bountiful, Theo.'

Theo laughed at seeing the tables turned upon him. 'Touché Madame.' he said, bowing as he spoke. 'You now wish me to parade my ignorance before a real musician. Well, I asked for it.' Turning to Beth, Theo said, 'Here's the deal: You will be patient and encouraging while I stumble through some Beethoven and Schumann and in return you will reward me with the embroidery I covet. Deal?' He stuck out his hand so as to strike a bargain.

Beth laughed and shook his hand to seal the deal. 'You'll get the worst of it.' she said. 'You've seriously overrated my needlework skills and if you play any Beethoven then I'm in awe. I never can play Beethoven convincingly.'

'I've no idea what your Beethoven playing abilities are, Beth. But don't be misled, ladies and gentlemen. I know for a fact that the beautiful outfit that Beth is wearing tonight is made entirely by her own fair hand, every stitch of it.' said Conrad.

'I think that's quite enough flattery.' said Drew. 'I've heard what sort of language emanates from my dear wife when she's sewing and it's not pretty, I can tell you. Bring out the coffee and let's be sensible.'

Emma and Hetty brought through the coffee and truffles. Emma gave a knowing nod to her parents, acknowledging the over-pink faces that may or may not be attributed to a little too much good wine.

'They've started round the piano and I know that my dad has brought a bottle of his precious single malt, so we might as well have a break before we tackle these last dishes.' said Emma. 'I'm catching a lift home later with mum and dad so there's no rush. Is Bobby picking you up?'

The chef had finished and left, leaving the two young ladies to finish off by themselves. Emma made good her promise of a break by bringing a pot of coffee to the table and some truffles which had been left for them.

'Bobby doesn't want his mum out late so he's staying with Toby. I'm getting a taxi when we finish.' said Hetty.

'We'll have this brew and then we'll crack on to get finished. Maybe we can share a taxi and get home before the clock strikes twelve and we turn into pumpkins. Maybe you can squeeze in a quick cup of cocoa before Bobby goes home.' Emma left the last comment hanging, suggesting that this might not be quite the full story.

Hetty laughed at her friend's delicacy. 'I'm in no rush, so we'll see.' She took a sip of her coffee and closed her eyes as she enjoyed the dreamy luxury of the truffle before she sat and looked earnestly at her friend. She took a moment to decide if she really wanted to pursue the conversation she was forming in her mind and then, after a small nod of decision, continued. 'You've been such a good friend to me, Emma. Particularly in the way that you've not pried and asked awkward questions. I'm really grateful to you for that, but I think it's only fair to tell you something about myself. If it wasn't for your kindness I don't think I'd have stayed here and then I'd never have met Bobby. Because of your friendship I managed to overcome my shyness and timidity and I've managed to settle down. There's no great conspiracy or secrecy, it's just that I wasn't ready to deal with things and talk about them. Until now, that is.' Emma said nothing to push or pry. She didn't expect details but just poured out the coffee and listened. 'Toby's dad was in the Rifles Regiment. He was one of the first troops when the regiment was newly formed. It was a tough life but I liked it, nevertheless. There was a real sense of community, we all looked out for each other. Jez loved it so much! He chose the Rifles because of their motto, "Swift and Bold." He'd have been right up at the front, totally fearless - heedless, you might say. He went on tour to Afghanistan. He never came back. Some of his friends made it back, at least physically intact if not mentally. Many came back with neither bodies nor minds intact. I'm not sure that Jez would have coped with that, but I guess that's what they all say. He never knew about Toby, he never knew that I was pregnant.

'It was never my intention to hide anything.' Hetty continued. 'Toby had never even heard of his dad and it never really came into conversation when he was a baby. If he ever asks I tell him and I'll make sure he knows all about his dad, but for now he's content and doesn't think about such things. I left barracks and stayed with my mum but, without being disrespectful, my mum was never one for home comforts and TLC. It was a place to stay, but I knew I'd have to leave sooner or later. I have a small army pension that I can draw upon unless I remarry and so I took out a map of the area I thought I might like and decided to move. Then I literally closed my eyes and stuck a pin in the map - and it brought me here.'

Initially Emma was moved to tears whilst listening to her friend's tragic story, but now she laughed heartily. 'You live here because you stuck a pin in a map? Who'd have thought it! I'm so glad it brought you here.' She gave her friend an affectionate hug. 'However, if your pin had landed elsewhere you might not be faced with the prospect of all these dishes. I'd better go and see if our esteemed diners want a final drink and then we'll get finished and get to bed. I'm shattered!'

The dinner guests had sagged a little. Shoes had been kicked off and ties loosened. Beth and Theo were sitting at the piano scrutinising some Schumann duets which they'd decided needed more preparation for a date to be named in the not too distant future. The prospect of more fine fare had lost its appeal and, in response to Emma's offer of drinks, it transpired that everybody now craved a regular mug of tea.

'Your duties are complete, so I'll come and make the tea.' insisted Hyacinth. 'If you can put the kettle on I'll finish off in the kitchen in the morning. I'll be through to the kitchen in just a moment and, if you're ready, we'll get you girls home. I'm so thankful for your hard work tonight, you've made it a real success, but you've done more than enough and it's time you went to bed.'

'It's been a real pleasure. I've thoroughly enjoyed the experience.' said Emma.

Henrietta had already donned her apron and was elbow deep in a bowl of soapy water when Hyacinth walked into the kitchen.

'Whatever are you doing in the sink? These can all go into the dishwasher!' said Hyacinth.

'It's your best Spode tableware. We didn't want it to get chipped or to have the pattern fade.' said Hetty.

'Nonsense. These can go in the dishwasher tomorrow. Now you get your things if you're ready for home and Conrad will call your taxi.' said Hyacinth. She pressed her point home by physically removing Hetty's apron and pulling her away from the sink. 'I'll go and get Conrad now. I know he wants to thank you and to say goodbye.'

She returned to the kitchen, this time with Conrad, who was holding two splendid bouquets of flowers and two envelopes with a generous tip for the impromptu waitresses.

Hetty and Emma remonstrated that they'd already had their wages but it fell upon deaf ears. Conrad shook their hands and thanked them for all they'd done to make his birthday so special. After calling their taxi home and thanking them again he returned to his guests. When he rejoined his friends Theo and Beth had given up on the Schumann but had promised to practise so as to try again, agreeing that it merited another evening's get-together.

'I can't match the standard of hospitality that we've enjoyed tonight, but it would be lovely if we could all spend another evening together. Theo and I will then give Schumann's "Oriental Pictures" the attention that it deserves.' said Beth.

This plan was heartily agreed upon and the group settled on the sofas with their mugs of tea. The conversation meandered around the mutually favoured topics of music and art and the good wines were adding a metaphysical element to the discussion. Conversation was still in full flow at midnight when the taxis arrived to take the guests home. Hearty handshakes and hugs with promises of happy evenings to come were exchanged. As the parties dispersed a similar vein of conversation flowed between the respective couples: It was pleasant to find mutual friends with overlapping interests and it was a welcome relief to talk about the more pleasant aspects of the artistic world after the shock of the theft and the discovery of a throttled museum curator.

Chapter Thirteen

DCI Monroe, Inspector Argyle, DCI James and Sgt Maddox all sat in the meeting room requisitioned by Monroe in the Manchester Met Police HQ. As a senior officer of the Art and Antique Squad who deemed matters ripe for a little intervention.

'It seems to me that we now have an overlap of interests.' Argyle said. 'It's highly likely that this Dutch chap was Monroe's man for the old Turner theft and so we can't exclude the possibility that he was also behind this current Constable situation. The fact that we now have a corpse on our hands raises the stakes significantly. James, what are the facts of this murder? What do we know?'

'Precious little I'm afraid, Sir,.' said James. 'We know that he was throttled with some heavy duty picture wire and we know that the murderer wore cotton gloves. It's not too far to leap to the conclusion that he used the cotton gloves that are usually worn when handling the fragile paintings in the archives. They're readily available, along with the wire that was used to kill him. Whether the murder was premeditated and Rick was lured to his death, or whether a clandestine meeting went wrong and opportunity offered these things we can't know. We are pretty confident that the victim knew his assailant. It's hard to imagine a stranger finding their way into the Whitworth archives and then stumbling upon Rick to kill him there. If the meeting was arranged by either of the parties at the museum, which seems likely, then it's also likely that it's a colleague we're looking at. But we can't really be

148

sure of anything, it's all conjecture. There are endless possibilities.'

'We all know that it's unlikely to have been a chance meeting. We'll work on the premise that it was someone known to the victim and somebody linked to the Whitworth. I imagine that this whittles the list down to a starkly limited number of suspects.' said Monroe.

'I'm afraid that's not the case at all.' said Argyle. 'The museum community is very fluid with circles continually overlapping. Although there's the expected territorial precociousness there is an underlying sense of community which leads to a certain amount of overlap. It's already known that Rick often wandered into the Whitworth at will and the same can also be said of the Whitworth staff wandering freely around MAG to see various colleagues. James' brother-in-law made regular visits to MAG, as did Scott Malkin. These places are generally open to the public but even when closed, or entering restricted access areas, visiting curators would have open and unremarked access. Even that's not the full extent of it. There's quite a crowd of peripheral associates and officials. Members of the committee can freely come and go and there's also a long list of "Friends" made up from particularly interested and loyal members of the public. Of course their access is less open but there are bound to be some members who have been involved since Domesday who will have privileges. There's no saying that one or two of these who joined the ranks years ago didn't do so with a long term goal that wasn't altruistic and in line with the official manifesto.'

'Fair enough. Since there is a legitimate link, maybe you should all get your heads together to work through this list. I'll see if I can get Baskeyfield reassigned to the case to lend a helping hand. I'll leave the murder for you to chase up and you can keep me posted. Now, Monroe, what can you tell me about your status on the historic Turner case? Where does this murder leave you?' said Argyle.

'At a complete dead end, if you'll pardon the expression.' said Monroe. The complete lack of any further details highlighted his sense of utter defeat.

'If you don't mind me saying, Sir. I'm not convinced that's quite the case.' said Maddox, blushing at his own audacity. James beamed at his protégé and encouraged him to continue. 'If it was Rick who was behind both of the thefts then he can't have been working on his own. I don't mean Finn, he was just the errand boy. Rick was obviously working with somebody in his own sphere because that somebody murdered him in the gallery. Finn can't have done it, even if for a moment we think he might have, because he's still unconscious in a hospital bed. We've all agreed that it's somebody who can easily gain admittance to the Whitworth archives. If it wasn't a museum type they'd meet in a totally different venue, there are lots of dark corners in the city. Anyway, it can't have been Finn, so whoever it was they were in the same league as Rick, I think, and are still at large. All of this is my long-winded way of saying that you still have a lead out there and so you might still find your Turner after all.'

'I wish you were right. In fact I'd like to hope that you are right, but "hope" isn't a word that enters my vocabulary much these days.' said Monroe. 'I'm almost one hundred percent certain that Rick was my man for the Turner, but any hope of finding the painting tragically died with him, I'm afraid.'

'Doesn't his death give you unlimited access to his life? You can search everywhere now! It's a high price to pay for a painting though, isn't it?' said James.

'You can approach the police in Holland and get them to start a search in his office and rooms back at home. You'll have to liaise with the Dutch authorities but they should cooperate. If the Turner is anywhere it's most likely back there.' said Argyle.

'And if they find it?' asked Monroe. 'Do you honestly think they'll just hand it back? There's a loophole in Dutch law that means that if a stolen piece remains undiscovered in a person's possession for more than thirty years it becomes legally theirs. No doubt this was Rick's plan. He's not that many years off, relatively speaking. If they keep quiet about it, within a decade they've got another treasure in their collection and then we can never get it back!'

'I thought the law was that no convicted criminal could profit from their crime. You can't do a stint in prison and then legitimately dig up your buried treasure for a cosy retirement.' said Maddox.

'That's quite correct - in this country.' said Monroe. 'I accept the fact that the Turner was originally stolen from England which could pose quite a legal conundrum. But once those sorts of lawyers get involved the debate could go on forever.

The value of the Turner couldn't justify the long term expense. No matter how highly we value the art intrinsically the maths just doesn't work out. It'd be the sort of case that would never end, whilst lining certain barristers' pockets nicely along the way. It'd just be quietly forgotten.'

Seeing the gloom on Maddox's face Monroe said, 'It's a depressing reality isn't it? I know it feels unjust but it'd be out of our hands. Let's try and stay positive and hope that it doesn't come to that. However, we do have a murderer to catch and murder is wrong however you look at it. Let's concentrate on catching a killer and maybe we'll stumble onto a couple of paintings while we're at it.'

This signified the end of the meeting. Monroe and James agreed that the task before them was daunting but acknowledged that good, old fashioned legwork could achieve miracles, even if it was long and arduous. Knowing that there was no time like the present they allocated lists and leads agreeing to keep each other up to date with progress.

The first port of call for Maddox was a trip to the hospital to see if Finn's testimony might be anywhere on the horizon. His return to consciousness could provide a massive short cut to some vital evidence. It was to be hoped that a severe bashing had knocked some sense into him. Although he might be in pretty deep trouble, it was nothing compared to murder. Cooperation in giving the key to a murder enquiry would go a long way in alleviating punishment for his presumed part in the Constable theft.

As Maddox walked along the hospital corridor it was evident that the constable on duty was just recovering his composure. There had obviously been a recent disturbance of the long, unnatural peace that encompassed the patient.

'What's going on?' asked Maddox. 'Is everything alright?'

'The lad came round for a brief minute or two, but he's sedated again and settled now. He went utterly crackers!'

Just as Maddox was about to ask for particular details Scott came out of Finn's room looking terrified to the core. Not wishing to risk missing any small detail Maddox told Scott to wait for him and to not leave his sight. He then returned his attention to the constable.

'Did he say anything? Did you get a word out of him?' Maddox said.

'I heard him suddenly yell, just out of the blue. When I got into the room he was sitting bolt upright and yelling incoherently. He calmed down a bit when he saw Scott sitting there and kept grasping at him. He started mumbling something about "Theo," whoever that is, and then he got all agitated again and started begging Scott to help him.'

Maddox was quick to deal with the situation. 'Sit down, right now. Write down absolutely everything that happened and everything you heard - even if you think it makes no sense at all. Did you or Scott ask him any questions?'

'Scott asked him what he meant when he begged for help, but by this time he was going all crazy again. The nurse had come into the room at this point and strictly forbade us to question him. She then gave him an injection and he was soon out of it all again.'

'Write it down, while it's still fresh in your mind. I'll come back to you in a bit, after I've had a chat with Scott.' Maddox then turned to Scott. 'You look like you've had a bit of a shock. Let's go and get a cup of tea. I don't suppose they do all those fancy coffees in the hospital canteen, but a tea bag's a tea bag wherever you go. No doubt it'll cost a small fortune but I'll put it in my report as expenses. I'd say that this was an emergency.'

In the canteen Scott sipped his tea and his ruffled feathers gradually began to settle.

'I'd been sitting there all morning; Theo doesn't seem to mind and things are still a bit unsettled at the museum.' Scott said. 'I'd been wittering away about anything and everything. I think I'd been talking about my mum. She made this really nice tea loaf with some Tippy Assam tea from a recipe that your mum gave her. I try to keep away from the topic of art and the museum but it's hard to keep rambling on. I forgot where my train of thought was leading and said that I'd taken some in to work and how much everybody had liked it. My mum was really chuffed about that.

'For a moment Finn opened his eyes and mumbled quietly.' Scott said. 'Then, all of a sudden he sat up and got more and more upset. Before I knew what was going on he was raving mad. He looked absolutely petrified. He then looked at me and seemed to recognise me. He calmed down for a minute then, but not for long. He started grabbing hold of me and begging me to help him, then the nurse shooed me away and took over. She must have given him something because he just sank back in his bed again and was fast asleep, or unconscious - whatever he is now.'

'Did you notice him rouse before you mentioned the museum?' asked Maddox.

'No. He was completely out of it until I forgot what I was saying and slipped. It's all my fault again, isn't it? No matter how much I try and do the right thing it always winds up causing trouble. I thought I was being a good friend, sitting there gabbling on. The nurses said it's good and can sometimes bring them back. They said it'd help Finn to hear a friendly voice and that people who are unconscious can often hear everything that's going on around them. Some people have remembered everything when they've come round. I've gone and messed that up too! He's in a worse state now than he was before. It'd have been better for him if he'd been left in some peace and quiet.

'Nonsense. Don't be so pessimistic!' said Maddox. 'You want him to wake up, don't you? When he did come round he was bound to be in a bit of a state as he took a real pasting. But that wasn't your fault, was it? Not unless you put him in the rubbish skip.'

Scott jumped at the suggestion. 'Of course I didn't! How can you even say so?'

'There you are then. If you didn't beat up your old chum - and I'm sure you didn't, how can you be responsible for his state of mind now? We want him to wake up and come to his senses, even if it is a bit traumatic for him. Then he can help us sort out all of this mess.' This seemed to reassure Scott and he relaxed a little. 'You'll see I'm right.' continued Maddox. 'Now, do me a favour. Find somewhere quiet and write everything that happened down, and I mean absolutely everything. Go home if you want, you can say I told you to. Don't leave out the tiniest detail, even if it's utter nonsense. We can't know what's important and what isn't at this stage, so it's better to have too much information than too little. Now you get off and do that because I need all of my courage to face up to the Ward Sister and ask to take the nurse off the ward for a bit to get her side of the story.'

'Good luck to you.' laughed Scott, but with little sign of jollity. 'You're a braver man than I am if you dare try that. She's an absolute battle-axe!'

With such gloomy portents Scott went to gather his thoughts and left Maddox to his doom.

An informal gathering had been arranged in the usual rendezvous of Beth's kitchen. Here James and Maddox could pool their findings and the sense of being off-timetable helped them to think more freely. It also meant that they got decent and regular brews with the addition of a plentiful supply of cake. It also meant that Beth could join in the discussion and DCI Benedict James always valued his twin sister's input. She had a flair for viewing things from what she described as "the domestic angle" and, as every villain also had an everyday persona it was a surprisingly revealing viewpoint.

'You were in on the action then, Maddox! Fancy your mum's Tippy Assam tea loaf sparking off the young villain.' said James.

'Excuse me, Benji. Did you say Tippy Assam tea loaf?' asked Beth.

'I did indeed. Does that give you insight into a breakthrough clue?' said Benedict.

'No.' Beth laughed. 'But it does make me wonder how news travels so fast. That's my own recipe. I made it for the WI last week and I gave my recipe to Eileen for her tearoom.'

'Mum did say that she got the recipe from someone in the WI. She doesn't claim intellectual copyright.' said Maddox, hasty to make amends.

'Steady on, Beth. Good food is for sharing! And you know that the WI upholds mutual friendship and education.' said Benedict.

'Oh, I'm not guarding trade secrets. You should know me better than that. I'm just surprised at how quickly it's done the rounds. It is delicious. The strong, malty tea and dark muscovado makes a winning combination. I've got some here if you want to try some.' said Beth.

'That's more like it. In the name of research we'll all have a slice.' said Benedict.

Beth set to slicing and buttering the fruit loaf and the conversation returned to more serious matters.

'I hardly know what to make of Finn's outburst.' said Benedict. 'What are the main points we should be considering?'

'The nurse doubted whether we could put any weight upon anything that Finn said then. She explained that, in layman's terms, as the neurons reconnect after their shaking they can fire off in any direction while the brain tries to piece things together again.' said Maddox. 'Finn just shouted Theo's name a few times, with intermittent ramblings, then clutched at Scott and begged for help. It's all very melodramatic. The nurse said that he saw Scott and told him that they were a team, and then begged him to help him and save him. Make of that what you will.'

'It's so frustrating that he was sedated again. He might have calmed down and then told you all you need to know.' said Beth.

'I'm told it's not just a matter of emotional trauma that concerns the medical staff if he gets agitated. The nurse was concerned about his physical fragility. The swelling on his brain had reduced as he lay quiet but this brief moment of fraught consciousness has made his brain rather inflamed again. They need to keep him quiet so as to let his body go through the natural healing process as best it can. There's not much more that they can do at this stage and any complications can soon become serious where the brain is involved.' explained Maddox.

'Do we attempt to follow any potential leads from what he said? Is there anything we can infer from Finn's ramblings or do we discount it all as rubbish?' said Beth.

'There's no way such ramblings and incoherent outbursts can hold any official sway or be remotely considered as evidence. Maybe he shouted Theo's name because he started to piece together recent events, starting with the impromptu tour Theo gave him. Perhaps he was shouting out as he remembered Theo squeezing the life out of him and tipping him into the dustbin.' said Benedict.

'Goodness, I'm so glad he didn't just randomly shout out Drew's name!' said Beth.

'What can we guess from when he recognised Scott?' asked Maddox. 'Was he begging a friend to help him and reminding him of their ties of friendship before Scott turned over a new leaf?'

'Or was he referring to a more recent partnership in crime?' continued Beth.

'As things stand we can have no way of guessing. We certainly can't go haring off casting aspersions based on the ramblings of a semiconscious petty crook.' said Benedict. 'However, I'm not willing to discount any thread or lead. We can't afford to totally ignore anything. We'll have to just quietly bear all of these things in mind and see what fits together as we follow the breadcrumbs.' said Benedict. 'Speaking of breadcrumbs, it appears that I only have crumbs on my plate. You can at least remedy that problem Beth. Dish up the tea, in all its forms please.'

'If you're having seconds I'll call Drew through. We can't let him miss out on a helping.' said Beth. She banged on the silver service bell to summon Drew through to the kitchen. Knowing that the bell heralded food or drink, usually both, Drew was prompt in cleaning his brushes and joining the party in the kitchen.

'This won't do, you know.' said Benedict. 'We can't allow this case to beat us, we've a reputation as a team to maintain. I know that Monroe said that these cases can go on for years, decades even, but I'm not prepared to accept that. We're a dynamic team and we can crack this. Let's have another go at things, now we're properly fortified. We need to try a different angle. We need to be more abstract in our thinking; this is an art case after all. Beth, I know you'll have set your mind to this. What are your thoughts?'

'I have been thinking about this a lot.' said Beth. 'I'm not sure that my train of thought is particularly helpful though, I'm afraid.'

'Never mind about that, this is unofficial.' said Benedict. 'We're just throwing ideas around. Let's get the creative juices flowing and see what follows.'

'My mind has been whirring ever since we went to that marvellous dinner party at Hyacinth's for Conrad's birthday.' said Beth.

'My mind has been whirring ever since I discovered that Conrad Jefferson was closely linked to the Whitworth art gallery and a prominent member of the committee, but we'll let that lie for now.' said Benedict.

'You must follow your own lines of enquiry, Benji.' said Beth. 'You said you wanted some abstract thinking and so here are my thoughts. I've been trying to find out about historic art thefts. It was our discussion of the parallel timelines of art, literature and music while were having coffee and truffles. Somehow that got me thinking about historic art crimes.'

'You obviously attend very different parties to me.' laughed Maddox.

'I'll admit that it was an unusual one.' said Drew.

'It was a rare treat to indulge in such chatter and to play piano with Theo. I'm really looking forward to our next get-together.' said Beth. 'After that evening I've become fascinated with the subject of art crimes and I've read of some really bizarre accounts. Did you know that a Von Gogh was stolen in a very similar heist to the Constable theft? That got me thinking. I'm not quite sure what it's made me think but I've a funny feeling that it might help in the end.'

'I know all about your "funny feelings" and I know better than to ignore them.' said Benedict. 'You must follow the train of thought as you think fit, don't ignore your gut instinct. Sometimes we call it a hunch, but it's the start of a half, faint thought and when it's fully formed it becomes a sensible fact that was just waiting to mature in your mind. If you need any help you know that you only have to ask.'

'Drew is a bottomless pit of knowledge, so I keep pestering him for information. I've got plenty of text books to go at too. There is just one thing that I want to know.' said Beth.

'What's that, Beth?' asked Benedict.

'What is the exact size of the stolen artwork?' said Beth.

'You're asking me for the exact proportions of the missing piece?' asked Benedict. 'Why on earth do you want to know that?'

'I really don't know why I'm asking, but I want to know nevertheless. Don't give me a vague idea. I want the exact proportions.' said Beth.

'I've got a good idea off the top of my head, but if you leave it with me I can tell you exactly.' said Drew. 'I'll go back through my talk for the WI and check, it's on my laptop so I'll find it easily enough without bothering them at the museum.'

James and Maddox exchanged confused glances and then shrugged their shoulders. No doubt all would become clear eventually.

Chapter Fourteen

Monroe and Inspector Baskeyfield had dedicated the entire morning to searching through Diederick van der Molen's city apartment and office space in the gallery. It was decided that three policeman would be a case of "too many cooks spoil the broth" and so DCI James had brought the investigation back to the Whitworth. A fragile peace of sorts had returned to the museum and the staff had resumed their usual work load in an effort to soldier on. The skylight which had been damaged to gain entry for the break-in had been replaced and what little fire damage there was had been repaired and decorated. Although the calm atmosphere was brittle, at least a superficial veneer of normality reigned. The fact that the everyday manner exhibited was a little unconvincing passed unremarked and everyone was happy to follow suit, a person could only be shocked and aghast for so long. Admittedly there was an extra strain whenever Brian was on duty. Although he rarely spoke a word his punctilious and overbearing manner was unnerving. Nevertheless it was borne patiently. Who could blame him? If "once bitten, twice shy" was a maxim then the repercussions of being "bitten" twice could hardly be imagined, especially when Brian's strong sense of duty was added into the equation. If truth be told it was Theo's excessive good humour that really rankled. His frenzied jocundity could only be tolerated in very short doses. No doubt he felt that it was incumbent upon him to restore a sense of team work and to rekindle the joy of the vocation which knitted them together. Nevertheless, it was oppressive. It actually came as a relief when Theo's temper fractured at the interruption caused by DCI James questioning everyone yet again.

'How the hell are we supposed to ever get any work done?' Theo thundered. 'As if it isn't enough to have the very bricks and mortar violated. My collection has dwindled and my colleagues too! When we finally start to find some sense of rhythm again there's always some bloody copper who's bound to break the flow!'

Once the energy of his outburst had dissipated Theo sagged and apologised for his outburst.

'Oh, don't mind me.' said James. 'Best to vent it, get it off your chest. I grant you that we do keep turning up, like the proverbial bad penny. It must be annoying for you, but just remember that we are pursuing a common cause at the end of the day.'

'Of course you are, and I am grateful. I just feel so desperate! I'm not at all sure how I'm supposed to play this out. Do we carry on as usual, as far as we can, or do we throw our hands in the air and surrender? I have to admit that I feel like just giving in, but that can't be right - can it? Nothing feels right.' said Theo.

'The best solution to this would be perfect closure. Let's catch a killer and maybe find a painting while we're at it. You'll feel better then, I guarantee it.' said James

'I wish that could be the case.' said Theo. 'As far as catching a killer goes, I wouldn't know where on earth to start. However, I suspect that the

Constable is lost on some rubbish heap. I cherish your enthusiasm, but I'm afraid it's over optimistic.'

'Excuse me for interrupting,' said Sally. 'But I really do need to ask you something. She hovered nervously next to DCI James and appeared to be gathering her courage and her thoughts. 'Is it true that Rick really stole from MAG all those years ago? Could he have been behind all the trouble here?'

'We really can't say for sure but I'd suggest that it's highly likely. It's the best scenario we can think of that will explain all of these recent events. The timing certainly fits.' said James.

'Is that why he was killed?' Sally shuddered visibly as she asked the awful question.

'At present we can only presume so.' said James.

Sally took the statement in. 'How awful! It's just not worth it, is it? We spend our adult lives believing how valuable and priceless these treasures are, but nothing is worth a human life, is it? What on earth are we doing here? Pussy-footing around some blobs of pigment on a stretch of canvas. It's ludicrous!'

Theo took Sally in his arms as she fought back the tears. 'I'm sorry, that's my melancholy rubbing off on you. You've put up with my maudlin moods at home and now my depression has brought you down.' he said.

'Try not to get too bogged down with it all.' said James. 'Some of what you say is true but don't lose the intrinsic worth of the art you know and love. Hold on to the value of the heritage. Let the anger you have fuel you into helping me get to the bottom of this business.'

Sally gently nodded her head and slipped away leaving Theo to talk with the Inspector.

'How can I help you?' Theo asked. 'I realise that sounds cliché but I really do want to help, despite my tantrums.'

'Tiresome as it is I need you to cast your mind back to that day, yet again.' said James. 'Try and remember any tiny little thing, and I really mean any little thing, that didn't ring true. Forget about the lads descending upon the museum as they did - that's an obvious factor. Consider anything from the more mundane elements of the day of the robbery.'

'I think I understand you but I really have nothing else to add. I'll keep thinking on it though.'

'Consider the smouldering fire. Somebody must have had time and leisure to set that up. It wasn't a haphazard affair. How was that managed without comment or notice? It may not have been a stranger or anything so conspicuous, but somebody ostensibly going about their legitimate business, but on reflection something was a little out of place.'

'You said to cast aside the lads turning up, but what about Rick? Who knows what he was up to before anybody saw him? Even so, nothing springs to mind. I'll bear it in mind and chat to the others. And in the mean time?'

'In the mean time I'll just keep putting one foot in front of the other. I'll let my feet take me to chat to Brian, he's desperate to have a hand in clearing this up as a matter of conscience. Where can I find him?'

'Now there's a man in need of professional help. He's pacing about the place like a caged tiger. He's here somewhere but it's a matter of chance where he'll be at any given moment. He's terrified that something catastrophic is going to happen under his nose again and he's bursting for a chance to prove his worth. Of course there's nothing that he can do, but you try and tell him that.'

'I'll go and rescue the poor chap. But heaven save me from his terrible tea!'

DCI James found the fretful security guard pacing the corridors of the upper storey. He looked tired out.

'Good morning, Sir.' said Brian on recognising the police officer.

James noticed that the security guard had to forcibly stop himself from standing to attention and saluting. It was a textbook example of somebody nervously wrung out and reverting back into old habits for security and solace.

'How are you getting along?' Brian asked.

'I'm not "getting along" at all if truth be told. But for my sake keep that to yourself.' said James. Although he'd made the comment out of kindness and in an attempt to build some camaraderie with the man, placing himself in a vulnerable light to ease the blighted guard's ego, James realised that this was in fact the bald truth. Such bonhomie that James hoped to establish wasn't really an act of charity but was a reflection of the blatant fact that they were both in the same boat. James too felt utterly helpless whilst havoc was being wreaked under his very nose and he hadn't a clue about who might be at the heart of it all. A deep respect for this soldier welled up inside James and he relented.

'Let's go and get a brew. I'll ask Theo to be on the alert to relieve you and I'd like you and me to get our thinking caps on again.'

'If you think that'll be all right, I could do with a break. I have to admit that these walls are closing in on me and I feel like I'm going mad trying to think of what I can do to help.'

James already regretted his impulse to indulge in strong tea and seeing an opportunity to forego the penance he suggested a breath of fresh air.

'It might blow the cobwebs away.' admitted Brian. 'You never know, it might blow a few wisps of inspiration into my head too.'

As they walked together they discussed the case.

'I've gone through all of the security footage for two days previous to each of the tragedies to see if there was anything that could help us there. I haven't missed a second and I can assure you that I can see nothing to give us a clue, not a single thing made me stop and wonder.' said Brian.

James now understood why the guard looked so utterly fatigued. The poor guy probably hadn't slept properly for days but had watched and re-watched endlessly dull security footage over and again.

'The trouble is that I've a very uncomfortable thought growing in my mind.' Brian continued.

'What's that, Brian? What's troubling you?'

'I can vouch for everybody who is on camera and you don't need to tell me what that means, do you?'

'I see that we're both working from the same song sheet here, Brian. It's unsettling, I know. Nevertheless, you're right.'

Holding their conversation outside of the museum lent a conspiratorial air to the discussion. Brian continued in a confidential tone.

'The awful thing is that it now means that I'm starting to suspect people that I've known and liked for years. If I've got the wrong end of the stick I'll have wronged some really nice people who have only ever been good to me, and are innocent to boot. Of course, they don't know what I'm thinking - but I do. It feels really mucky!'

'Welcome to my world.' said James. 'My only offer of consolation is that, if it catches a killer, it's worth it. The tar you've painted and marred your friends with soon washes away. Trust me, it really does.'

'I can just about cope with labelling my friends and colleagues as thieves but contemplating that they could be murderers makes my mind recoil.'

'Let's not throw a complete blanket of suspicion then. Let's narrow it down.' suggested James. 'First of all, let's think about the fire alarms. Somebody had to carefully construct a controlled fire. I seriously doubt it could have been prepared in a rush. It's possible that one of the youths organised it, but I have to admit that it doesn't strike me as their style. I'm not even sure it's something that they're capable of. I know that you say you can vouch for who is shown on the security footage but think about it logically. Who was seen loitering around the security lodge or approaching it and not leaving for some time without an obvious reason. If there's a valid reason then we can soon find it out and clear their name.'

'There are certain blind spots so not every movement is seen in a clear trajectory. A figure can get lost for a time and then reappear on a different camera. It's not much of a gap but it's fair to say that the security lodge was never a main source of concern. Most of the camera angles would have been based around entrances, exits and the collections. It's inevitable that certain pathways of movement will leave gaps which can't be linked together.'

'Just fire off some of the anomalies as a starting point.'

'Sally can be seen entering the ladies toilets. Obviously there aren't any cameras in there but it's a good ten minutes before she reappears. It looks like she was crying when she went in so that would explain her delay.'

'And why do you think she was crying?'

'Oh, there's no surprise there. Theo had been particularly testy that afternoon. Despite his charming manner he was furious when those lads turned up. Sally had defended Scott, saying that he couldn't be to blame. It's likely they'd had a bit of a spat. Theo can be like that sometimes, but they'd made it up later because Theo said that he was going to Sally's for dinner that night.'

James was sure that the museum staff had no idea of how much the security guards could see and infer from what the cameras showed. They probably forgot that the cameras were there at all for the most part.

'Go on. What other discrepancies have you found?'

'I presume that we're only thinking of the afternoon, otherwise the timing of the fire doesn't work out, does it?'

'I'm not sure of anything right now, so just keep it rolling around and don't worry too much about specifics. If something rings a bell we'll scrutinise it then.'

Brian nodded and continued to consider all he'd viewed so many times over the past few days.

'Of course, that Dutch chap came when the lads were in. When Drew was showing the boys around the archives Theo had a long chat with him. They wandered off camera for about five minutes and then reappeared still looking engrossed in conversation. I have to admit that they didn't seem too happy with each other, but that could just be Theo's temper after the invasion of the youths. I gather from Drew that the Dutch gent kept missing the opportunity of seeing him in the archives. Theo seemed to be pointing in the direction of the archives at times during the conversation and I guess the visiting youths figured heavily in the conversation.'

'Excellent. This is the stuff that I need to hear, so I can build a picture of what was going on that day. Can you keep going?'

They'd been walking around the grounds of the museum and had come across a bench pleasantly situated in a grove of shrubbery. Brian took a seat and continued to cast his mind back through the footage he now knew so well.

'Earlier in the day, about mid-morning, Mr Jefferson called in with some paperwork for Theo to sign. Because of his business connections he's helping to oversee some of the building work. He knows and uses the contractors regularly so he's helping to liaise with them. In fact, it was by his recommendation that this particular building firm got the contract with the museum. They're good too, I'll give them that. I've never known a firm of builders be so tidy in the workplace.'

'What did Jefferson do?'

'He found Theo in his office and, as far as I can tell, asked for some papers to be signed. I'd say that Theo hadn't expected to see Mr Jefferson but was pleased nevertheless. The paperwork didn't take many minutes and Mr Jefferson soon left Theo in his office. On his way out he spoke to some of the builders. He's always good with people. He looked around the atrium and the skylight and the builder seemed to be showing him what progress they were making. He seemed very eager to please - no doubt grateful for the recommendation and the business. Is this sort of stuff helpful?'

'I've no idea at present but it's usually seemingly inconsequential details that clinch a case. What about at the end of the day?'

'I've looked at the start of the shift, starting from when I took over at 18.00 hours. Theo was looking for the day guard, or that's how it seemed. Sometimes he'll chat to us on the change over. It's usual for him to do a quick tour of the museum before the handover. Theo goes into the security lodge but comes out straight away. He must have seen that the guard wasn't there because he then goes to find him elsewhere. Within a minute or so they're both back on camera chatting away together. All the others had gone home by then, and then Theo left too, presumably to have dinner with Sally.'

'You're an absolute treasure, Brian. You've saved my Sergeant hours and hours of trouble. I can't thank you enough.' said James. 'The only thing I think we can do now is to hand over the footage to the techies in our IT department. They won't need to watch it through but they can put it through some clever software they have. The trouble is we'll have to wait our turn for them to get to it, so thanks to you I can still keep working and thinking. Once again, thank you for all the trouble you've gone to. Now, do me a favour and have a rest. You can't do this all by yourself and you look like you're about done in.'

Brian smiled and shrugged. 'If willingness and effort were all that was needed I'd have this licked. I can't begin to imagine how the painting theft was pulled off and as far as murder goes - I'm stumped.'

'We'll get there one step at a time, don't you worry. If I could ask you for one more favour I'd be grateful.'

'Just say the word. I feel useless enough as it is so I'll do anything I can.'

'First of all if you can gather together all of the discs with the footage from the two days in question, and maybe a day before just to be on the safe side. After that can you give me a basic schematic of where all of the cameras are situated around the gallery? A rough sketch will do - just enough to give me the gist of things. After that try and switch your brain off a bit and get some rest.'

The two shook hands. Brian returned to his fevered pacing and James made for the Manchester Met for his meeting with Monroe.

'I hope you've had a more productive morning than I have.' said Monroe. 'Baskeyfield and I have been through Rick's things like a nurse combing for nits. Other than discovering the fact that it seems that the Dutch are excessively tidy I've nothing to show for my efforts. It's obvious that Rick kept work and home distinctly separate. There's nothing to give any hints about his private life at work, and I have to say that there's very little of that in his apartment either. Neither does anything work related seep into his domestic quarters. His desk is obsessively tidy. One would almost question if he actually did any work there - not a paperclip is out of place. That fact alone unnerves me and makes me convinced that he's guilty of something. You've got to be covering your tracks to be so painfully organised. It's aggressively tidy. However you look at it there's nothing to link him to any stolen artwork at any point, either now or historical.' James shook his head in commiseration and Monroe continued. 'The lab have got his laptop in the queue so we've that last shred of hope for some sign, but I'm not optimistic. He was careful. I can't think he'd leave any evidence of shipping of valuables or suggestion of a sale after seeing his filing methods.'

'That's what's bugging me about this case.' said James. 'Everything is hidden in plain sight. Whatever's going on, it's a tight network and I'm continually fighting the sensation that everything I need to know is right under my nose.'

'It's funny that you should say that - not that I'm laughing at all, as you can see. I'd not realised until you just said it, but I feel exactly the same. I'm convinced that I'm being watched and somebody is laughing up their sleeve as they watch us stumble over clues everywhere we walk.'

'It's not a nice feeling, is it?' said James. 'What's Baskeyfield up to now? Can you keep him on the case for a bit?'

'I haven't asked yet. Goodness knows we need all the help we can get but how can I justify keeping him when I hardly know what to tell him to do next? Nevertheless, I'm going to keep him regardless and plead ignorance when it comes to protocol. I've sent him for one last look around Rick's office before the gallery clear it out.'

James smiled at a classic tactic. Manpower was always in short supply and he was surprised at the levels of deviousness he himself had employed to get some desperately needed help. He was grateful for Maddox and was pleasantly surprised that he was legitimately assigned to work with him.

Their conversation was interrupted by the ringing of James's mobile phone. The caller ID showed that Forbes had something to say. Glancing at Monroe to register that he needed to take the call he waited for Monroe's nod before hitting the green phone icon.

'Forbes, tell me you've something of interest to report. I need a lifeline.' said James. It was evident that this might be the case as James listened with growing attention. 'I'll get to you as soon as I can. Can you wait for me?' It appeared that the caller could wait and after expressing his thanks James ended the call.

'Something to go on?' asked Monroe.

'Who knows?' replied James. 'But I'm not proud and I'll clutch at anything to get a hold on this case. I think I'll give Maddox a call and ask him to meet me at the forensic lab. It'll be good for him to see all aspects of the case and, if there's anything of interest, I don't want him to miss out. Sorry to bail on our meeting like this, but I'd better get over there straight away.'

'Just let me know how you get on. Maybe next time we meet we'll have a bit more to say to each other.'

Forbes was sitting at his ease drinking coffee in the anteroom to the lab. Through the glass Rick van der Molen lay on a metal dissecting table. After being uncovered in every way imaginable he was now decorously covered with a sheet. Maddox glanced nervously at the inert body wondering what gruesome sights awaited him. Seeing the young Sergeant's apprehension Forbes explained.

'In many ways there's nothing new for you to see. There's no doubt that he was strangled with the wire as we saw. Nevertheless, there is something that I think you should look at.' Forbes said. He drained his mug and got up to lead the way to the body.

'Ordinarily I wouldn't give such a thing a second thought, but what do you make of this?'

Forbes drew back the sheet to reveal the left arm and on turning the palm upwards he pointed out a small tattoo on the pale white skin of the inner forearm.

'A tattoo?' asked James.

'Yes, a tattoo.' said Forbes. 'I know that it seems like everybody has one these days but this gent just didn't strike me as the type.'

'You never can tell with these arty types.' said Maddox.

'Well, that's rather the point I think.' said Forbes. 'It's your job to fathom these things out but, from experience, I've noted that the repressed arty types tend toward grand and marvellous works of art on their body. This specimen is rather understated, hardly worth having at all. Nor is this the place I'd usually expect to find such a design.'

'I know what you mean.' said James. 'Those small, monotone designs tend to be either on your wrist or neck, or maybe on the shoulder or ankle. What exactly is this design, do you think?'

In the exact centre of the fleshy part of the inner forearm was a small, black design of three small blobs which tapered outwards to a thin point, almost like a speech mark or a paisley shape. The marks were placed face inward and tapered outwards whilst forming a flowing circle as a whole. The complete design spanned only an inch or so.

'It's a bit like the Yin-Yang but there's no Yang, or Yin - whichever is in the centre. And there are three shapes, not two.' said Maddox. 'Is it religious? Three often means trinity or something.'

'That's a very good point.' said James. 'I've never come across it before. It's a bit boring really, isn't it? Not like some of these Chinese designs or Celtic knots. It's a bit on the functional side, don't you think?'

'Maybe it's nothing but I thought you should see it. I've emailed a photo of it to you but I thought you'd better have a good look at it in locus.' said Forbes.

'Quite right too, thank you.' said James. 'It is in an unusual place. If he wore a short sleeved shirt it'd be in plain view, or even if he rolled his shirt sleeves up a bit. It's sort of hidden, but not really.'

'From what I gather I don't think this guy ever rolled his sleeves up or wore a short sleeved top.' said Maddox.

'You're right. I can't imagine he ever relaxed on holiday, lounging around in a tee shirt. Maybe he thought that this was hidden away.' said James.

'Why would he need to hide it at all?' asked Maddox. 'Nobody is shocked by tattoos anymore. They're quite the norm. Perhaps he just thought it looked good there. There's no accounting for taste.'

'Perhaps you're right, but it still feels wrong. It's a very work-a-day design slapped inartistically on a semi accessible part of the body. Can you tell how long ago he got the tattoo?' said James.

'I'd say it was quite an old tattoo.The edges blur as the ink spreads under the skin and the ink fades and starts to take on a blue hue over time. You can get them re-inked but this looks quite old.' said Forbes.

'He was in England some years ago, maybe he got it then. It's a long shot but we've got to check it out. That's you fixed up for tomorrow at least then, Maddox.' said James. 'You can see the sights and check out all of the tattoo parlours. Show them the design and also a photo of Rick, explaining that he would have been considerably younger when he got the tattoo. I'll send a picture to Monroe on the off-chance it means anything to him, he's the art specialist after all. I'll copy Argyle into the message too - maybe he'll have come across something like it.'

Forbes placed a conciliatory arm around Maddox's shoulders. 'Sorry I've got you a few miles of legwork from this.' said Forbes. 'Think of it as an educational trip. You're bound to see lots of new and exciting things on your rounds.'

Maddox just rolled his eyes and went to get his reference picture from Forbes's printer.

Chapter Fifteen

The cakes for the end of the meeting were exceptional. It was Nicola's turn on the rota as tea hostess for Mossleigh WI and she had excelled all previous records by decorating each cupcake with buttercream, piping each cake to look like a Chrysanthemum. As the village Florist the floral theme was in character and it seemed a shame to bite into the creation. Nevertheless, after only a brief struggle everyone tucked in heartily.

'These cakes are artistic wonders.' said Kirsty. 'How can buttercream be made to look so floral?'

'Nicola assures me that they're really easy, you just need a specific piping nozzle.' said Beth.

'Well, I wouldn't dare try it - no matter how marvellous the piping nozzle.'

'Kirsty, is Carlton especially busy at the moment? Do you think he could spare us some time to help out on a case?' asked Beth.

'Is this another covert operation? Either way, I'm sure he'll squeeze you in somehow. I know he enjoys your little challenges.'

'I don't know that it needs to be secretive. I just think we need to get ahead with this case and if Carlton can help us queue jump in the tech department, who knows what we might find.'

'I'll tell him to call you so that you can arrange a convenient time amongst yourselves.'

Beth was prevented from explaining further by Hyacinth joining them.

'I really enjoyed your dinner party.' Beth said. 'It was a rare treat. Exquisite food, good friends and congenial conversation. It was heavenly! I can't attempt to out-do your hospitality but if you can cope with a less exalted menu I'd like to get us all together again. I've been practising the Schumann so I'm as prepared as I'll ever be.'

'Don't be silly, it was a special occasion. Ordinarily Conrad has to make do with cheese on toast or cottage pie. I agree that we should get together, though. Let's get everybody's diaries together and meet as soon as possible. However, in the mean time I have another proposition that might interest you.' said Hyacinth.

'This sounds intriguing.' said Beth.

'Some time ago Theo opened the museum up to a group who refer to themselves as "The Historical Stitching Society." They used to meet each week at the Whitworth but of course had to stop when the renovations began.'

'That sounds quite marvellous.' said Beth. 'What do they do to warrant such a title?'

'It's obvious enough really.' said Hyacinth. 'They collaborate their efforts to produce reproductions of famous historical textiles. The museum seemed the perfect venue for such a group. Surely the point of a place such as the Whitworth is to serve the community. I believe they're currently working on recreating the William Morris "Acanthus" pattern in a massive tapestry rug. You'd love it! Most of the dirty work is finished at the gallery and Conrad and Theo both agree that the gallery needs using again, to breathe some life into the place. It can't be opened to the general public for exhibitions yet, it's not ready for that, but certain rooms can be used and we think they should be as soon as possible.'

'I certainly hope that all of the "dirty work" has finished there.' said Beth, with meaning. 'You're right, some life does need injecting into the place. A bit of normality and "business as usual" would be good for everyone. Of course, you're also right in thinking that I'd be interested. Is the group open to new members? Maybe I could fit it in after I finish teaching, even if I'm a bit late. I'd love to join in.'

'I thought you would. I go to make tea as I can't sew for toffee, though I wish I could. I can just about sew a button on, but William Morris tapestry is beyond me. I can make a decent brew, however, so at least I can be involved somehow - and making a good cup of tea for the workers is helping one way or another. I love just being there in the midst of it all. I've really missed it while the gallery has been closed and I'll be thrilled to go back.' said Hyacinth.

'I've just remembered reading about a similar society in the Victorian era.' said Beth. 'The wife of a silk dyer set up a group to recreate the Bayeux Tapestry. The only problem was that the museum which provided the reference had censored the original and had covered all the naked men on the borders of the tapestry with clothing - and so they stitched pants on all of them!'

'How bizarre! At least that was more likely to suit their Victorian sensibilities.' said Hyacinth. 'Our group shouldn't have those sorts of worries at present. Even "The Strawberry Thief" should pass Victorian scrutiny.'

Mae called the meeting back to business and so the ladies made their way back to their seats. Although there wasn't any pressing business, the Croquet Crown now being over for this year, there was always a significant pile of correspondence to get through. As Beth sat her mind wandered from the various notices and the business in hand and she mused over the prospect of visiting the Whitworth again. It was strange how history kept creeping into the topic of the gallery and the whole seedy business of the missing Constable, and now a gruesome death, too. In an attempt to bring her attention back to the meeting in hand she shrugged off further thought by acknowledging to herself that art history was inevitably a large part of any gallery or museum.

The meeting was soon over and after a brief chat with a few members as people found their coats and walked to the door Beth made her way home. On entering the kitchen she met her brother, Sgt Maddox and her husband deep in conversation. There was tea in the pot and so, after hanging her coat on the back of the chair, she sat and joined them.

'So, you say that one of the tattooists you visited has a vague recollection of this image and might be able to shed some light on it?' asked James.

Knowing that the question was directed to him Maddox answered, 'Yes, actually a couple out of the many. Who knew there were so many tattoo parlours in Manchester! However, they're going to check their records to be certain of their facts and then will get back to me.'

'Two tattooists say they recognise it?' asked James. 'How is that possible? You wouldn't get it done twice, would you?'

'You could get it re-inked, so that could explain it. Either that or two people have the same tattoo.' said Maddox.

'Or at least two people have the same tattoo. There could be others that we don't know about.' said Beth.

'As if we haven't got enough to get through.' said James. 'Let's concentrate on the one we know of for now and we'll meet anything else that comes as we go along. We can consider the others after we've figured this one out. We'll keep our focus tight for now. What else did you learn?'

'I've learned not to judge a book by its cover, even when that cover is quite alarming.' said Maddox. 'I've met all sorts and, although they're pretty scary to look at, on the whole they're as nice and polite as you'd wish to meet. I've seen so many piercings and some haven't got an inch of flesh that hasn't been tattooed but, I have to admit, they were more helpful and polite than many so called "respectable" types I've dealt with. However, I don't expect that's quite what you're asking me. If you want to know what I've learned relating to this case I'd better refer to my notes.' After a brief reminder from his notebook Maddox continued. 'Nearly all of the tattooists I spoke to said that this particular tattoo is old. Not only did they say so because of the colour of the ink - a black which had aged into a blueish hue, but also because of the quality of the ink. Apparently, despite the growth in popularity of tattoos the quality of the inks today is quite poor in comparison to old school tattoos. There's a much wider choice of colour today but the vibrant colours don't last anything like the old inks. Most of the black inks they use today would fade before they turn to this shade of blue. Every tattooist I spoke to reckons that this tattoo is probably from the '80s but is definitely more than ten years old.'

'That's very interesting. You did a good scientific research today. What about the tattooists that specifically recognised the design?'

'One seemed to think he did this design a couple of years ago. He thinks he did it from scratch too - he remembered thinking that it was a very bland design. We'll just bear this in mind for now and discount it as not being our man - it's too recent to be his tattoo. The tattooist is going to try and find the records so we might get a name. We can but hope. The other chap said he has an idea that he did this when he first opened up his business decades ago. He remembers that it was one of his first jobs and was glad that it was relatively simple. He says it'll take him some time to dig around for his old records but they'll be around somewhere. He'll let me know when he finds something.'

'That sounds encouraging.' said James. 'Let's hope that he gets back to you with some solid facts.'

'What does the fact that somebody else has this tattoo mean, then? Will that be helpful?' asked Beth.

'It has the potential to help but we can hardly request that everybody roll their sleeves up, can we?' said James. 'How many people just might have a tattoo? It'd be like searching for a needle in a haystack! I think that, at present, such information just gives us a false lead and false hope. We'll just have to keep it in mind for future reference.'

'Let's hope that the tattooist really did recognise the pattern and that it is the same one he did all those years ago. It's a strange design! What can it represent?' said Beth.

'I still say it looks like a strange adaptation of the yin-yang image. I think it's a clandestine group of some sort.' said Maddox. He seemed to be quite enjoying the prospect of infiltrating an underground cult. The others took a more matter of fact approach to the matter.

'It's all about perspective, isn't it?' said Drew. 'It could mean any number of things if you look at it from a different viewpoint.'

'Are there any Masonic symbols that look like that?' asked Maddox, determined to keep the matter intriguing. 'Don't they have a penchant for triangles?'

'It's a fair comment, Maddox.' said James. 'However it's usually triangles and compasses rather than blobs.'

'Let's have a look at the photo. Maybe a layman will see something different.' said Drew. James pulled up an image on his mobile and, after a moment's thought, Drew rushed off to his studio with only a brief explanation that he'd be back in a moment.

'Is it a paw print, maybe?' said Beth. 'They look a bit like the pads on Noodle's paw, but three isn't the right number and the composition isn't right.'

Drew came back into the kitchen with a brush, some paper and a bottle of ink.

'I'm almost certain that they are brushstrokes.' he said. Seeing incredulity on his friend's faces he continued to explain. 'I realise that I'm staring at brushstrokes all day long and so my perceptual set will predispose me to see that in the image, but it would make sense. Don't you think so? I'll show you.'

They moved aside to give him room to demonstrate his ideas at the table.

'This is a standard watercolour sable.' Drew said. 'It loads up the liquid in the base of the brush head and then the brush fibres taper to a fine point. If you give more pressure at the start of the stroke you dump a block of colour and then, as you release the weight off the brush, you can sweep the bristles to get a flowing line on the page. This ink gives a more solid colour than watercolour paint and you can see that the tattoo representation is a simplification of the overall effect. You can't expect a tattoo to have exactly the same fluidity as an actual brush. The fact there are three might mean something else but I'd bet on it being a brushstroke.'

'It would make sense, wouldn't it? said Beth. 'Rick's life revolved around art.'

'If you were going to have an arty tattoo, wouldn't you have something a bit more pretty than this?' said Maddox. 'I know that the tattooists say that tattoo designs have moved on considerably since this one would have been done, but surely they weren't all this uninspiring even in the '80s.'

'Let's combine the Masonic affiliation with threes to the icon of a brushstroke and maybe we're onto something.' said James. 'It'd be like a stamp of membership to some sort of group maybe? The first Masons were branded with a simple icon as a rite of passage and as a sign of lifelong membership. I wonder if there's a branch within the Arts?' James looked at Drew for confirmation of such a theory.

'Don't look at me!' Drew started to roll back his shirt sleeves to expose plain, unmarked flesh. 'If there is any such organisation I know nothing about it.'

James patted his brother-in-law's shoulder reassuringly. 'I know you haven't got a tattoo there Drew. I've been to enough of your famous barbecues and seen you in a tee shirt, turning sausages, to know that. I just wondered if you had any ideas.'

Drew merely shook his head and insisted complete ignorance on the subject.

'I'll bet your friend Conrad Jefferson would know something about such a group if one existed. It'd be just to his fancy to belong to an elite art society. He doesn't mind blurring the edges of the law, either.' said Maddox.

'Poor Conrad.' said Drew. 'He always does excite suspicion. I've only ever known him dally with accounts - and then only once.'

'You mean he only got caught once.' said James. 'I have to agree with Maddox. I wouldn't be surprised if Jefferson wouldn't be flattered to join some inner arty circle.'

'We don't know anything for sure yet.' said Beth. 'Let's not get too carried away with mystery and intrigue. It could have been something from Rick's student days - a member of a would-be underground life drawing class. You know, like "The Dead Poets Society." A bit affected maybe, but certainly not criminal.'

'It's very moderate-minded of you, Beth, and you may well be right. However, I can't afford to ignore any slight chance of a clue.' Turning to Maddox James adopted a business demeanour implying that he was ready for action. 'Maddox, can you chase up the tattooist for his records and see the other chap who did the more recent tattoo. See if he can remember anything else - we'll have to start clutching at straws. I'll go and see Monroe and put the scenario to him. He may have seen this design or heard of something like it. Monroe is desperate to make a case against Rick so I'll see if he can come up with any ideas too. They're bound to know about nefarious art groups. At least it's a start.'

James looked at Maddox and signalled that it was time to leave. They said goodnight and the two policemen walked to the car.

'I'll give you a lift home. We should leave these good people in peace. At the end of the day it's our problem, though I doubt Beth sees it that way.' said James.

As Beth cleared the mugs away she and Drew continued to discuss the matter.

'Do you really think that tattoo design is a brush stroke? asked Beth.

'It seems logical. What else could it be?' said Drew. 'If I'm honest Beth, I don't really care. I don't share your desire to chase down every clue and solve every loose end. I find the whole business sickening. I can live with a piece of artwork being stolen, although I disapprove of it of course. Much as I love the concept of artistic heritage, at the end of the day it's just pigment on paper. A human life is a very different matter. Nothing is worth that cost. It's utterly ridiculous! In the cold light of day no painting is worth that much.'

Beth leaned over and gave Drew a kiss. 'You're such a treasure. If only the rest of the world thought as you did.' She reaffirmed the sentiment with a hearty hug. 'The trouble is that not everyone is as sensible as you are and I'm not content to let that be. However, at this given moment in time the only thing that I can do is to finish my needlework. Let's go and be comfortable in the lounge so that I can do some sewing and we'll see what unfolds.'

Drew marvelled at the woman he loved but also gave his head a shake. It confused him to think that his wife would consider taking on the criminal classes in a heartbeat but could then put matters to one side for the sake of a bit of stem stitch.

'I thought you'd finished that design on a larger canvas.' said Drew.

Beth had been working on a representation of an illuminated manuscript from the Lindisfarne Gospels. It was a design that Beth had faithfully traced onto a large piece of linen and painstakingly stitched for months. He'd understood that she was ready for something different and yet here were the familiar sepia coloured threads again.

'I've finished the first work but I thought I'd do a quick miniature as an experiment.' said Beth.

'An experiment? It's a long process for an experiment!'

'You'll see.' said Beth, with a twinkle in her eye.

Drew knew better than to pry and decided to let matters rest, for the present at least. Beth threaded her needle and Drew picked up his book.

Chapter Sixteen

Carlton was the centre of attention as he connected power leads, hard drives and other technical paraphernalia. He conveyed the atmosphere of an alchemist setting out his chemical apparatus and the twinkle in his eye suggested that he was certain of creating pure gold.

'I know that we've worked under the radar in the past, but this is a legitimate service that you're providing. You can put in an invoice for services rendered, although I'm hoping that you'll quote "mates rates" on this one.' said James.

Carlton waved aside the prospect of payment and opened the lid of his laptop.

'The security guard was correct when he said that he couldn't see any anomalies.' said Carlton but the smirk that was breaking through indicated that this wasn't the end of the story. 'The poor chap could've saved himself a few dreary, sleepless nights as the human eye would never have been able to spot it.'

The question that was in everybody's mind was, "Spot what?" but the point was so glaringly obvious that nobody bothered to voice it. Instead, DCI James, Sgt Maddox, Drew and Beth all leaned in a little closer.

'There's no doubt all the security footage looks like "business as usual," even at more than a mere glance but that really isn't the case at all.' said Carlton. 'I'm not sure that what I've discovered will bring you any closer to finding a painting or a murderer but, although it looks like a lot of ad-hoc wandering to our eyes, I'm afraid that the camera does indeed tell lies. In actual fact there is a lot of repeated movement which in real life simply can't have happened. Nobody ever walks in exactly the same way, using the same number of steps with the same body motions and yet this is exactly what we have on these discs.

'You mean that the recording is actually old footage copied and pasted onto these recordings?' asked Maddox.

'It's a little more sophisticated than that, but in a nutshell - yes.' said Carlton.

'You say sophisticated.' said James. 'Exactly how sophisticated? Would you need to be a professional to make that false recording?'

'Oh, no! Most YouTubers would have the appropriate software. It doesn't take too much to get to grips with the programme if you're reasonably computer literate. After that it's just time and effort. Anybody with basic editing software could pull it off.' said Carlton. 'Finding it is another story though.'

'I'll ask you to write an official report with all the jargon of course, but would you distil it down into terms that we mortals could understand just for now.' said James.

Carlton responded with a nod and explained. 'There's so much security footage out there that it's physically impossible to view it all and scrutinise it. Gait recognition programmes have been developed to find common stances that occur in situations such as carrying a weapon or planting a bomb so as to quickly comb through the footage and flag any potential threats. It's still in the developmental stages at present, however it has been suggested that there are similarities in walking patterns, strides and body posture when a person is carrying a concealed weapon or walking away from making a drop. These common denominators are referred to as "human gait DNA" and when superimposed over security film the algorithms can detect potentially dangerous situations, whereas a team of observers would never get through the material in time. I took a chance and ran your footage through this process, thinking it might flag up a few clues. What I didn't expect was for it to find absolute carbon copies of movement, alike in every minuscule detail. It's irrelevant that sometimes a figure is walking in the opposite direction or is set against a different background. It's simply not possible for a human to replicate movement so consistently in such microscopic detail.'

'How are they walking in the opposite direction? And, who exactly are "they"?' asked James.

'Flipping an image can be done in a single click. Superimposing the video is more involved. You'd have to do quite a bit of editing and green-screen work, but it's still manageable.' said Carlton. 'Actually, there are some bits when the video does seem a bit ropey but you'd have to know to look for it before you'd notice it. The poor quality of the security cameras helped there, it's a bit grainy and that covers a multitude of cinematic sins. As far as who is altered, I'd say that pretty much everybody at the gallery has been given the treatment. In each of your cases a good hour or so is repeated footage one way or another.'

'You'd have to have access to the security suite which means that it has to be an inside job.' said Drew. 'We thought that was the case before but now it's an absolute certainty. There's no possible alternative. Who else could help themselves to a long term loan of a security disc except one of us?' The realisation that one of his colleagues, maybe even a friend, was a thief and probably also a murder was obviously repellent and Drew looked physically sickened.

'My friend Brian is going to be very upset when he realises how he's been duped.' said James.' Understanding his brother-in-law's predicament he laid a hand gently on Drew's shoulder. 'The only way to clear suspicion is to cast it on everybody and then, by a process of elimination, clear those who are innocent and see who is left.'

'Who on the staff has such technical skills?' asked Maddox. 'Alternatively, who is utterly incapable of such technical wizardry?'

As Drew was the only one who could guess at such things everybody fixed their attention on him. At first he shrugged his shoulders and shook his head, but realising that he at least needed to make an attempt for the sake of progress he started to search his mind.

'Unless I'm very much mistaken, I doubt that either of the regular security guards could manage such stuff.' Drew began. 'As far as I'm aware they work from a crib sheet and press button A or button B as required but don't think beyond that point - or can't think beyond it. I know they usually have to call Theo in when the computer has frozen and their flow chart of what to do doesn't clear the problem.'

'So could Theo manage it?' asked Beth.

'He's reasonably computer savvy, but whether that stretches to video editing I couldn't say.' said Drew.

'We don't imagine that Finn or his cronies could manage it - or do we?' asked Maddox.

'I think that anyone in their age group could make a good go of it. They were all born with a computer mouse in their hand.' said Maddox.

'Scott has a graphics tablet and "pen," not a mouse. That much I do know.' said Drew. 'Actually, I think he has a YouTube channel too. He posts time lapse videos of his artwork - the ones he can own up to.'

James gave Drew a searching gaze and when Drew realised the implications of what he'd just said he jumped to save his young friend's reputation.

'I know you think that clinches it, but it doesn't!' said Drew. 'Everyone of his peer group has a YouTube channel. They all make videos - even if they've really got nothing to show or say. Vlogging is like writing a diary to them. They just film it on their phone and upload it - even if it's drivel.'

'Nevertheless, we can't ignore it. You know that, Drew.' said James. 'Let's look at it from another angle. Every investigating officer is always told to consider three elements: Location, Victim and Offender. In both the theft and the murder the location is the same, the art gallery. The victim is linked to the world of art and museums - that much is obvious as the stolen item is a piece of art. So far the elements keep on overlapping. Let's now consider the potential offender.' At this point James came to an abrupt stop. Remembering his role as mentor to Maddox he turned to his protégé and began a lesson in deduction. 'Maddox, I know you've been cramming the police manual. What can you tell us about any possible motive in either of these cases?'

Maddox blushed now that his aspirations for career progression had been revealed but James soon reassured him that he wasn't in for a ribbing. Taking hold of the opportunity to further his education Maddox cautiously began to compose a hypothesis.

'Of course, we can only make an educated guess about the offender. What could the motive behind the murder be?' he began. 'Sex and revenge are the most common motives but an art related crime is unlikely to be sex related. The pure thrill of the crime is also unlikely. Revenge is always a possibility if the murder is linked to the theft but the prospect of gain is the most obvious motive, I think.'

'Surely that's universal in this case? Isn't anybody liable to benefit from owning a Constable?' said Beth.

'Yes, they are - if they know what to do with it. Would you know how to shift a great master without getting caught?' said James.

'Let's consider the aspect of time. The artwork has always been there, so what's changed? Why now?' said James. 'We know that a painting was stolen years ago and our victim was a likely candidate, but it didn't get him murdered back then, so what's new? Although both thefts were in the art circles of the Manchester galleries this case has a very different feel to it.'

'It's a different museum and no doubt the staff will have changed many times since then.' said Drew.

'That's a line of enquiry that we haven't yet pursued.' said James. 'Maddox, we need to dig around in the records to see who was in the staff or on the periphery of the Whitworth and MAG at the time of the first theft and see who's still on the scene now. However we also need to think about what's new - why now? One fresh face that I am sure of is our young friend Scott. I know you won't like it, Drew, but I'm afraid he's in for a grilling.'

The office space wasn't adequate for four grown men to be comfortably seated. Nevertheless DCI James, Sgt Maddox and CI Argyle managed to find a surface to rest on in DCI Monroe's office. Monroe sat in his own chair behind his desk with Argyle facing him on the only other allocated chair. James had requisitioned a chair from the corridor, positioning himself next to Argyle, and Maddox rested in a semi-standing position on the window ledge. They were all scrutinising the photograph of the tattoo that Forbes had pointed out on Rick van der Molen's body.

'It's less than inspiring, isn't it?' said Argyle. It was a rhetorical question as nobody could possibly disagree. 'You seem to favour the trinity chain of thought, don't you, James? What do you think, Monroe?'

'I agree that it's definitely something to do with threes. The only tattoos that are preoccupied with the significance of threes that I've ever heard of are the Triads in Hong Kong and China. There was a big crack down in the Seventies. The British police force and the civil service were largely in the pocket of such gangs - half of the force was in their pay. They were mainly associated with prostitution and drugs but a good deal of bribery and black market dealings were also part of their stock in trade.' said Monroe.

'Good grief, you're right!' said Argyle. 'We should be thinking of triads not trinity. There used to be, and most probably still is, a Chinese triad that specialised in the theft of art and antiquities. They'd lure young, vulnerable kids into their net and use them to transport stolen goods. Once you were a member you never got out alive. They were branded with a tattoo on the soles of their feet. It was a more sophisticated affair than this design but I seem to remember that the design was based around a triangular shape.'

While Argyle was explaining about the gang Maddox was searching the internet and looking for an image on his phone. He handed it to Argyle asking which one it might be.

'I've never personally seen one but I read of a few of these examples.' Argyle pointed to some particular images. 'Each group has a kanji set inside a triangle. I heard of the orchid being used as it represented perfection, harmony and elegance. This might be appropriate to the world of art but their world was really a very different story. As ever, the bottom line was the fact that millions of pounds were at risk and they'd pay any price to keep their assets, no matter how gruesome the outcome. Betrayal inevitably resulted in violent death. They made their example plain to see so that everybody got the message to toe the line.'

'Our design seems quite a schoolboy rendition by comparison. Do you honestly think it can be related? It hardly seems feasible!' said James.

'I agree that these look like simplified brush marks.' said Monroe. 'But combine that with the fact that there are three of them forming a symbol and a masterpiece has gone missing - and now we also have a violent murder on our hands. Don't forget that Rick was under suspicion himself. The incontrovertible facts point to this almost childish tattoo having sinister connotations. It may not be a Chinese Triad, it could even be a sort of copy cat attempt, but it's a convincing line of thought. I'd say we'd got a gang of one sort or another on our hands.'

'When you put it like that it makes sense, but it sounds ludicrous nevertheless.' said James. 'It's the sort of thing you'd read about in a boys' adventure story.'

'It might sound like that at first, but I assure you that no mere boy would get past the first chapter.' said Monroe.

Maddox had been plucking up courage to join in the discussion and as his seniors paused to contemplate the seriousness of what they might be dealing with he found the lull he'd been waiting for.

'I know you've explained about a Chinese gang that specialises in art theft and murder, but we're not in China now. What does this mean for us specifically?' he asked.

'We can only guess at the moment.' said Monroe. 'However, even if it's a pale comparison I think we've an unpleasant organisation on our hands. It's apparent that they are organised - it's the only explanation for how successful the theft, or thefts, have been. Now there is a murder we have to take the prospect seriously. They obviously mean business, whether we think their tattoo is silly or not.'

'The tattoo Rick had is old, maybe even decades old. That would put him in his student days. Perhaps he got lured in as a student. It's a time when he'd be ripe to join in daring escapades and elite organisations, especially if they offer you the prospect of position and power in a world that's notoriously difficult to get on in. I suspect he wouldn't have been made fully aware of the cost until it was too late.' said James.

'Does this take the heat off Scott?' asked Maddox.

'I'm not so sure that it does.' said Monroe. 'He's ripe for the picking just now. He's vulnerable and idealistic. Maybe he's keen to make his own mark, more than mere spray paint on a wall. He's already been in trouble - he's the perfect candidate! He'd only be at the bottom of the food chain in the organisation now but he's perfectly placed to be used like a pawn on a chess board. He'd have to show his commitment and earn his right to enter, with promises of reward and advancement. What better way than to give access to the gallery - and for what?

A mere sketch! It's the action rather than the actual item, like a rite of passage or an initiation. It's just a token, that's the message here I think.'

'They could have stolen anything, so why stay at a mere trifle?' said Argyle.

'But didn't you say that this often happened? Art has been stolen purely because it was the only thing they knew to take.' said Maddox.

Monroe nodded. 'Yes, that's still a possibility. It's all supposition and theory, but we have to view matters in the light of all the information we have available and, on balance, I think we're looking at the gesture rather than the actual value of the item stolen. That and the fact that murder is now in the equation.'

On the way back to Mossleigh James and Maddox discussed the case.

'Do you honestly think that this Triad theory is viable, Sir?' asked Maddox.

'I don't know that it isn't viable.' said James. 'As such we have no alternative but to consider it as an option. It may not seem at home to our experience to date but the theory withstands scrutiny and we'll have to pursue the enquiries. In the meantime you need to delve back into the employment records of the academic arts scene at the time just before and up to the time that the MAG theft was discovered.'

'Do you have anybody in mind?'

'I'm not sure that I have any firm suspicions but I've a funny feeling that when you come up with something - and I'm certain that you will - I'm sure I won't be surprised. It seems uncanny that Conrad

Jefferson is in the art clique. He'd be just the type to find it flattering to belong to some elite group. He'd never get his own hands dirty, of course. Nevertheless I have no doubt that he'd be quite at home to turning a blind eye to the less pleasant part of belonging to such a scene. So long as he gets to feel important and clever he'd be involved somehow. Didn't Monroe tell us that one of the motives for stealing or acquiring stolen art was to gain a sense of conferred power and culture? That'd be just like Jefferson.'

'You really don't like him, do you Sir?'

'Whatever gives you that impression?' James laughed at the transparency of his feeling against Jefferson. 'I know that he seems like a really nice guy - and I do like the veneer that he presents to the world. It's just that in this game you never do trust that first impression, at least not with types like Jefferson. He's too clever for his own good! People like Jefferson are never satisfied with what the world legitimately has to offer. He doesn't need money or possessions but he does need a challenge, and he thrives on power and control. Running an architectural company and studying art in his spare time won't be enough. You mark my words, there's always more than meets the eye with men like Jefferson.'

'And what about Scott?'

'Ah yes, Scott. He's the new kid on the block and it's funny how things turn sour now that he's on the scene. I've been nice to young Scott until now but I think it's time I gave him my full attention. I've let you talk to him so as not to spook the kid but I think

I'm guilty of shielding him for Drew's sake. I promised Baskeyfield that I'd be impartial and it's true that I've not stinted on Drew but I've let him affect my attention to his friend. Scott is just as likely to be motivated by the possibility of prestige and acceptance, even if it's in less exalted circles than Jefferson's - it's all relative.'

'It's time to get down to business.' continued James. 'My sister is hatching a plan but she's keeping her cards close to her chest and so we'll have to carry on in our own fashion. Let's see what tomorrow brings.'

Maddox pulled in at Mossleigh police station where James had left his own car. After bidding James goodbye and then posting the keys into the police station letter box Maddox walked to Henrietta's and James drove home in his own car. Every case required a good measure of dull routine enquiry and a generous helping of luck. James knew that, if they just kept following their noses, in time they'd smell the scent of a lead. At present there was no tangible scent but his nose was definitely beginning to feel the first signs of a twitch.

Chapter Seventeen

It was Mossleigh WI's turn on the watering timetable. The date for the announcement of the winner was imminent and there was no knowing when a judge might visit, so everything still had to be looking its best. Watering took place early in the morning and then later in the evening so that, should the weather turn particularly hot, the petals and leaves wouldn't scorch. Mercifully the summer had been mostly dry so at least they weren't dealing with soaked and rotten foliage. Usually a bit of dead-heading as you watered did the job. After her last pupil Beth shared a quick ham sandwich with Drew and reached for her shoes to walk to the village hall to rendezvous with the other volunteers.

'I think I'll come with you.' said Drew. 'I know I'm not a member of the WI - obviously - but another pair of hands won't go amiss, I'm sure. I've been staring at my drawing board all day and I don't seem to be getting much further on. I just can't seem to concentrate. It's a good job that Conrad isn't in too much of a rush for this painting. I could do with a break and a bit of fresh air.'

Beth and Drew walked hand in hand in the cool evening. They took the scenic route through The Green and walked by the lake rather than walking down Main Street to make the most of their short walk together. Quite a crowd had gathered outside the community hall. Everyone carried watering cans and large bottles and a queue was forming for the outside tap so that the various vessels could be filled. Beth saw Kirsty on the edge of the crowd. She had a clipboard in her hand and was directing waterers to various locations. Carlton had obviously had the same inclination as Drew and walked over to say hello.

'There are plenty of hands on deck tonight. We'll be done in an hour if we don't dally. Why don't you and Beth come for a drink as soon as you're done?' Carlton said.

Drew agreed and went to tell Beth the change in the arrangements for the evening. The team of waterers marched off to the stipulated locations and, as Carlton had predicted, the job was soon done. Volunteers could either deliver all the dead flower heads to Kirsty to add to her own compost heap or they could take them home with them and dispose of them however they chose. Kirsty said it was worth her time waiting for the few who did bring their collections to her as it was rich substance for her compost. Beth opted to wait at the community hall with Kirsty while the men walked back to prepare drinks and nibbles. By the time they were joined by the ladies glasses of Kirsty's home-brewed Elderflower wine were poured and a cheeseboard awaited them. The night was still mild and they opted to sit outside in Kirsty's beautiful garden surrounded by flowers and twinkling garden lights.

'Do you think we'll win?' asked Beth.

'Who can tell?' said Kirsty. 'We've put on a good show and I don't think we could have done better, but I guess we'll just have to wait and see.'

'How is your brother getting on with the case?' asked Carlton. 'Did my discovery help at all?'

'I don't know what progress he's made but it's solidified what were vague suspicions into facts. I guess that's progress of sorts.' said Beth. 'I can just about grasp bits being mirrored, although you think they'd look wrong, but what on earth is green screen?'

'Flipping a stationary image is easy and it's not too much trickier with a video image. You're right that the architecture and doors would be mirrored but if you're not really looking for it it wouldn't be noticed. After all, you're just watching people walking to and fro as they go about their business between bouts of seeing nothing at all.' said Carlton. 'Green screening is a special effects technique where you can select certain aspects and then overlay them to new images. You screen off any background with a backdrop, ideally a green cloth. The back drop eliminates any background noise making it easier to select a single moving figure. Without the screen you have to deselect all sorts of background details which is very time consuming. The computer software can do it for you to a point. The tool is called a magic wand and it selects what it thinks you need to transplant but if there's lots of background detail it can't differentiate between background and foreground. It gets particularly tricky with enclosed sections such as in-between arms and legs, and with a moving image this would be a nightmare. However, if you screen off the background a couple of clicks of the mouse should do it. After that all you do is superimpose the clip onto a different static background image.'

'So in the context of the gallery if a plain cloth, such as a builders dust sheet, blanked off a wall or corridor, somebody walking in corridor A could be made to look like they were walking in corridor B?' asked Drew.

'Yes, that's exactly so.' said Carlton. 'That way the footage doesn't look too repetitive so as to raise suspicion. They are walking down different corridors and in different directions and the repetitious movements don't look too fishy. It's very clever.'

'It shows planning and forethought.' said Drew. 'Murder is nasty enough but to plan it so meticulously is particularly disturbing - and I'm working alongside someone with such a devious mind. It's terrifying!'

'It shows that the theft was planned meticulously but it doesn't necessarily follow that the murder was premeditated.' said Beth.

'I'm not sure that I find that altogether reassuring, but I'll take what comfort I can get. I hope this all gets cleared up soon. I don't like going to the gallery myself and I'm definitely not at all happy about you going tomorrow Beth.' said Drew.

'I appreciate your concern.' said Beth, giving Drew's hand a squeeze. 'But just think about it. In the first place I'll be in a group the whole time and we both know that we have absolutely nothing to do with any theft. The police may not know that as a categorical fact, although I don't think we're under particular suspicion, but we know it - and better still, so does the murderer. So why bother with us? We're no threat and so we're not worth noticing.'

Beth's argument was convincing but Drew didn't seem entirely satisfied.

'What else can we do?' Beth continued. 'We can't lock ourselves away. I hope we do get to the bottom of it but we can't hide indefinitely. I'm sure I'll be quite safe and I really would like to go.'

Drew shrugged his shoulders. He accepted Beth's point but that didn't mean that he had to like it.

'What's happening at the gallery to tempt you, Beth?' asked Kirsty.

'I'm going to the Historical Stitching Society. Do you remember, Hyacinth invited me when we were at the last WI meeting?' said Beth.

'Oh I remember.' said Kirsty. 'I almost wish I could sew just so that I could come along. It all sounds very jolly. What historical theme will you be stitching? If you were sewing illustrations from Gerard's Herbal I might be tempted to pick up a needle no matter how many times I stabbed myself.'

Beth laughed. She'd seen Kirsty's attempts at sewing a missing button and could only watch for a couple of seconds before she offered to take over.

'I think the group are working on a William Morris design but I'm taking my Celtic embroidery along. I can't presume to butt in at my first meeting and I really do want to get this finished for Theo. I'm holding a little party next week and I want to give it to him then. Actually, I have two to show him and then he can pick his favourite. I can't think why he wants one at all so I'd rather he chose himself.' said Beth.

'Who wouldn't want one? They're beautiful!' said Kirsty.

To hide her embarrassment Beth reached for her cardigan. The night was getting colder but as she turned she realised that she'd left it at home. It was suggested that they move inside but as it was getting late Beth and Drew said it was time to go. Drew gave Beth his jumper and they started the short walk home, walking slowly to make the most of the lovely evening.

DCI James had been on his way to interview Scott when he'd got the call from the hospital notifying him that Finn was now fully conscious and seemed well enough to manage a short interview. Scott would have to wait. It would do him good to sweat a bit. Knowing that Maddox would want to join in, not to mention the fact that he'd appreciate a break from poring over employment records, he'd called to arrange to meet him at the hospital.

The doctor wanted a brief word with James before he interviewed Finn.

'He seems pretty well in himself.' the doctor said. 'Can you believe that when he came round he calmly asked for some paracetamol as he said he'd got a bit of a headache? He must have the mother of all headaches! At first he couldn't remember what had happened and didn't know why he was in hospital but as he slowly gathered his wits it's all coming back to him. He probably wishes that he was unconscious again, he must feel pretty rough. After about half an hour he asked to speak to the police. I guessed you'd want to speak to him first so I got the call put to you.' James expressed his thanks in a gesture and the doctor continued. 'I said that he seems remarkably well, but don't let that deceive you. The brain is a fragile thing and his has had a pretty bad shaking. You can only speak to him for a limited time. I insist that a nurse be present for the whole interview and if she thinks the patient has had enough then you have to stop, no matter how inconvenient it is to you. And if the patient says he's had enough then that's the final word.'

James agreed to the terms. What else could he do? The nurse escorted him and Maddox to Finn's room and stood by the door to keep an eye on proceedings.

'Are you the police?' asked Finn.

'That's right. I understand you asked to speak to us?' said James. 'However, you must be careful not to overtax yourself. Take your time, we can always come back.'

'Oh, I'm fine. I've just got a bit of a headache. Though, now I come to think about it I'm not surprised. My throat's sore too.' To add meaning to the statement Finn gingerly felt his neck where signs of bruising still showed.

'You're in good hands here and you'll soon be right as rain.' said James. 'I gather you particularly asked to see us so do you mind if I record this conversation? My sergeant here will take notes and ask you to sign them but my shorthand is shocking and his handwriting is terrible. It'd take the strain off us all if I could record us chatting.'

Finn gave his assent and was eager to get talking. He began to recount his tale with plentiful sips of juice to help his sore throat. His vocal cords did sound like they'd had a throttling but other than the frequent sips Finn didn't appear to consider it.

'At first I didn't know why I was here.' he began. 'I felt so knocked about and couldn't think why but then it came flooding back to me.'

'So why are you in hospital?' asked James.

'Because that bloke at the museum strangled me and threw me in the tip.'

'Which man?' asked James. He pulled a picture of Theo, from his profile on the gallery's website, onto his mobile and showed it to Finn.

Finn shook his head. 'No not him, but I do remember his face.'

James was confused and found another picture and showed Finn.

'Yes, I think that was him.'

'Was he alone when you were attacked?'

'I don't know. I couldn't say for sure.'

'Now why would this man attack you?'

This question stunned Finn and he suddenly looked confused. However, James wasn't convinced that this amnesia was authentic.

James continued to question Finn. 'Where have you met him before? You say from the museum but you don't strike me as an art lover. Why would you see him there?'

Finn only responded with silence.

'Let me tell you what I do know.' continued James. 'Maybe that will help you piece things together. I know that you and your pals decided to thrust yourself into the Whitworth Art Gallery and were treated to a private tour. I also know that later that night a painting was stolen from the archives - a cloud study to be exact. It was the sketch that had been pointed out to you only hours earlier. Does this help jog your memory?'

Finn looked confused again but this time it was obviously a feigned confusion. It was a well practised closed-off look that had obviously been perfected during many previous interviews with the police and it indicated that he had nothing further to say. Finn had taken himself down a cul-de-sac and hadn't realised, until it was too late, where the conclusion of his story would take him. He knew that silence had served him well in the past and was now the only option open to him. James knew better than to keep hammering on this closed door, especially with a vulnerable patient.

'Never mind. Don't you worry yourself about it.' said James. 'I'm sure things will piece together in good time.' Deciding to pick up the threads of a different theme James changed his tone and casually asked, 'What about your friend Scott? Do you see much of him these days?'

Finn practically harrumphed at the question. 'He thinks he's too good for me now he's got in with the posh lot.'

'I don't know about that. He's proved himself to be a good friend while you've been having a nice little sleep here.'

Finn looked to question James at this new information.

'Oh, yes.' said James. 'Scott has sat by your bedside for hours. The nurses said it would help if you could hear a familiar voice and so Scott has sat chatting away to thin air for hours on end in the hope that it might bring you back.'

'He always did witter on when nobody was listening.' said Scott. He looked like he was grateful nevertheless. Then remembrance dawned on him. 'I remember him sitting here! I tried to tell him what had happened but I got so confused.' Realising again the awkward ground that he heading toward he trailed off by mumbling that he couldn't remember any more. Amnesia was a safe haven and so he resorted to it once again.

James could see that the nurse was starting to get fidgety and realised that his time was almost up.

'I don't want you to over-do things but do you feel that you could write a brief line or two explaining a few details of your attack? Just the basics. If you could then sign it that would be really helpful.'

Finn said he felt quite up to the task and readily took up the paper and pen that Maddox gave to him.

'I've written "Rick" but I don't know his full name and I've written what I can remember of the Whitworth when I came to for a short while. It's not a very full description but it's the best that I can manage.' said Finn.

'Now you just concentrate on getting better and I'll sort it out, don't you worry yourself about anything' said James in his best bedside manner.

After more reassurance to the patient James led the way into the corridor. Before Maddox could speak James gestured for him to stay silent. Without any further clue James marched to the hospital canteen and bought a coffee for himself and a tea for Maddox, along with several sachets of sugar for his sweet-toothed protégé.

Bursting to break the silence Maddox said, 'Well, that's pretty damning. Who'd have thought Rick was capable of murder, or at least attempted murder? I wouldn't have thought him strong enough! It doesn't help us much now though, does it? I don't think he killed himself!'

All the tension drained from James. His whole body sagged.

'What this gives us is precisely nothing. It's all a mare's nest!' said James. 'It doesn't matter that some of the details don't add up - some of the timings don't quite work out - because in his present condition nothing he says is admissible in court. Even then, it's no good at all to us. His brain is completely addled!'

'I know it won't do as evidence but Finn seems pretty clear about what happened to him, even if he clammed up when it didn't suit him. It does give us some answers though.' said Maddox.

James just sadly shook his head and handed Maddox the statement that Finn had written out. Maddox looked at it and couldn't believe his eyes.

'Is he taking the mickey?' asked Maddox.

'I don't think so. No, I really don't think he is.'

On the page were a series of meaningless squiggles written with great gusto but conveying absolutely nothing vaguely recognisable as a letter, let alone a constructed word or sentence.

'When I asked Finn to check it through and sign it he didn't seem the least bit embarrassed or fazed. He happily signed it - or at least thought he did. I'm convinced he thinks he's done a good job of it. I know he's not the most academic youth but he's not so illiterate as that.' said James.

'What's going on?'

'I have absolutely no idea. We'd better go and ask the doctor.'

The doctor wasn't surprised in the least.

'When I asked you to come it was primarily for the benefit of my patient, although I knew you'd want to know that he was conscious and see him for yourself. He'd asked to see you but you already know that anything he says is inadmissible and you can surely guess that he'd be bound to be confused.' he explained.

'What about the random scribble?' asked Maddox.

'It's just another indication that his brain isn't quite firing on all cylinders yet, if it ever will. He may well make a full recovery - eventually. However, as it stands just now things are still healing. He may honestly think that he's remembered and written a comprehensive account of his experience but it doesn't mean he's got it right. The brain is an extremely complex organ but it's childishly simple to explain.' said the doctor. 'While all the neurological pathways are connecting after the shaking the brain took they're continually firing and misfiring. He'll feel like he can solve all the world's problems and become a mathematical genius into the bargain. It will all seem so glaringly clear as his brain is sparking but at the same time he probably won't be able to coordinate his thoughts to tie his own shoelaces. If he can dress himself and put food into his mouth he'll have made good progress. However, he could be shoving his socks into his mouth and mashed potato on his feet and be unaware of his mistake. I've got great hopes that he will make a full recovery, but it will take time. You can't rush the healing process, we just have to keep him comfortable and let his body do the work.'

The interview was soon over and Maddox and James stood in the car park mulling over what they'd just heard.

'So that was an utter waste of time.' said Maddox.

'Quite possibly, but it still had to be done. Perhaps Rick could have been involved, in fact it's likely that he was. It's just another breadcrumb to pick up along to road. Don't lose heart, we're a formidable team.' said James. Brightening up he turned his attention to other matters. 'Let's see how an hour or so of waiting has softened Scott. We'll see what he has to say for himself. I'll meet you at the station and we'll give him our full attention. Monroe has cleared an interview room for us. Give me half an hour or so and then come in with coffee and smiles. You can play "good cop" once he's had a bit of the stern side of me.'

It may only have been an hour or two that Scott had been kept waiting but he looked like he'd been sitting in the waiting room for a week. As soon as James entered the room Scott jumped to his feet.

'Inspector James, thank God you're back. I've been dying to go to the loo for ages but this plod won't let me go!'

'Steady on, that's no way to refer to a police officer.' said James. 'He's only doing as he's been told.'

Scott looked abashed. 'I do apologise.' This was directed to the police officer who had been standing guard. Turning back to James he continued, 'I'm getting stressed and I really need to go. It's making me slip back into my old ways. I haven't done anything wrong and yet I'm locked in this room like a convict and can't even go to the bathroom.'

James allowed Scott to make the necessary trip, explaining that maybe the police officer had overstepped what was required in his orders but was only doing what he thought best. As Scott passed through the door James gave a wink to the police officer and said he could leave once he'd seen Scott back.

'Tell me about your YouTube channel.' said James.

This obviously threw Scott off his guard completely.

'You made me sit here all this time to ask me about my YouTube channel?'

'I asked you to wait here so that I could ask you a number of questions. Telling me about your channel will make a good start. Assume that I know nothing whatsoever about the subject - and make it easy for me to understand.'

'I've just got a few videos of my artwork on there. I don't do anything else. I really don't get vlogging. Who wants to listen to somebody chattering on and on about nothing? I used to earn a bit of money from it but not now. All the rules for monetisation have changed.'

'Where do you film this artwork then? Do you film as you paint?'

'I used to film anywhere I could. I don't film any more. Since I've been at the gallery I've stopped with the graffiti.'

'You mean since you got prosecuted.' This wasn't a question. James wanted to strip away the flummery and get down to brass tacks.

Scott just nodded.

'You'll notice that this little chat is unofficial.' said James. 'I'm not taking statements and I'm not recording. I have no interest in historical graffiti cases but I do need you to tell me how you filmed and edited your material.'

Scott thought a moment before he answered. Once he'd decided to be totally honest with the Inspector he sat up straight and then answered with confidence.

'I filmed myself painting wherever I happened to be, on location you could say. In the edit I made sure that I cropped out any landmarks that could pinpoint where I'd been. For the most part you'd just see the wall on screen but some of the edges of the film are blurred if I thought it would be noticeable as a specific place that could easily be traced.'

'Did you screen off the area so you could select it for editing? I think they call it green-screening. Did you do that?'

'No there wouldn't have been time. I had to work fast - I'm sure you can understand why.'

James merely nodded.

'There was no need, either.' Scott continued. 'The wall did the job for me. I didn't need to deselect or magic wand anything out because the image was cropped and it was easy enough to blur the edges. I thought it made the film look better too, it gives a sort of blurred vignette.'

'I almost want to ask what a vignette is but I'll leave that for a time when I can take a personal interest. Now let's talk about your friend Finn. Have you been to see him recently?'

Scott looked ashamed and lowered his head. His voice was lower too as he answered. 'No. I've hardly been recently. I'm not doing any good, in fact I think I'm making it worse.'

'You're referring to his brief, but dramatic return to consciousness I think.'

'Yes. I forgot where my ramblings were taking me. It's hard work to chatter away endlessly whilst avoiding touchy subjects - they crop up more than you imagine. I thought I was helping but I really wasn't at all.'

'Had he shown any signs of returning to consciousness before that?'

'No.'

'What about since then?'

'No. I haven't been much since then, but no - just that one time.'

At this point they were joined by Maddox who came in carrying a tray of drinks. As Maddox handed a can of cola to Scott the young lad looked relieved to be included in the round of drinks - and not merely for the sake of quenching his thirst. He beamed his gratitude for such a show of camaraderie.

'I think we're almost done here, but if we've got a drink we'll carry on chatting for a bit.' said James. 'Can you give me any idea of where Finn might have been hiding before we found him?'

'I've absolutely no idea. He certainly hasn't been home - Brad and Leighton would have known. Neither was he in any of his usual haunts. I'm out of touch with all that now, he'd have changed them since I was in his good books. The others would know though and they couldn't find him.' said Scott.

'I should probably now tell you that Finn has properly returned to consciousness.' said James.

'Has he?' said Scott. 'That's great news! How is he?'

'Bearing in mind what he's gone through he's in remarkable shape. He's a bit confused just now but it's thought that he's likely to make a full recovery in time.' said James.

'Can I visit him?'

'No, that's out of the question. He's a key witness, so you can't be talking to him.'

'That makes it sounds like I'd be conspiring with him. But I suppose I take your point. Can he remember who attacked him?'

'He thinks he can but I can't rely on what he says, even if he thinks he's telling the truth. I do think that he can remember more than he's letting on, though. He has very selective bouts of amnesia.'

'He's such a fool! Even if he hadn't had his head knocked about he wouldn't understand the trouble he's in. He's bound to be cagey about the theft just out of habit, but he'd never realise that he's in much bigger trouble for colluding with a murder.'

At this point Scott abruptly stopped speaking and looked directly at James. 'He doesn't know that though, does he? He was in over his head when he got involved in the break-in, without being bright enough to know it. Once he realises that somebody has actually died - even if he doesn't realise how close he was to that being him, he might start to understand that he needs to tell you everything. You have to tell him!'

'Give me chance.' said James. 'He'd only just come round. I'm not going to give him such a shock the minute he wakes up. The doctor would have me suspended for misconduct! And, as I said, he really is quite confused, so I'm not sure he could help us much at the moment anyway. It'll keep. Let's give him time to get his head together and then we'll see. In the meantime we'll have to do without Finn's help and that's why you're here.'

Maddox handed round a packet of ginger nuts to endorse the friendly atmosphere.

'Had you ever met Rick before you were at the Whitworth, or did you ever meet him outside of your work there?' asked James.

'I'd never have met anybody like Rick before I started community service at the gallery. I mixed in far less exalted circles before then. That's what made Finn so mad and started all this trouble.'

'Did Finn ever come to the gallery before that day?'

'Not that I know of. I can only guess why he came at all on that day, but who knows what he's been up to. I'm out of the loop so I would be the last to know.'

'We've finished our tea party so I guess we'd better get back to work.' said James.' I'll probably have some more questions for you so don't go too far away.'

'I've nowhere else to go, don't worry.' said Scott.

Chapter Eighteen

Beth had decided that it was futile for her to attempt to emulate even a minute shadow of the finery that Hyacinth had managed for Conrad's birthday party. Instead she wisely stayed within her own usual remit and opted for a homey supper, stipulating that the dress code be casual. When her friends first arrived they were greeted with a scaled down, domestic alternative to hors d'oeuvres. The recipe had originally stipulated Cheddar cheese for Cheddar and Chutney tarts but, in deference to the county of her residence she'd changed this to Cheshire cheese. Because of the sharper taste of the cheese she'd also changed the chutney to her own apple and apricot chutney which she'd made at the start of the summer. If there was any specific theme to the supper it had unwittingly developed into an homage to apples. Supper usually implies a wintry feel and, although Beth chose to use the slow cooker to make a hotpot for convenience, she had resorted to various additions of apple to keep the menu light.

The party was cheery enough on the surface but there was a barely distinguishable tension beneath the surface of joviality. Drew poured everybody a glass of cider which covered some gaps in conversation. Nevertheless, Beth couldn't escape the feeling that there was a dampener to the evening but couldn't locate the source. Doubling her efforts as hostess she rallied the conversation and moved the group to the dining table. Ordinarily they'd have chatted leisurely before being seated to begin the meal but, as chatter wasn't flowing naturally, Beth thought it best to move on with proceedings.

'I thought you'd said that this was to be an informal supper, we should be in the kitchen.' said Hyacinth. 'I'm all out of sorts sitting here at the dining table.'

Beth laughed. 'I wanted to make at least a little effort at creating a sense of occasion. Although, in truth it's because I didn't particularly want you sitting looking at the dishes. I never could wash as I cook. Don't worry, you'll soon relax once you get to the bottom of that glass of cider.'

Seeing his cue Drew topped up everyone's glass. For the main meal Beth placed a large casserole dish of pulled pork and Bramley apple hotpot into the centre of the table. To keep the meal on the lighter side there were warm baguettes with butter and rocket salad alongside the casserole instead of layering potatoes into the slow cooker. As the group settled into congenial conversation and the hotpot decreased down the sides of the dish the bread and sauce became more of a fondue scenario and the guests relaxed into familiar chatter. Nobody seemed in a hurry to leave the table and Beth kept up a steady replenishment of warm bread and butter whilst Drew kept the cider flowing.

Drew thought that now would be a good time to ask if any of his artistic friends knew anything about the unusual tattoo design that was causing so much consternation.

'Here's a rough sketch of the design.' Drew explained. 'Did anyone see this on Rick's forearm? Have you ever seen anything like it before?'

Nobody could recollect ever having seen it.

'You used have a tattoo, didn't you, Conrad?' said Hyacinth.

Conrad looked deeply embarrassed at this revelation.

'I don't know why you're blushing, Conrad.' said Sally. 'Theo's got loads! It's quite normal in these degenerate days.'

'Oh, I'm not blushing because I had a tattoo per se.' said Conrad. 'It's more the what and the why that makes me cringe.'

'Do tell!' said Sally. 'I can't imagine you ever doing anything cringeworthy.'

At first Conrad was reluctant but popular opinion demanded that he share his secret. He rolled up his shirt sleeve to reveal his inner forearm - the same spot where Rick's tattoo was situated.

'It was during a stupid student phase.' he said. 'I'm embarrassed by my own pomposity. I studied Architectural Drawing for my degree but I hung around with the Arts and Classics students. A group of us all had the same tattoo. If I'm honest I never really understood the reason and the symbolism behind it - everybody else seemed to. I just tagged along wanting to fit in. It was some sort of Chinese calligraphy resting over a symbol that I had no clue about but I thought it was super cool at the time. Lord, I could die at the thought of it now! I felt that I was so cultured at the time but years later, although not all that many years later if truth be told, I realised how utterly ludicrous it was. In fact I became convinced that I'd got something from a take-away menu on my arm forever. I couldn't shake off the conviction that I'd got a tattoo saying "chicken chow mein" with me for the rest of my life. As soon as laser removal looked like it was a valid option I had it removed. It took a few goes but you can hardly tell there was a tattoo there at all now. It just doesn't tan so well on that spot, that's all.'

Conrad sat back and resigned himself to his friends' laughter and jibes.

'Yours are pretty decent on the whole, Theo.' said Sally. 'Show them yours. Here, start with this one.'

Sally began to unbutton Theo's shirt but he shook her off.

'Oh no, Theo! You're going to have to bare all now.' said Conrad. 'It's only fair now you've had a laugh at my expense. It's your turn now.'

Theo looked sheepish but eventually succumbed knowing that the tide was against him. He undid a few of his shirt buttons so as to expose the back of his shoulder.

'Well now, that does show commitment.' said Drew.

Theo was embarrassed in the extreme but stoically bore his friend's inspection and only barely guarded amazement at the artwork embedded in his skin. His shoulder sported an excellent, if simplified, copy of Salisbury Cathedral with a token tree, cloud and the formation of a rainbow rounding off the design. All the elements combined in such a grouping made it instantly recognisable.

'Good grief, it's the Constable!' said Conrad.

Theo visibly cringed at this exclamation but sat still as his friends pored over his shoulder looking at the image.

'It's quite marvellous, actually.' said Drew. 'I'll bet there isn't another tattoo like it in the world. I knew you were a devotee, Theo, but this is quite something.'

Oblivious to Theo's discomfiture Sally blundered ahead to increase his shame.

'He's got another! Show them your other one, Theo. They'll recognise that design too.'

Enough was enough. Theo had taken enough humiliation and wasn't prepared to go any further.

'I don't intend to strip, Sally!' he said. 'I think these good people have seen enough of my skin, inked or otherwise.' Theo's tone had sufficient steel behind it for even Sally to know that he'd had enough.

In order to cover the awkwardness Beth jumped into the conversation. 'I'll never have a tattoo.' she said. 'It's not that I disapprove, it's just that I have a really low pain threshold. I also have a deep seated horror of exposing flesh to a complete stranger.'

'You are funny.' said Hyacinth.

'I could never have a tattoo, purely because I can't imagine living with the same image for my entire life.' said Drew.

'But you could have it removed.' said Conrad.

'You can now, yes, but you'd hardly have a tattoo in the sure knowledge that you'll soon want it gone.' said Drew.

'I guess not.' said Conrad. 'But I'm so glad that I could get rid of mine even though, at the time, I was convinced that I'd wear it as a badge of honour for all eternity.' Conrad shuddered at the recollection of his foolish arrogance.

'What on earth did you do all the time, when you hung around with these cultural types?' asked Beth. 'Drew, you were an art student and I don't remember you having the option of getting a clan tattoo.'

'That's because I didn't hang around with the arty set.' said Drew. 'I might have been an art student but once I was outside of the studio I was with you all of the time.'

'How romantic!' said Sally.

'Well, Beth, you saved him from the pain of getting a stupid tattoo and then having that pain all over again to get it removed.' said Conrad. 'You've got a good woman if she'll save you from such folly - but I guess you know that already, eh, Drew?'

'Seriously though, what on earth did you all do?' asked Beth.

'Hardly anything at all, if my memory serves me right.' said Conrad. 'We just floated about looking like we knew it all. We'd go to private viewings in obscure art galleries, listen to music and poetry recitals. All of this was in a fog of cheap wine and cheap cigarettes - with a few dodgy smokes in between.'

'Conrad! You never told me about that.' Hyacinth's merry tone reassured her husband that he wasn't in too much trouble.

'Would it spoil my reputation still further if I confessed to you all that I merely pretended to smoke. In fact, I pretended pretty much everything with that set. I knew absolutely nothing about the art and literature they waxed lyrical on. I just nodded and tried not to look stupid.'

'That doesn't sound like the Conrad we know.' said Theo.

'I was a late developer, you might say. In fact, I think it was the desire to know all of these hidden things - which seemed to be so open to them - that drove me to study and learn so much of these subjects that I was so drawn to. When I look back now, I'm quite sure that they were as clueless as I was. I'm convinced that none of them knew what they were talking about. It was all bravado, they just bluffed more convincingly.' said Conrad.

They all agreed that this was so often the case and found that it was more usual that those who really did know their stuff didn't bother to shout about it because they were sufficiently absorbed with their own thoughts and hadn't the need to wear all of their medals at once. It was to be pitied that this was rare enough in adults let alone in the younger scene.

'Beth, speaking of knowing your stuff, let's see if you've been practising the Schumann as you said you would.' said Theo.

'Oh goodness. Now I'm going to have to bluff my way through.' said Beth. 'Won't you have dessert first?'

'No. We all need a breather. Let's play piano while we digest that lovely supper. We'll enjoy dessert all the more if we let supper settle and make a bit of room. No excuses, let's go play.' said Theo.

It was agreed unanimously that this was a good plan and so they all squeezed into Beth's music room. Conrad and Hyacinth occupied the small sofa, Drew took the office chair at Beth's desk, Sally sat on the floor and the two pianists just about managed to share the piano stool.

'I hope I've got it right. I am playing the treble, aren't I?' asked Beth.

'Whichever you prefer. I'll take either.' said Theo.

'Crikey! Are there no limits to your prowess?' said Beth.

'Well, I could pretend that I can sight read either, but after our conversation about bluffing your way through the arts I really ought to own up. I've played both parts a few times over the years so it's already in my fingers. I wish I could sight read in five flats but I won't pretend I can.' said Theo.

This revelation earned Theo a hearty punch on the arm.

'I hope you've got a dead arm now.' said Beth. 'That might slow you down a bit.'

The duet went well. After a couple of false starts while the two performers got the measure of each other's body language for the slight rubato of the music, their understanding soon grew to fluidly taking page turns at a slight nod of the head. It was as much a pleasure to watch as it was to listen. The impromptu pieces were composed by Schumann to convey the exoticism of a set of traditional Arabian stories and it was easy to get carried away by the rich harmonies which exuded Eastern mysticism.

Rousing applause rewarded the final echoes of the closing bar. After taking a bow together Beth brought proceedings back in the domestic arena.

'The only antidote to so much German Romanticism is apple pie and cream.' she said. 'Unbend yourselves from these cramped seating arrangements and go through to the lounge. I'll bring dessert and tea through in just a moment.'

Theo and Beth had indeed set the correct tone and, after a little rest to aid digestion, everybody was ready for the next course. She served up some puff pastry apple tartlets with clotted cream and took them through for people to eat as they sat on easy chairs. However, the awkward tension had returned to the party. Beth noticed now that the negative influence emanated from Sally and Theo, but especially from Sally. She noticed that although the sofa was available they chose not to sit together but maintained a chilly veneer towards each other. As Beth poured out the tea Theo absentmindedly rummaged through the sewing basket which was next to his chair. This was obviously a displacement activity which Theo used in attempt to cover the rift.

'Theo, you've uncovered my surprise.' said Beth.

'Is this the embroidery you promised me?' said Theo. 'Can I see it now?'

'Actually there are two. I wanted you to have a choice. I've almost finished the second - I was hoping to get it finished tomorrow night at the Historical Stitching Society.' said Beth. 'There's a larger one which is about A4 size and then I've done a miniature which is a bit bigger than A6. Please choose whichever you prefer, size is irrelevant and doesn't necessarily imply more or less work.'

'Can I really choose either one?' said Theo.

'Of course. Whichever you like best.'

'And you're sure you won't accept any payment?'

'Certainly not! I wouldn't know what to charge and I couldn't charge a friend. I would have got it framed for you if I'd known which one to give you. My usual framer gets the tension just right when stretching the canvas, but you know best which style of frame you like and I imagine you know all there is to know about stretching a canvas.'

'I wouldn't hear of you framing it. It's generous enough to give me the embroidery free of charge without going to the cost of framing it too. I'm so thrilled, thank you. If you think you'll finish it tomorrow, when can I collect it?'

This last comment especially disgusted Sally and she even tutted aloud at Theo's hasty impatience.

'Oh, I don't mind at all.' said Beth. She was a little flustered by the evident animosity between them and had no idea what could have caused it. 'I'll get Drew to bring it to the gallery as soon as I've ironed it. I'd prefer to do that myself at least. There's a bit of knack to it so that you don't flatten the stitching. I am so glad you like them. Which one will it be?'

Theo chose the smaller of the embroideries insisting that this was his particular choice rather than a false sense of humility preventing him from taking the larger one.

The party atmosphere never quite recovered and soon the guests made their excuses and left for home. As Beth and Drew loaded the dishwasher they discussed the evening, deciding that Theo and Sally had had a lover's tiff.

'I've been dreading this.' said Drew. 'With Theo's history of fast paced relationships I knew it was inevitable. Even so, I did think they seemed happy enough recently and I hoped we'd be spared. It's going to be unpleasant at the gallery, that much I do know - as if things there weren't bad enough!'

Adopting the ethos that "sufficient unto the day is the evil thereof," knowing full well that there was nothing he could do about Theo's tempestuous love life Drew shrugged his shoulders and sat contentedly with a whisky in one hand and with his free hand he stroked Beth's hair as she lay with her head resting on his lap until it was time for bed.

The one glass of whisky had progressed to two or three and even Beth had partaken of a glass or two as they'd sat chatting into the night. When Beth's twin brother knocked on the door the next morning and let himself in they were still sipping tea at the kitchen table in their dressing gowns.

'Is today a holiday?' he asked.

'We're enjoying the perks of the freelance work ethic.' said Drew. 'I'm not at the gallery today, thank goodness, so I'll just work a bit later tonight. I've not got too much on so there's no rush.'

'We had a bit of a supper party last night.' explained Beth. 'Conrad, Hyacinth, Theo and Sally came. It was jolly enough for the most part but Drew and I think that Theo and Sally have had a row. The atmosphere was really strained at times.'

'I think I can help you there.' said Benedict. 'Theo came to see me the other day. He's asked if it's OK with us for him to fly out to Amsterdam next week. He was keen to specify that he really shouldn't need to ask but with so much suspicion hanging over everybody's head he didn't know the protocol. He's after Rick's old job.'

'What? Why on earth would he do that? He's spent his whole career building up the Whitworth.' said Drew.

'Theo says that the whole affair has made a mockery of his lifelong passion and it's sickened him to the heart.' said Benedict. 'He said he needed a change. In fact he said he'd go and be a plumber if he could but the art world is the only world he knows - he has no other skills. However, as he isn't fit for any other line of work he wants as much of a change as he can get. It's obvious that Rick's job will be up for grabs and he reckons he has as much chance as anyone so he wants to go for an interview next week.'

'But where does that leave Sally?' asked Beth.

'That's the root of your problem last night. Where indeed does that leave Sally? It's obvious that it does indeed leave her out of the equation.' said Benedict.

'She must be so upset. Poor thing.' said Beth.

'She's being foolish, not that I blame her. She knew what Theo was like.' said Drew. 'It's always been career first with Theo and then women can come and go without much regret, as far as he is concerned. Knowing Theo he'd think he was doing Sally a good turn by giving her a chance of promotion at the Whitworth as he vacates his position. He'd even put in a good word for her and think he was being gentlemanly.'

'It's the same, sad story. She probably thought it would be different with her. She'll realise her mistake now, of course.' said Beth. 'She must have been fuming all last night. They probably wouldn't have even come if it hadn't been planned in advance. They could have cancelled, we'd have understood. They needn't have gone through the whole charade.'

'That's the British way though, isn't it?' said Drew. 'Brave face to the world. Stiff upper lip and all that. He's sick of Constable though, that's understandable.'

'He'll have to get rid of that tattoo!' said Beth.

Beth and Drew burst out laughing. Seeing that the joke needed explaining to Benedict they recounted the unveiling of Theo's tattoo the previous evening.

'How very strange.' said Benedict.

'Actually, Conrad used to have a tattoo, years ago.' said Beth. 'He regretted it pretty soon afterwards; the folly of youth scenario. He actually became convinced that the tattoo really must have said "chicken chow mein" despite his original pretensions.'

'Chicken chow mein? What was the tattoo?' asked Benedict.

'Conrad said he was in with a pompous cultural set, in his student days. They all had this supposedly deeply symbolic tattoo on their inner arms.' said Beth. Seeing her brother's intense interest she added. 'It sounded nothing like the one that Rick had. There are probably loads of different tattoos drawn on people's inside forearms. He said he never understood what it was meant to represent but just went along with the crowd. The egotistical arrogance of it makes him cringe now and so he had it removed as soon as he could.'

'I can't imagine Conrad Jefferson being swept along by any crowd.' said Benedict.

'We said that too. He reckons he was a late developer.' said Drew.

'We all thought that the inner forearm was a strange place for a tattoo. Maddox says that most tattoos are on the outer arm because it's less painful there. Apparently the tattooists advise it on less tender areas - not that many listen to their advice.' said Benedict.

'Is Theo allowed to fly to Amsterdam?' asked Drew.

'I explained that we have no cause to stop him.' said Benedict. 'Everyone is innocent until proven guilty. But we do need him to keep us informed of his whereabouts as it's inevitable that we'll need to keep coming back to him - and everybody else - with more questions.'

'Poor Sally.' said Beth.

Chapter Nineteen

Brad and Leighton sat fidgeting as DCI James shuffled his paperwork and Sgt Maddox handed them each a can of cola. Brad wore his hoodie right over his eyes and made the small table shake as he bounced on the soles of his feet and jerked his knees repeatedly. Leighton wore a baseball cap but evidently couldn't decide which way he would wear it and so, between sips from the can and adjustments of his jacket zip, he alternated the peak of his cap from front to back and then round again. It took all of Maddox's self control not to laugh and even James found that all of this nervous activity was beginning to set his own nerves on edge.

'Just to clarify,' began James. 'You're here under your own volition, out of the goodness of your hearts, to help me with my enquiries. You'll notice that I'm not taking any statements and you're free to go whenever you choose. However, I hope that you'll be patient with me and stay until I can't think of anything else to ask you.'

The jittery duo nodded and made a show of sitting at their ease, although it was patently obvious that they were desperately uncomfortable. No doubt they'd been in similar interview rooms under very different circumstances. Not wanting them to drift into an automatic refuge of silence James made a last attempt to help the lads to relax.

'Any time you want a break or a drink just say the word. I'm always ready for a coffee myself.' said James.

Right on cue Maddox handed his supervisor a strong, black coffee. He then drew up a chair and stretched out his legs as he sipped his own sweet tea. James began the interview with some general facts that he was sure of. After that he could only hope that they'd help to fill in a few gaps.

'I know that you were persuaded, against your better judgement I suspect, to visit the Whitworth and then the Manchester Art Gallery for a bit of an art history lesson.' said James. 'You were quite a while with your tour of the Whitworth, Finn being very keen to learn, but then you hardly stayed to be polite at the MAG. Why was that?'

As deputy leader, or even head now that Finn was out of action, Brad was to be the spokesman. Knowing it was his place to speak he braced himself for this newfound responsibility.

'We just did what Finn said.'

It wasn't the best of beginnings for his future career.

James wanted to ask if they always and only did whatever Finn told them to do but knew that the answer would undoubtedly be "yes" and didn't want to undermine Brad's brittle command. Instead he merely nodded his head in encouragement to expand on this further. James had often found that silence was a wonderful tool because nervous people always felt inclined to fill it, and when carried away with thoughtless chatter they say more than they initially intend.

'Neither of us wanted to go.' said Brad. He looked at Leighton for him to confirm this simple truth. A switch of the cap signified agreement and

Brad continued. 'Finn made it clear that we'd get a beating if we left before he was ready. I asked him why we had to go and he said it'd be funny to see Scott squirm. This didn't make any sense though as before he'd said that he wasn't bothered about Scott any more cos he'd got bigger fish to fry now. All the same I could tell he enjoyed making Scott suffer.'

'And why go to MAG? You hardly stayed a minute.' asked James.

'Finn said we'd have to go for the look of the thing but it was no fun as Scott wasn't there. He said it was boring and so we left. I wasn't complaining.' said Brad.

'Didn't Finn think the Whitworth was boring?' asked James.

'Yeah, he did but he said we had to go. He said we could remind Scott of his old friends but that isn't the main reason he went. I don't know why he went, though.' said Brad.

Sensing that this was starting to go round in circles James picked up the end of a different thread.

'Have you any idea where Finn was hiding before he was found?' asked James. Sensing that this might be touching on sensitive information that Brad might want to keep secret, James reminded him that this was off the record. 'We've got him now so it hardly matters, it might just help fill in a few details.'

'He wasn't in any of his usual digs. If he was we'd have found him. It's a good job for him that he wasn't, otherwise he'd be in a worse state than he is now.' said Brad.

James wasn't sure how much of this was bravado but could feel the strength of Brad's resentment.

'Why is that?' James asked.

'Finn had used us and then cut us out.' said Leighton. Their ill usage loosened his tongue. 'He broke the code and he should pay.'

'And what is your code?' asked James.

'All for one and one for all.' said Leighton. He looked embarrassed when speaking this out loud but there was a gleam of pride within his shy admission which dared DCI James to mock him.

'The Three Musketeers, I've read that. Is that you three?' said James.

'We're the three Muskehounds and Scott was Dogtanian.' said Leighton.

'The Muskehounds? Dogtanian?' asked James.

Leighton just nodded.

Feeling that he'd somehow lost his way in a cultural divide James decided he'd better leave it at that. He understood the parallel enough to get the gist even if he couldn't figure out where dogs came into the equation.

'So is it pistols at dawn for Finn's treachery?' asked James.

A slight nod of the baseball cap, facing backwards this time, assured James that revenge was on their mind.

'Do you think Scott was in on Finn's plan?' James continued.

'Dunno.' said Brad. 'I don't think so because Finn was desperate to make Scott suffer for ditching us - but I don't know. He could've been. Not that Finn would tell us.'

'Maybe Finn thought he was moving up in the world too. How far would he go? Could he kill someone?' asked James.

'He's dished out some pretty bad beatings when he's really riled.' said Leighton, but he clammed up quickly when he thought about the thrashings he'd dealt out himself, bearing in mind that he was now sitting in a police station.

Seeing Leighton's thoughts as clearly as if they were typed on his forehead James got the picture, but sticking to the task in hand he moved on to yet another line of enquiry.

'Do you think Finn had been to the Whitworth before? Or, had you ever been there before?' James asked.

'We didn't know where we were going, we'd not been there before. We just followed Finn and were told to stay with him until he said so.' said Brad.

'Did Finn find his way there easily enough? Do you know that part of the city?'

'We never go to that end of town.' said Brad. 'But Finn got there OK. At least he didn't get us lost.'

After a little more desultory chat James thanked the lads for their help and Maddox escorted them out of the station. On his return James decided that they'd earned a visit to the canteen.

'All that fidgeting has put me on edge. I could do with an espresso.' said James.

'I know what you mean, I'm all stressed out!' said Maddox. 'And yet, what good has it done us? They didn't tell us anything we didn't already know.'

'I'm not so sure about that. They didn't tell us in words but they did reveal some interesting information. I don't think they can even formulate thoughts themselves but they've helped us more than a little.'

'What did they reveal?'

'It's obvious that Finn had been to the gallery before, he found his way easily enough even though they were off their usual map. Those two lads are new to that part of the city but it's obvious that Finn is familiar with the route. We also know that, apart from the happy by-product of making Scott suffer, Finn's main purpose was something more substantial. Brad and Leighton can sense that Finn has moved into a new set and that punishing Scott wasn't the reason for the visit. They themselves admit that Finn's usual redress would normally be much more direct, it's obvious that they're not unfamiliar with such rough justice. They even acknowledge that Finn now has bigger fish to fry.'

At this comment James started to chuckle.

'What's so funny about that?'

'It's funny how this case keeps turning in on itself and always seems to come back to art. On the night that the painting was stolen I was listening to a talk which featured Dutch paintings of a fishmonger and then chatted about it whilst eating fish and chips. Now my suspects are talking about frying fish. I just think there's a poetic symmetry to all of this.'

'Are Brad and Leighton suspects?'

'I think they still are, but I have to admit they're not high up on my list. I don't think they're very high on anybody's list, poor chaps.'

'I didn't think that Scott had such a violent past. They really are quite a brutal bunch.'

'Scott never was quite in the original set, though I don't think he was an angel. You remember they said that Scott was Dogtanian, he was added in to the edge of the group. If you've read the story you'll recall that d'Artagnan never was a Musketeer. Although, where dogs come into it I can't imagine!'

'It was a cartoon on TV when I was a kid. It's based on The Three Musketeers but they were dogs, not people.' laughed Maddox.

'I knew we were all speaking English back there but we were definitely speaking a different language. How very strange, I got the gist though. We know that Brad and Leighton fight like dogs. Whether they're directly linked in all this or not I do think that we need to give these ruffians a bit more attention. I'm sure they'd be quite happy to take on a bit of dirty work. It wouldn't do to miss them out of our reckoning. There's steel behind their stupidity and it's obvious that they're not averse to violence. They'd be open to the prospect of promotion if given half the chance.'

Beth had been a little nervous when she first joined the group but the ladies, and gentlemen too, of the Historical Stitching Society were friendly and welcoming and Beth was soon at her ease. Some of the members worked on smaller, individual projects making outfits for local historical groups or small items of decorative embroidery for houses of historical interest. Not surprisingly many original specimens had not survived the rigours of time and so replicas were always in demand to lend an authentic air for visiting enthusiasts. Beth joined this group as she worked to complete her own embroidery but couldn't refrain from frequent visits over to the large table where a group worked in collaboration on a larger project. On the table lay a large canvas on which the William Morris Acanthus pattern was slowly taking shape. Each worked on a section that would gradually meet in the middle. In between the general chatter reference was made to tension, stitch formation and other technical issues to ensure that the separate efforts would create a unified whole.

Sally wandered in and out throughout the evening but came and sat with the group during their allocated tea break. Beth had gathered that Theo and Conrad were in the building but that Hyacinth was not.

'Where is Hyacinth?' Beth asked. 'I thought she came to help with the refreshments.'

'She's at home, ill. ' said Sally. 'In fact, that's why I'm here. You'd have been enjoying homemade cakes if Hyacinth was in charge. As it is you'll have to make do with a packet of custard creams.'

'Do you know what's the matter?'

'I don't know exactly what's wrong but I gather she's really poorly. Conrad had to come to help Theo look over the new security arrangements but he's dashing off as soon as he's done. I don't think she's well at all.'

Beth really wanted to offer Sally her sympathy over her troubles with Theo. It was obvious that, but for Hyacinth's illness, she wouldn't have been there at all. Sally did little to hide her disgust at being there with Theo out of hours. However Sally was a proud woman and Beth suspected that she wouldn't appreciate sympathy and so quietly went back to her stitching.

Drew wasn't due in at the gallery and so on the following morning Beth left him to his breakfast and drove to see Hyacinth, planning to meet him back at home for lunch. Conrad made a pot of lemon and ginger tea and carried it with him as he escorted Beth to his wife who was in bed but eagerly awaiting the visit from her friend.

'Beth, I'm so pleased to see you.' said Hyacinth.

'How are you?' asked Beth. 'You do look poorly. Can I do anything to help?'

'Just you being here is a big help. I'm so glad you came!'

'Well, if it's as easy as that I'm entirely at your disposal. This is the easiest nursing I've ever done. Sitting chatting and drinking tea is no hardship to me.'

'But it does take out of your time and I am grateful.'

Beth realised that such a small gesture, just visiting a friend, might not be such a small thing after all. She had forgotten just how isolated Hyacinth was because she never made any fuss about it. Conrad was out so much with all of his business concerns, her son lived abroad and her house, beautiful as it was, was not surrounded by friendly neighbours who nipped in for a cup of sugar or a brew and a quick chat.

'What's the problem?' asked Beth. 'Do you have the flu or sickness?'

Hyacinth was reluctant to answer at first and so Beth urged her friend to make use of her in any way possible.

'I'm afraid you're in a rush and I don't want to keep you.' said Hyacinth. Beth looked alarmed but Hyacinth quickly dispelled any significant worry. 'Oh, it's nothing sinister. In fact, I feel quite stupid when I think of saying it out loud.'

'Don't be silly! Just tell me and we'll see what we can do.'

'The doctor has just left and he thinks I'm exhausted mentally more than physically, although there are physical symptoms. He says that I'm suffering from stress. How embarrassing.'

'It's not embarrassing at all. You carry so much on your shoulders and you never complain or share the load. It's time you made a bit more use of your friends. You do so much for us, it's only fair we help in return. Can you articulate what it is that you're worrying about?'

'I know it sounds silly. Of course, it isn't anything executive - Conrad deals with all that sort of thing and he doesn't get stressed. Nevertheless, I do think that the doctor is right. I think it's mostly to do with all this business at the gallery.'

Beth nodded her agreement and now fully understood the foundation of her friend's troubles.

'It's bringing us all down.' said Beth.

'Yes, but not everybody is married to a convicted criminal.'

'He's hardly in this category!'

'I know that, and I'm glad that you think so too, but he's bound to be under suspicion to those who don't properly know him.'

Beth blushed a little to know that her brother was numbered among that group.

'Conrad knows it too.' continued Hyacinth. 'I can tell it's getting to him. He tries to hide it but he just isn't himself at all. He's really on edge. Poor Conrad, he's got enough to worry about without all of this.'

'What other worries? Can you tell me?'

'Conrad says it's all in a day's work and nothing to worry about but his business interests aren't doing half so well as they should. I suppose that business is bound to have its ups and downs but it's a pretty steep down and it's getting to us both. All this trouble at the gallery just adds insult to injury because that's normally where Conrad would go to relax.'

'That's funny, it's where Drew goes to work.'

'How strange life is. Conrad always says that it does him good to feed his mind after staring at mathematical figures all day, and so he goes to see artistic figures to put him back on an even keel. All this worry has made me ill and that's doing nobody any good - but I can't help worrying. It's silly of me to have let it get me down so much.'

Hyacinth tried to hide her embarrassment by covering her face with her hands.

'Nonsense!' said Beth. 'We're not machines. Drew and I can barely concentrate on our work. Drew's just glad that Conrad isn't pushing for this artwork - though now I know why I'm sorry about that. Drew just can't seem to get down to work. I actually found him crying at his easel the other day because it's all too much for him. We both had a bit of a weep in the end.'

'At least Drew knows he's not under suspicion. You're brother is the investigating officer and that must be a comfort to you both.'

'I'm not sure that's entirely the case, in fact that in itself is an added pressure. It's all a matter of perspective.'

'Yes, and when our sense of perspective breaks down it seems that we quickly follow suit.'

At this point Hyacinth could no longer hold back the tears. After more tea and chat the friends exchanged hugs and encouragement until, with further promise of support, Beth said goodbye.

Feeling glad that she was to be welcomed back at home by the familiar face of her husband Beth walked expectantly towards the house. Instead of being greeted by a hug and a smile she found that the back door was locked. Once inside the kitchen the only welcome that awaited her was a hastily written note.

"Gone to the Whitworth. Tell you when I get back."

The lack of any preface or kiss at the end told her that all was not well. Other than that she could only wonder and wait.

Chapter Twenty

Drew had no clear idea of what was going on when he'd received the call from his brother in law telling him to get to the Whitworth as a matter of urgency. Benedict gave no details. On arrival Drew was met by a crowd of police and the all too familiar forensics team. However, it was James who pressed through the crowd to meet him.

'Dear God, Drew. This is totally out of control now and I have to say that I've had enough. I'm tired of being played for a fool and now I'm angry. You have to help me! I need a fresh pair of eyes to help me to make sense of this.'

'Just slow down, Benji. What's going on?'

Realising that he was racing too far ahead James checked himself and caused Drew to stand still with him.

'I'm so very sorry, Drew. I've got a real shock for you. It's very, very bad news.' Drew braced himself for the bombshell. 'It's Sally.' Unwilling to guess at the worst Drew merely looked at James. 'Yes, Drew. She's dead. She's been murdered.'

Drew dropped his head into his hands and stifled a sob. Then he gathered himself and looked earnestly at his brother in law.

'Is it the same murderer?' he asked.

'I think that's a safe assumption. It's the same modus operandi.' said James.

Understanding the full implication of this sentence Drew merely nodded. It was obvious that Sally had been strangled.

'Here?' asked Drew.

James said that this was the case.

'And what on earth can I do?' said Drew.

'Forbes thinks that there's something weird about the crime scene. If you think you can stomach it I'd like you to have a look. He reckons it's been staged but we simply can't grasp the thinking behind it. Someone is playing games with me and I don't like being made a fool of. This isn't a game and it has to stop! Will you look?' said James.

Drew gave just one decisive nod of the head. This wasn't a scene he'd relish viewing but he wanted at least to try to help, and so he followed James and walked towards the archives. Drew had a strong sense of déjà vu but there was no mystery to that, he really had been there before. Under exactly the same circumstances he'd walked to see the scene of Rick's last few tortured moments. The similarities to what he saw now were obvious. Sally lay in contorted pose with the same horrific injury to her throat, in almost exactly the same spot in the room. There were some differences, however. Although it couldn't be said that Sally looked at peace there was less collateral damage than he'd seen at Rick's scene of death. There was no profusion of blood. Only at the site of the wound had there been any bleeding and it was apparent that she'd put up less of a fight. Drew could only hope that this meant that she'd suffered less. There were no signs of a struggle and no overturned chairs, but there was a sense of disarray and clutter that was barely perceptible.

Forbes stood to meet James and Drew as they hovered on the threshold.

'Just stay there, we're going over the whole scene again.' said Forbes. 'Something doesn't feel right, apart from the obvious. We're keeping the room clear until we've gone over it all again.' Turning to Drew he continued, 'Something feels odd about the placement of the furniture. What do you make of it?'

'It feels messy.' said Drew. 'Not in the sense that it's been trashed, but disarranged or disordered.'

'But that's just it.' said Forbes. 'It's not disarranged. I'm sure that it's been particularly arranged so as to be out of place. Look at these chairs - they're in a perfect line. Why? Or take that red cardigan. Nobody knows who it belongs to, so why is it folded onto the back of that chair? The chairs at the back aren't tucked under the table as they should be but are all against the back wall. I've never seen anything like it and I have to admit that it's creeping me out.'

'We need an artist's eye here, I think, Drew.' said James. 'Can you manage to detach yourself from the horror before you? Don't think about the subject matter but take it in as a whole. Step back and look at it in an abstract sense then tell me what you see.'

With no further idea but to try and help Drew stepped back and squinted at the scene before him as he would when sizing up a landscape to be painted "en plein air." On both hands he extended his thumb and forefinger to form the corners of an imaginary rectangle in an attempt to crop out the scene as for a canvas. As he did so signs of comprehension grew upon his countenance.

'What is it, Drew?' asked James.

'I hardly know. I've got a vague sensation that it's a staged sense of perspective.' said Drew. He took up his squinting again and nodded to himself. Yes, he was sure now. 'Can you get a wide angled photo of this room? I think it would be easier to explain if you could see it in 2D.'

Without a word Forbes jumped to the task and was soon linking the camera to his laptop to download the image.

'Do you say that nobody can account for that red cardigan?' asked Drew.

'Nobody knows who it could belong to. It certainly wasn't Sally's. Everybody said she hated red and never wore that colour. It's the wrong size too. We've gone over it for prints and DNA but there's none we recognise. I'd say it's never been worn but has been well thumbed on a shop hanger.' said Forbes.

'I think I have an idea.' said Drew. 'It's outlandish, but everything has lost any sense of reality so I don't see why my theory shouldn't hold. Can we take the laptop somewhere else so that I can talk you through it?'

Drew didn't want to contaminate the scene and that was ostensibly why he suggested finding another room. There was no shame in admitting that he didn't want to chat over theories next to the dead body of his dear friend and colleague but Drew hadn't the emotional energy to explain all of that, not that any such explanation was necessary. The three men found a quiet table and clustered around the laptop eager to get to the bottom of this eerie arrangement of furniture in the archives and hopefully also get to the bottom of who had killed dear Sally.

'I think it's all about creating a sense of perspective. It's what an artist would create in 2D to create a 3D flow, but in actual 3D the effect feels weird. I think I'm right and the cardigan clinches it.' said Drew.

Seeing that the others had no clue what he was talking about Drew explained the principle from the beginning.

'An artist uses all sorts of techniques to create a three dimensional effect and to draw your eye around a picture. When you look at a painting your eye is manipulated so that you see what the artist wants you to see. More detail is painted in specific areas to give particular focal points, whereas background areas remain more sketchy. Artists would often place items purely to move your eye around the canvas. Colours tend to get lighter as you progress to the background, giving the effect of distance in addition to following lines of perspective.' Drew now referred to the picture on the laptop. 'Do you see how these chairs move the eye to the focal point - which unfortunately is Sally. Once you accept the idea that the furniture is moved to act as perspective guides you can then accept the fact that these chairs at the back of the room are all pushed back as far as the room will allow to give a further sense of depth.'

'And what about the red cardigan?' asked Forbes.

'Ah, this is where it gets even more creepy.' said Drew. 'I said that colours become lighter as you progress towards the horizon line and so conversely they get darker in the foreground to bring it really forward. Tints of red and green are very effective, even when mixed amongst other colours. However, in Constable's day it was common practice to add a splash of red in the foreground. The smallest dab of red animates the whole canvas. Examples of the devices that Constable used include a red gypsy shawl, a cluster of poppies and the collar on a horse. It's unlikely that such horse equipment would have been bright red but it was altered for a particular artistic effect. I think the most pertinent example for our purposes would be Constable's painting of Willy Lott's cottage. In the bottom right hand corner of the painting is a figure wearing a bright red top. If this cardigan doesn't belong to anybody here I think it's safe to assume that it was placed and I can only guess that this is the reason why.'

'You're saying that the crime scene has been staged in the manner of a Constable painting?' said Forbes.

'One from the same period at least, but yes. The subject matter is a very different story but the principle is there.' said Drew.

'I've never heard anything like it. Now that is creepy!' said Forbes. 'So, you're looking for an artist, James.'

'Or somebody who knows about art.' said Drew, keen to keep himself out of the reckoning.

'Which doesn't particularly tell us anything that we didn't already know.' said James. 'However, it does clarify our thoughts. I do think that the net is beginning to close about the culprit. I'm certainly instigating martial law. I know that everyone is innocent until proven guilty but until I know that everyone is safe this place is closed until further notice - and that now includes staff as well as the general public. It's gloves off and no holds barred.'

Drew couldn't remember ever having seen his brother in law looking so angry. He was a formidable force when even tempered and so he suspected that the murderer had now met his match.

Drew and James had agreed to meet back at Drew's house so that they, along with Beth, could talk matters over together. Maddox was to join them once he'd collected his notes. Before that James planned to take a detour to see Finn in hospital. Finn was perhaps well enough to have gone home but there was nobody there to care for him and, of course, he was a suspect in a burglary case which was becoming increasingly alarming. As such it was thought best to keep him under supervision, in all respects, at the hospital. It was better than a police cell at least.

When James finally arrived he found Drew eating his dinner alone in the kitchen, although that was something of an over statement. Drew merely pushed the food around his plate having no appetite to eat.

'Where's Beth?' asked James.

'She's in her music room. For weeks now she's been reading up on historical art thefts but since I told her about Sally she hasn't been able to tear herself away. I'll go and get her now. She won't want to miss anything now you're here.'

When Drew and Beth returned to the kitchen Maddox had also arrived. James had made himself busy and four mugs were waiting at the kitchen table. Soon each mug found an appropriate owner and discussion could begin.

'I think I'll open up the conversation with a few obvious truths.' said James. 'I refuse to accept my lot and resign myself to the statistic of yet another unsolved art theft. We've two murders and an attempted murder to deal with now and in that regard my record is unblemished. I don't intend for that to change now. If we put our heads together we can beat this villain. His luck is about to run out!

'I think we all know that this is a three horse race.' continued James. 'The "who-dunnit" will soon make itself apparent. I've a feeling that the "where-is-it" has always been our biggest problem.'

'I may be able to help you there.' said Beth. 'I haven't fully formulated my thoughts and I'm not ready to commit to anything just yet but I've a hunch that I'm on the right track.'

'That's very reassuring.' said James. 'I won't force your hand but you know I'm relying on your alternative approach to help me out.'

'Tell of your three horse race, Benji.' said Drew. 'It may seem obvious to you but I can't imagine anyone doing these things.'

'I will presently.' James replied. 'First I'd like to confirm a hunch of my own by asking Maddox to tell us his findings from the employment records of the Whitworth and MAG.'

Maddox rolled his eyes at the remembrance of the pages and pages of employment records he'd ploughed through. 'I'd never make an historian.' he said. 'They must spend their whole lives screening reams of paperwork. It's like searching for a needle in a haystack.'

'Nevertheless, I trust you've found a needle.' said James.

'A few actually, although I know you'd have preferred just one.' said Maddox. 'I'll save you the agony of hearing about the whole payroll. Riveting as that might be in itself it didn't shed any light on our situation. However, the rostrum of Friends and students on placement in the general gallery scene was very interesting. Just as you suspected, a few familiar names did crop up. We know that Rick did a placement at MAG during his student days when he was working on his Masters. In the year before that Theo did some voluntary work at the Whitworth and about six months later Conrad Jefferson signed up as a Friend to both galleries. Looking at the calendar of the academic year there is an overlap where all three could have been in the same artistic circles for a period of a few months. It's highly likely they'd have met.'

'Jefferson did say that he'd hung around with a so called "cultural set" when he was a student. He said he went to private viewings too.' said Drew.

'And he had a tattoo in exactly the same place as Rick. They must have all met at some point. These arty types are so cliquey' said James. He glanced at Drew and murmured a short apology. 'Arty circles always seem to overlap. It's politely referred to as networking but it's war beneath the veneer as people vie for notice and advancement.'

'I resent that remark!' said Drew. 'I'm just glad that I studied outside of Manchester. I never did manage to hobnob but nobody would believe it if my student days overlapped with theirs.'

'You didn't play the game.' said James. 'You're too nice a chap for all that self advancement - though you've done OK for yourself nevertheless. Besides, as I remember things, you were too absorbed with my twin sister at about that time.'

Drew and Benji exchanged a smile, remembering the early days of their friendship. Of course, Benji was right because Beth had been at the heart of all that occupied Drew's thoughts at that time.

'Once again I've unwittingly saved you from trouble.' said Beth.

A despairing sigh from Maddox regained their attention.

'Those who live in glass houses shouldn't throw stones.' said James. 'I've seen the way you look at Hetty. Don't think you're immune.'

They all laughed and then turned their minds once more to the unpleasant business in hand.

'Of course Rick is now out of the running and so we have our three horse race.' said James. 'Drew and Beth, you'll have to put your personal considerations to one side. I know you're friends with both Theo and Conrad but you must let the facts speak for themselves.' Seeing that they understood him James continued. 'We've known from the start that Theo is a prime suspect.'

'But it's destroying him!' Drew interrupted. 'He's devastated. His life's work is in ruins and, although his approach to a relationship with Sally differs greatly from a manner which we would agree with, in his own way he is very fond of Sally. Or rather, he was. You can see in his face that he's a broken man.'

'Nevertheless, he has to be considered. He has unlimited access to all areas of the gallery at all times.' said James.

'Then why bother with all of this fuss?' said Drew.

'Who can tell what goes through a person's mind?' said James.

'Let's take it as read then, and move on. What about the other two horses?' said Beth.

'The next candidate is obviously Jefferson.' said James. 'I know that Drew and Beth are bewitched by him but there's more to him than meets the eye. Years in the force have given me a nose for a crook - and Jefferson is one to the core. He also has the means to commit these crimes. He has a finger in every pie and he's clever enough to help himself.'

'I agree that either of these could be involved in the theft. But murder?' said Maddox. 'Do you honestly think that either of them are capable of murder?'

'Anybody is capable of murder. You don't have to be a policeman to know that. Years of psychology research has shown that, with the right trigger, we're all capable. The threshold for each individual is different and, thank God, the vast majority of us don't get pushed to that point. Fear and the protection of those you hold dear would be enough for any man but sadly a bit of Constable will do for another, or so it would seem.' said James.

'I can see how Theo and Conrad at least had the opportunity for the theft. They both have access to the museum, the security footage is at their fingertips, and they both have the brains to orchestrate it to their advantage.' said Beth. 'But who is the third dark horse?'

James knew in his own mind that he was playing for time because even he lacked the courage to blatantly accuse Drew's favourite protégé and so he gave a long preface to his thoughts.

'Let's look at this logically and see who is left.' James began. 'Although there are others in the museum circles who have access to the building and security lodge most lack the necessary skills. Brian might surprise us with his computer skills but never in a thousand years would he stage a murder scene to represent the mechanics of an old master. Non of the ancillary staff could.

'Whereas I could stage the scene but haven't the computer skills to doctor the footage - nor could I murder any of my colleagues but I hope that doesn't need stating.' interjected Drew.

'Exactly.' said James. He knew that it was time to lay all of his cards on the table. James took a deep breath and then took the plunge. Very quietly he said, 'However, your young friend now has all of these skills at his command.'

'Scott? You can't be serious!' said Drew.

'And why not?' said Beth. Drew looked at Beth as though she'd shot him through the heart. She laid her hand gently on her husband's arm and said,

'Benji said that we must put our personal concerns to one side. Let Scott face the spotlight as you have done. If he's as true as you believe him to be he'll stand the test.'

'I'm sure he's innocent. 'said Drew. 'But I'm not sure he's strong enough to stand all of this. If nobody else is found to be guilty and Scott isn't actually proved to be innocent it'll finish him.'

James stayed true to his course and continued. 'Viewing matters objectively he could have done it. He obviously has the editing skills. Now he also has the artistic knowledge and he does have obvious links to Finn. We have been led to believe that those old ties are broken but we only have Scott's word. Do we know for sure? Maybe he wanted to introduce his old friend to a new level.'

'But how does this help us progress any further forward?' said Maddox. 'We suspected these very same people right at the start and, two murders later, we still have no evidence. And what about motive? I can see that any one of these three would have had the means but I'm struggling to see any motive. Although I have to be honest here and say that I've struggled with that from the start too. I can't comprehend why anyone would go to the trouble of stealing a painting that anyone can take a look at and nobody could easily sell, let alone kill for it.'

'If only everyone had your honest heart, Maddox.' said James. 'Let's look at the possible motives for each in turn. We'll start with Theo. He's spent his life building up this collection which has always been a passion of his. Maybe he decided it was time he had one for himself? Did he need some money? We're looking into his finances to find out. Or, maybe he was part of the same group that Rick belonged to and was under orders against his own inclination but was powerless to refuse. Maybe he was involved in the theft from MAG all those years ago but this time, for whatever reason, matters didn't progress so smoothly.'

'Whatever you suggest sounds so far-fetched. Either Theo was part of an illicit gang or he was overwhelmed by a craving to bask in the glory of a masterpiece in the privacy of his own living room. Didn't your police specialist say that art crimes were never really about the art after all but were a form of quick collateral?' said Maddox.

'It does sound like a movie, doesn't it? These are just theories to be put to the test.' said James. 'Let's carry on, no matter how ludicrous it seems. Let's move our attention to Jefferson. It'd be just to his fancy to belong to some dubious art underworld. He'd steal, whether for himself or to order, of that I have no doubt.'

'And he had a tattoo in the same place as Rick.' said Maddox.

'Is it likely that he'd steal for money? Is he as rich as he makes out?' said James.

'I do know that his business interests are struggling.' said Beth. Seeing the surprise on everyone's face she recounted her time at Hyacinth's bedside. 'Conrad has reassured Hyacinth that's it's perfectly in the run of the normal ups and downs of business but she did admit that the combined worry of business and the trouble at the gallery was getting to both of them. Hyacinth said that Conrad just wasn't acting like his usual self these days and that worried her more than the financial concerns.'

'Would he know how to sell it on, though?' said Maddox.

'Who knows what contacts Jefferson made on the inside?' said James. 'You can be sure that he only moves in the highest circles, whether out in civilian life or inside a prison. Some people trade information for a packet of cigarettes but that will not have been Jefferson's métier.'

'What about Scott?' asked Drew. 'What possible motive could he have? He couldn't shift a painting on the black market and he certainly doesn't move in influential circles.'

'That young man is a quick learner. He'd soon know to talk to Rick or anyone else in that line if the inclination suited him. He's clever and astute and we don't really know for certain whether he'd use that brain of his for good or ill. He's well placed to make use of his old friends and also to make his way with a new set. If it suited Scott's purpose to mix with the wrong crowd in the new world he found himself in he'd certainly be up to the task. Maybe you weren't the only one to take him under their wing, Drew. Perhaps Scott was more than ready to prove his worth to less honourable souls than yours.' said James.

'Perhaps Scott thought it would grant him acceptance into an elite artistic society which was less savoury than the one Drew knows. 'Weren't we told that art was sometimes stolen to provide a sort of status symbol?' said Maddox.

'Who on earth could he brag about it to?' said Drew 'You've seen where he lives. They'd be more impressed if he nicked a Playstation!'

'His old friends maybe, but his new set?' said James.

'He doesn't have a new set!' said Drew. Realising the futility of his remonstrance he sighed. 'I guess I'll have to let you find that out for yourself.' Beth smiled at Drew encouragingly to confirm that this is what she'd meant in her earlier statement. Drew was still troubled though. 'Unless Forbes uncovers any evidence we're at stalemate until we find the painting. I do hope it's not in a rubbish heap somewhere, otherwise suspicion will be hanging over all our heads indefinitely.'

'I don't hold out much hope for forensics opening any new lines of enquiry. Any evidence that is at the murder scene has every right to be there. No doubt Theo's DNA will be all over Sally's body, if you bear in mind their relationship, and trace evidence is bound to occur simply because she'd have been in working contact with Conrad and Scott on a regular basis.' said James.

'So it really does come down to "where is it" before we can say "who-dunnit" doesn't it?' said Maddox.

'Unless we get an unexpected lucky break, I believe so.' said James. 'Which now brings us to you, Beth. What have you got up your sleeve?'

'I wasn't being unduly modest when I said that I hardly know. I've been looking at historical cases for inspiration but nothing seemed to ring a bell. However, just before you arrived I came across a case in which the artwork has never been found and conspiracy still rages about the stolen piece. Something about the story has caught my attention and yet I hardly know what or why.' said Beth. 'Recently those who are still searching thought that they knew where it was hidden only to find that, in past generations, somebody got there before them and now the piece is missing again. I can't say why it's grabbed my attention and before I could properly think about it you came and I've lost my train of thought. Leave it with me and I'll have another think. Don't get too excited but I do have the beginning of a shadow of an idea. It's not much I know, but I hope it will help eventually, once I've gathered my thoughts again. Don't be disappointed if it's all nothing in the end.'

'I know how you work, Beth.' said James. 'And I know not to ignore it when you pick up a scent. Trust your instincts and call me if there's anything I can do to help. I can even take you to Argyle to see if he can help. He might even offer you a job.'

Beth waved away her brother's jest. He was always trying to get her employed for her sleuthing skills. However, Beth knew that it would be all wrong. Her instincts ran in an unusual vein where imperceptible parallels in her domestic world led her to conclusions via very abstract avenues. She knew that, if she was required to work to schedule, it would kill any inspiration she had. She knew where she worked best and enjoyed it all the more for that. Their grandmother had been content to work in obscurity during the war years at Bletchley Park and had then, after helping to save the world, to remain sworn to secrecy and to employ her skills in unknown ways as she raised her family. No tinge of resentment was ever evident and Beth was proud to follow in her footsteps. She didn't need an official accolade. Benedict always said that he lacked the strength to work in such anonymity. It was no effort to Beth, in fact it was a positive joy to her, so why upset matters? Benedict was happy to take the official line and Beth was genuinely happy to remain in the background. They were a perfect team, so why look for change?

Chapter Twenty One

DCI James and Sgt Maddox sat together with DCI Monroe in Monroe's office discussing the case.

'Our problem is that we have too many theories and not a single shred of evidence.' said James. 'The one witness we do have can't be trusted to know what he's on about and even if he is telling the truth it can't possibly stand up in court.'

'Is this the lad who just about survived a beating?' asked Monroe. 'What does he have to say for himself?'

'He says he's convinced that Rick is to blame for his beating but now thinks that there was somebody else on the scene, although he can't or won't say who. He's still very cagey about the theft, though. Now that he knows about the murders he's a bit more vocal and admits that he's visited the Whitworth more than once and met Rick there. It wouldn't take them long to get the measure of each other. He says that he originally sauntered over there to teach Scott a lesson but after that he suffers from a convenient bout of amnesia.' said James.

'If Rick did have the Constable then it's gone the same way as the Turner. We won't be seeing either of them on exhibition again.' said Monroe.

'There had to be another person who had a hand in the burglary but Finn seems genuinely afraid and hides behind his forgetfulness. Perhaps he thinks he'll be attacked again but won't be so lucky next time. I can't get him to see sense. He'd be much safer if he told us everything and helped us to catch whoever it is.' said James. 'Then he'd be out of harm's way. Instead of helping us catch them, whenever the conversation touches upon this other person he either says he can't remember or complains of a headache. We can only hope that he'll see reason soon.'

'Idiot. He doesn't know what's good for him.' said Maddox.

'Do you think that the theory of a group working together holds water?' asked Monroe. 'Or does another motive ring true?'

'If I'm honest I don't have a clue.' said James. 'It is true that Jefferson isn't as securely affluent as we thought. He's in desperate need of a cash injection in his business.' said James. 'However, there's no hint of a sale, is there?'

'Not that I'm aware of, but that doesn't mean it hasn't happened. My network only spreads so far. What does Jefferson have to say about his financial status?' said Monroe.

'He doesn't seem fazed.' said James. 'Apparently it's all in a day's work according to Jefferson. He reckons that if things get too sticky he can approach his son who runs an offshoot company abroad. He's a cool customer, though. If his business was going to the wall he certainly wouldn't show any sign of weakness to me. His accountant wasn't much help either.'

'For what it's worth I'd be more inclined to look into the organisational line of enquiry.' said Monroe. 'It's obvious that we're dealing with professionals. I'll hazard a guess that this isn't their first crime and teamwork is the obvious reason for such a smooth operation.'

'I agree that we aren't working with a rookie but, if it's the same crew that stole your Turner all those years ago, why is it so messy this time?' said James.

'Somebody's bungled it.' said Maddox. 'Could it be Scott? He'd be new to this sort of thing. Maybe he's messed it up through inexperience.'

'You're right, it is messy this time. There's too much attention being brought to this case and you can be sure that certain people won't be happy about that.' said Monroe.

'Scott's frightened, that much is obvious. However, whether he's afraid of retribution or just afraid of being wrongly accused is impossible to tell.' said James.

'Couldn't we just politely ask everybody to roll their sleeves up for us? If we found a matching tattoo then it would clear the matter up quickly.' said Monroe.

James groaned at the constraints laid upon him. It was true that he could politely ask everybody to show their arms but that was as far as he could go. He didn't have sufficient evidence to insist, and even then it didn't really prove anything. Jefferson had had a tattoo removed which meant nothing and, even if Scott was in the gang now, it was unlikely that he'd be sufficiently integrated into the pecking order to have earned the right to have the tattoo. He knew they were clutching at straws. They were prevented from discussing matters further by the telephone on Monroe's desk ringing.

'Believe it or not, but Theo is downstairs and he's playing merry hell with the reception staff. He's in a rage and wants to see you. I don't think he's in the mood to oblige you with his shirt sleeves.'

James looked surprised but readily agreed to see Theo. 'Why don't you come with me? Perhaps you could ask him instead.'

The three policemen went to meet Theo in an interview room. Theo had demanded to see James but hadn't banked on having three policemen at his service.

'What the hell's going on, James?' Theo yelled. 'Is this the full force of the law being brought down upon me?'

'You tell me what's going on. You were the one who abused the receptionist and rudely demanded to see me.' said James. 'And so here I am.'

'You didn't need to come with an army at your back!' said Theo.

'Do be sensible, Theo.' said James. 'I was in a meeting when you rudely interrupted us and so we've brought the meeting to you. What's so urgent that you need to mistreat the staff?'

Theo's temper was up and he wasn't ready to calm down until he'd said his piece. 'You said I could go to Amsterdam. Now I'm almost under house arrest and can't go anywhere. I could lose this job offer because you're being so heavy handed. I need to go to this interview and now, because of you, I'm landlocked!'

'With all due respect it's not because of me, it's because of a murderer. There's a stolen masterpiece and two people are dead. Everybody has got to stay put until we find the culprit. You of all people should understand this.' said James.

Theo's eyes blazed with anger. 'Of course I know it.' he said. 'My life is in ruins. My career is over and my girlfriend is dead. This new job is a chance for a new start - and now you've killed that!'

'It can't be helped, Theo. We have to do whatever is needed and the sooner everyone helps us the quicker we'll get to the bottom of this and we can all get on with our lives.' said James.

'I have helped you and what do I get in return? Nothing!' said Theo. 'What more can I do?'

'Could you roll up your shirt sleeves?' said Monroe.

It was as though Theo had forgotten that anybody except himself and James were in the room and he jumped at the sound of another voice.

'What? What on earth are you on about?' said Theo.

'If you want to help us further, please would you roll up your shirt sleeves? I'd like to see your arms?' said Monroe.

'I've had enough of your stupid games.' Theo turned to leave but then made a last remark to James. 'When you've got something sensible to ask I'll do my best to comply. Until then I'd like to try and get the pieces of my life together. To start with I'd like you to get your stupid police constable to let me get inside my own gallery. I've some personal belongings there that I'd like to get. You can accompany me if you like, if you want to make sure I don't nick a painting while I'm at it.' This last remark was punctuated by a slam of the door as he left the interview room.

'You'd better get after him and escort him out of the building, Maddox.' said James. 'If you're feeling generous maybe you could go with him to assist him in collecting his belongings from the gallery. I'll meet you back at Mossleigh later tonight after I've had another word with Scott. You'd better run to catch Theo up.'

DCI James knocked on the door of Scott's flat and Mrs Malkin opened the door, keeping the chain on. James showed his badge in the small open gap and the door opened fully before he'd finished saying his name.

'I remember you from the Women's Institute talk.' said Mrs Malkin. She smiled at the remembrance of a happier time when life seemed to be taking a turn for the better. Reality soon swept back in again and her face regained a troubled expression. 'You'd better come in.'

'I wanted a quick word with Scott. Is he in?'

'Go on through. I'll go and put the kettle on.'

Scott was already walking towards James as he entered the small living room. He looked less than pleased to see James.

'I wanted to ask you a few more questions.' said James. 'Shall we sit here or would you prefer to talk elsewhere?'

'Let's get out of here.' said Scott.

James nodded and walked through to the kitchen. It was a tiny, square room that was immaculately clean. James suspected that the poor woman hadn't been able to sit still for weeks and had vented all of her nervous energy via the duster and the dishcloth.

'Mrs Malkin, I'll decline the tea if you don't mind and I'll take Scott out for a coffee.' said James. 'The lad looks like he needs a breath of fresh air. Now that the gallery is shut you must be sick of having him under your feet. We'll only be an hour or so, I'll get him out of your hair.'

Mrs Malkin smiled at James's kind tone but seemed nervous at the thought of Scott leaving her.

'We'll only be an hour.' James reassured her.

Scott unbent sufficiently to thank James for the consideration he had shown.

'It's nearly finished her.' said Scott. 'It was bad enough when I got the ASBO but now she's worried sick I'll get thrown into prison for murder. At least Brad and Leighton have kept away. Even so, she hardly dares to step out for the milk.'

'What can you tell me to help me, then? For all of our sakes let's get to the bottom of this.'

'How can I tell you what I don't know?'

'I think I'll be the best judge of what you think you know or don't know. Although, I have to admit that I don't know what drink you want.'

Scott laughed and asked for a flat white. James thought that this time last year Scott had probably never even heard of a flat white and would have asked for a cola. He knew that he was making trite assumptions but he also knew that such assumptions were rarely wrong. It showed how much Scott had embraced the new world he'd been introduced to. It was like learning which cutlery to use during a seven course meal without drawing attention to yourself.

Scott had adeptly suited himself to a different bracket of society, the question was how much had he left his old ways behind him?

'Did you know that Finn was already acquainted with the Whitworth before the night of the break-in?' James asked.

'No! Finn wouldn't want to be anywhere near the place. In fact I doubt he even knew it existed before I was there.'

'Exactly, and it was you that he was coming to see. Do you see what I'm saying here?'

'Of course I do and I don't know what I can say to convince you that I had nothing to do with the break in, or anything that happened after.'

Scott hid his face in his hands, overwhelmed by the implications.

'Have you got a tattoo?'

The question caught Scott completely by surprise and he stared at James.

'A tattoo? No. Why do you ask?'

'It's just in the course of my enquiries. Would you be willing to roll up your jumper sleeves to show me your arms?'

Without hesitation Scott pushed up his jumper sleeves to reveal bare flesh.

'My mum would kill me if I had a tattoo.' said Scott. 'I nearly got one on my back but I couldn't afford it and I knew mum would go mental.'

'Did you know that Rick had a tattoo?'

Scott shook his head but then seemed to lose his conviction. 'Now you come to mention it I remember hearing Drew talk about Rick having a tattoo but I didn't really pay attention. Is it important?'

James ignored the question and continued to ask another himself. 'Does Theo have a tattoo?'

'How should I know?'

Realising that this was a dead end James asked Scott about his relationship with Theo and Rick. 'Did you ever talk to them much outside of work?' he asked.

'I hardly spoke to Theo at work never mind outside of the gallery. I don't think he liked me much and I'm sure he regretted taking me on. Drew said it was nothing personal as Theo was tetchy with everyone while we were packing down the Constable collection. He was worried sick that something would get damaged. I only ever spoke to Rick that one time when Drew took me to MAG. Drew went home and I stayed at MAG because Theo was in such a temper. I only stayed about half an hour after Drew had gone though because I didn't know Rick and I felt awkward and in the way. I didn't go back to the Whitworth though, I went home. I couldn't face Theo any more that day.'

Scott looked embarrassed at being caught playing truant but, in the grand scheme of things, it was the least of his worries. After a few more cursory enquiries and the same number of dead ends James offered to take Scott home.

'I'll make my own way back if it's all the same to you.' said Scott. 'My mum's seen enough policemen recently and I could do with a quiet walk home. I don't like to leave mum but now I'm out I'll make the most of it and take my time and walk back. I need to clear my head.'

Maddox was waiting for James at Mossleigh police station but they were soon driving to Beth's to make use of the better facilities there. As James drove they caught up on each other's news, not that either of them had much to report.

'Theo was in such a temper but I did go with him to the gallery. He picked up some paperwork, a tie of his and his briefcase. I had a look inside the briefcase and I've made a list of everything he took home. His job interview letter and his passport were amongst the papers he took, I don't know if that's significant.' said Maddox.

'Was there anything other than paperwork?' James asked.

Maddox shook his head.

Not many minutes later they were seated at the familiar table in Beth's kitchen. Beth was pouring drinks and, after a summons from the silver service bell, Drew could be heard cleaning his brushes to come and join them.

'Beth, what have you got for us?' said James. 'A ray of hope would be a good start.'

'I have an idea. Will that do for starters?' said Beth.

'Anything will do for starters, I can't afford to be picky. What are you thinking?' said James.

'You know that I've been reading up on historical art thefts.' said Beth. 'I thought it might provide a pattern for our problem today. You were told that most art thefts aren't civilised and usually end up being quite base and are often brutal. Ours is no different as events have unfolded.'

'I'd forgotten that.' said Maddox. 'Because there was no fuss about the MAG theft I've been thinking that our case is out of the ordinary. That's not true though, is it? How awful.'

'There has to be a pattern.' continued Beth. 'We just have to find the right template. The most famous art theft of all time is the missing altar panel from Ghent Cathedral. In 1934 one of twelve panels went missing. Originally two were taken as a ransom for money. One panel was returned but the other, The Righteous Judges has never been found. The story is littered with conspiracy and intrigue and the investigation was either corrupt or inept. This artwork was highly prized, even Hitler desired it above all else, but the investigating commissioner only took a quick look at the case and instead of giving his attention to the loss of a famous piece of art he went to look into a burglary in a nearby cheese shop instead. Another officer used the typewriter which was used for the ransom note before bothering to check it for fingerprints. It was a real fiasco.'

'I hope you aren't insinuating malpractice here.' said James.

'No. I'm just telling you what I read. A retired police officer, Mortier, has made it his life's work but the panel is still missing to this day. If it's hidden away so successfully maybe it can help us find our missing piece.' said Beth.

'It all sounds very thrilling. Do go on.' said James.

'The original ransom note gave clues to the whereabouts of the panel and on his deathbed the organist of the cathedral, Goedertier, told his lawyer about the note. It said that the missing panel rested in a place where it couldn't be removed without raising suspicion. Later investigations suggest that it had been kept behind a panel in the organ loft where Goedertier played each week but it had been discovered and moved many years before the investigators found that part of the trail.' Beth continued, 'Goedertier told his wife that something misplaced could not be referred to as stolen and then hinted that, if it were down to him, he would restrict any searches to the vicinity of the cathedral. Mortier still receives clues to this day hinting to the whereabouts of the missing panel. The cathedral walls have been x-rayed but the panel still hasn't been found. Nevertheless, popular opinion still suggests that it is hidden in plain sight. Theories now include the extended church community rather than the cathedral alone.'

'The best place to hide a stolen car is in a car park.' said Maddox. 'The principle is the same.'

'Are you suggesting that the Constable is still in the museum?' asked Drew.

'If it isn't in a rubbish tip, which we have to accept as a possibility, and it hasn't been found in the usual channels for selling stolen art then it has to be considered as a viable possibility. Posterity shows us that the best place to hide a picture is with other pictures.' said Beth.

'But it's instantly recognisable.' said Drew. 'It would stand out like a sore thumb.'

'Not if it's hidden.' said Beth. 'I'm not suggesting that it's overtly on show but I do suspect that it's right under our noses if we have the wit to see it. It might be actually in the gallery or it may be "in the vicinity" as Goedertier suggested.'

All sorts of possibilities sprang to mind and options for searching the archives were discussed.

'I might be able to get a warrant to search the Whitworth.' said James. 'But as far as "in the vicinity" goes my hands are tied. I have to have compelling evidence before I can go nosing about people's private property.'

'Just hang fire on any searches for now.' said Beth. 'I have a few more ideas up my sleeve. I will need your official status when it comes to the last push but we'll make sure we have a clearer idea before we charge in.'

With little more than a vague inking of what further plans might entail the meeting broke up, once each were allocated to their particular tasks.

Chapter Twenty Two

Beth had particularly asked that the Historical Stitching Society be allowed to meet at the gallery and had asked her brother to accompany her in asking members to attend. Benedict had particularly reassured people that there was no cause for alarm and stipulated that life must carry on as best it could under the circumstances. He explained that a couple of policemen would be present as a token of reassurance and the security guard would also be on duty, however a group of people sitting sewing could not present any danger and so it would be a shame if they didn't meet as usual.

Benedict and Beth sat in Conrad's study as Beth explained that she hoped that both Conrad and Hyacinth would come to the group, indeed she was counting on Hyacinth to host the refreshments at break time and knew that Hyacinth would appreciate Conrad joining her. As they chatted Beth looked at Conrad's art collection and asked him to explain them to her.

'Would you please bring that little abstract to the group when you come?' asked Beth. 'I've been trying to explain a particular effect to the group and that perfectly illustrates my idea.'

Conrad agreed to bring the artwork and Beth and her brother left soon afterwards.

'Did you notice that all the other works are extremely large?' said Beth.

'That's because Jefferson has everything large, it's how he shows off.' said Benedict.

'Oh you do talk nonsense!' said Beth. 'Now take me to Scott's house please.'

Mrs Malkin was pleased to see Beth until she saw that she was accompanied by her brother.

'Take no notice of Benji.' said Beth. 'He's not here in his official capacity, so don't mind him. He can't help being a policeman so you'll have to be kind to him.'

Mrs Malkin laughed nervously. She didn't like to think that she could be unkind to anybody and so diligently fought her fear and prejudice.

'I've come to ask if you'll come to our little stitching group.' said Beth. Seeing a cross stitch sampler over the fire she walked over to admire it. 'Did you work this?'

Mrs Malkin blushed with pride. ' I did, many years ago. I haven't done any sewing for years. It's funny how you forget to pick up a needle, isn't it?'

Beth chattered on about sewing and art and was soon shown that other than a few photographs of Scott there were no other pictures in the house.

'Would you bring this with you when you come?' Beth asked. 'It's always good to see other people's work. I'd like to show the others.'

Mrs Malkin said that she wasn't sure if her sewing was up to scrutiny but hadn't the strength to withstand Beth's gentle but persevering insistence.

After that Beth felt that she'd exerted her influence as far as was necessary and left her brother to tell Scott that his presence was also required. When Scott asked James what on earth he was up to, dragging his mother along to the gallery, James at least had the decency to admit that he hadn't a clue.

Of course it was expected that Theo would open up the gallery and would remain for the duration of the evening. He'd been itching to get inside to get some work done and so he jumped at the chance.

'What exactly do you want me to do, Beth?' asked James. 'You can't call everyone to a sewing club and give me no idea what you're up to.'

'I told you that the Constable will be hidden in plain sight, if it's hidden at all. You can't issue a warrant without sufficient evidence but I might be able to give you a starting point. If my plan fails dismally we'll only have lost an evening so it's not so bad. But if I'm right in following a hunch then you'll need to have your men on stand-by.' said Beth.

'I think I can manage that.' said Benedict. 'Can't you give me anything more solid to go on?'

'I have nothing more solid in my own mind. Nevertheless, I have a feeling that this might just work.' said Beth. 'Have you got clearance to bring Finn along?'

'Yes, that's all sorted.' James nodded. 'And we've done a cursory search throughout the museum but nothing fitting your description has been seen. We'll keep looking though.'

Beth didn't appear concerned at this lack of progress.

'There's nothing more we can do until tomorrow night.' said Beth. 'If all of this is a complete mistake then I can only apologise. Even so, you should pick up a few tips on cross stitch and tent stitch.'

'Every day's a school day.' said Benedict.

The usual group continued working on the Acanthus pattern and Mrs Malkin looked on in undisguised admiration.

'How could you let me bring my little cross stitch and put it next to this wonder?' she said, looking accusingly at Beth.

'Nonsense.' said one of the stitchers. 'The technique is just the same, it's all in the design and that isn't of our making here. We're just working on a bigger scale. Cross stitch is very hard wearing so it's aptly suited to a large scale work like this.'

They then turned the design over and started to explain the structure of the stitch.

'I was always taught that it was rude to look at the back of someone's sewing.' said Beth.

'My mother always taught me that the back of your sewing should be as neat as the front.' said Mrs Malkin. 'In fact, when I had this sampler framed it was mounted inside out at first until I told them of their mistake.' Mrs Malkin actually beamed with pride.

Beth saw the opportunity that she'd been waiting for and seized the moment.

'Can you show us?' Beth asked. 'We're in an art gallery so all of the tools and skills are to hand to mount it back again. Do you mind?'

Mrs Malkin evidently did not mind and handed the framed embroidery to Beth, glowing with pleasure. Drew began to grasp what Beth's plan was and jumped into the conversation.

'If Scott hasn't yet learned how to stretch a canvas then I'll have something to say about it.' said

Drew. 'Scott can dismantle it and then re-stretch the fabric.'

Scott came forward, unsure of what was expected of him. Mrs Malkin actually giggled excitedly at the prospect of showing off her neat stitching and also giving her son the chance to showcase his newfound skills with canvas pliers. The group of stitchers were surprised at the turn their evening was taking but were more than happy to go with the flow and explore the mechanics of sewing and framing. There was an atmosphere of openness as members held up their stitching to be examined for neatness. Once the frame was dismantled there was no doubt that Mrs Malkin's stitching was the neatest so far.

Conrad began to sense that something deeper was afoot and eyed the group suspiciously. The stitchers were unaware of the tension in the room as they themselves were too absorbed in the topic of stitch tension.

'Scott's doing a grand job of re-stretching his mother's embroidery, Conrad. Lets give him a go on your painting.' said Drew.

'It's an original. I don't want it mucking about with.' said Conrad.

'Don't be so nervous. There are trained art conservationists here. Let the lad have a bit of apprenticeship experience.' said James.

'What on earth for?' said Conrad.

The atmosphere was charged now and it could explode with just a spark. Finn was getting edgy too but a look from James kept him rooted to the spot. As if oblivious to it all Beth carried on with her stitching inspection.

'Theo, you've got my embroidery here, haven't you? You were framing it. I want to show the ladies my stitching technique. Can I have it back a moment, please?' said Beth.

'I think it's here somewhere, but I don't know where. I haven't been here for days so I can't think where it is just now' said Theo.

'Please go and find it. I really want to show it here.' said Beth.

'I'll go in a minute, but I've already stapled it to the stretcher bars.'

Picking up the undertones of what was expected of him Conrad took up his painting and, throwing caution to the wind, thrust it on Scott.

'Go on, then. If we're having a workshop you might as well have a go at this. It's an original Kandinsky, so go gently won't you?' said Conrad.

By this point Conrad was almost removing the canvas from the frame himself. He looked at James and shrugged his shoulders. It was obvious that he had no real idea what was going on but nevertheless guessed what was required of him. Scott looked terrified at having to perform to an audience on such an original, but endeavoured to do as he was bidden.

'Don't worry, I'll help you with this one.' said Drew reassuringly.

'I know we're all a bit on edge being here at the gallery.' said Beth. 'Benji will go with you to find the embroidery, Theo.'

Swept along by the tide Theo went in search of the embroidery and brought it back to the group.

'I've already stapled it to the frame.' said Theo. 'I don't want to tear the fabric, so you'd better leave it on the frame.'

'Oh, it'll be fine.' said Beth. 'You're all professionals here. If you can see to a Constable then you needn't worry about a plain old Beth Williams original. I change frames all the time.'

Drew knew that this was a blatant lie. Beth was very careful about removing fabric from stretcher bars once it was fixed and she rarely allowed the fabric to be stapled. She usually stitched the back to keep the fabric taut and if one was ever stapled then it stayed put.

'You really shouldn't remove it, Beth. It would be detrimental to the fabric. You'll get holes and it could tear.' said Theo.

'Rubbish.' said Beth. 'It's quite robust. I'd like to show these ladies the technique I used on the back. My honour is at stake here next to Mrs Malkin's immaculate stitching.'

Beth glanced meaningfully at her brother and then leaned over to pick up the mounted embroidery.

'I can't allow it, Beth.' said Theo. 'You can't risk damaging the fabric out of mere curiosity. I'm a professional and I know, you'll have to trust me.' He picked up the embroidery and turned away. 'I'll leave you to your sewing group. I'm going to make the most of the time I have tonight. I've been locked out for days and I'm going to get some work done while I have the chance. I can't stand here inspecting backstitch.'

Beth gave her brother a decisive nod and then stepped away. Finn saw that trouble was brewing and stood up to leave.

'Sit down now!' James commanded.

Theo actually attempted to run but was prevented from escaping by Brian, the security guard.

'Theodore Hunter, I arrest you for aiding and abetting in the theft of a Constable paining and for the murders of Rick van der Molen and Sally Bickerton.' The rest of the caution that James gave was barely audible under Theo's tirade.

'Are you out of your mind?' Theo shouted. 'What on earth have you got to accuse me with? You have no evidence, this is madness!'

Once the attending officers had Theo in handcuffs James turned his attention to Finn.

'You'd better come along too.' James said. 'You're already under arrest for breaking and entering and burglary, let's hope you can help get yourself out of trouble by remembering something of use now.'

Once again James had to complete his address unheard. Finn was now hurling accusation and blame at Theo.

'Save it for when you're at the station.' said James.

Scott braced himself for similar treatment and Mrs Malkin collapsed in a chair. However, James walked past them both without notice. As Theo and Finn were being taken to the waiting police cars Beth seized her embroidery.

'The police may not be able to take this further without a warrant, but this is my embroidery - I made it. I can do what I damn well please!' said Beth. 'Pass those tools over, Scott.'

Beth attacked the staples with a screwdriver and soon the fabric was pulling away from the stretcher bars. Once the fabric was free Beth became more careful as she peeled away the fabric and turned the frame over, engrossed with what remained in the recess of the stretcher bars. Acid free tissue paper sat neatly folded on top of a piece of thin hardboard. Carefully unfolding the tissue paper Beth revealed a small watercolour study of a cloud formation. James rushed over to the table and was joined by Drew but Scott dropped into a chair and wept.

'You are all witness to the fact that this was in Theo's possession and that he was unwilling to have it revealed. The embroidery was given to him unmounted and he himself framed it here, where it has remained untouched until now. Nobody has been allowed access to the museum and so it's impossible that this has been tampered with after Theo himself assembled this frame. This has just been revealed to you all by Beth.' said James.

'Can I have my Kandinsky back now, please?' said Conrad. There was a glimmer of a smile behind his grimace. He knew he'd been put to the test but he took it in his stride.

It hardly mattered that Mossleigh hadn't managed to achieve the acclaimed Champion of Champions title in the Britain in Bloom awards.

They'd won Best Small Village and were quite content. More importantly, the community felt that they'd shared in playing their part in apprehending a murderer and solving a case of national importance. Even those who had played no part whatsoever in the investigation felt no embarrassment sharing in the glory of those who had been actively involved. Such was the sense of communal feeling. The details of the case were still to be clarified and the village at large waited to hear the final particulars of the mystery.

For a few days DCI James was unavailable, being in either interviews with Finn and Theo or in long meetings with Argyle and Monroe, who were desperate to find links to old cases in the new information that James had brought to light. It was doubtful whether they would ever find the Turner or quite get to the bottom of their case. It was a shame that Beth wasn't on their team too, but as a twin he recognised that he had access to certain privileges that they did not. As soon as matters settled James called everyone to a meeting, as those who had been under the cloud of suspicion would want the details of the case explaining to them. Brian was included of course. James was pleased that he got to play an active part at the close of the case, such involvement would bring much restoration of peace to the old soldier. Even Mrs Malkin was numbered among the group. She'd also suffered and had a right to fully understand the conclusion of events. The gallery was the perfect place to hold such a meeting. Hyacinth had been called upon to provide refreshments. She had made a plentiful supply of cakes and had taken the initiative to order in coffees as Sally had done before. A wave of sadness crept over the group as remembrance washed over them.

'How did you know it was Theo?' asked Scott.

'I didn't, not for sure.' answered Beth. 'We thought it might have been Theo right at the start but, as the case became darker we doubted that he was capable of such dreadful things.'

'Why did he kill Rick and Sally?' said Scott. 'It doesn't make any sense. I know he was mad about Constable, but surely Theo wasn't that mad. A sketch just isn't worth it, nothing is!'

'Events became increasingly complex the deeper Theo got into this mess. Perhaps it's better if I start at the beginning.' said James. 'Theo and Rick knew each other years ago. Even Conrad mixed in the same circles but, not being an art student, he wasn't quite so deep in their clique.'

'Thank God I studied Architecture.' said Conrad.

'They got involved in a group which orchestrated international art heists. It may be that they were initially unaware of the implications of their involvement, I guess that's something we'll never really know. However, once they were in they couldn't get out, even if they'd wanted to. We think they were part of a theft at MAG years ago. It wasn't noticed for years and then, decades later, it was time for a similar operation at the Whitworth.' said James. 'They didn't handle matters so smoothly this time. They were unable to rely on the previous method which was more surreptitious because everything was being documented for storage. Also Drew kept on revisiting items to photograph them for his talk to the WI. It wasn't the best time but they were under orders and so they had to get creative. Finn had started to make a habit of loitering around the museum to annoy Scott but, until it suited his purpose, Theo hadn't allowed Finn inside. It was too good an opportunity to miss and so they made use of Finn who was keen to score one over on Scott and it would also make it easier for Theo to lay the blame on Scott.'

'I said he didn't like me!' said Scott. 'Now do you believe me?'

'It wasn't a matter of personal dislike. He just made use of you when it suited his purpose.' said James.

'If they were part of the same group why did Theo kill Rick?' asked Drew.

'They were part of the same team until Theo decided to go solo.' said James.

'He wanted the Constable for himself!' said Conrad.

'Initially he wanted to keep it out of the hands of those who'd ordered him to take it. It was a collection that had taken his whole career to amass. That feeling soon gave way to the idea that he might even keep it for himself.' said James.

'And Rick was sent to get Theo back in line.' said Conrad.

James nodded. 'Then Theo saw that, with Rick out of the way, any knowledge of the whereabouts of the painting could conveniently die with Rick. Now Theo could quietly keep the painting for himself.

'But surely he'd know that everyone would now be looking for a murderer?' said Scott.

'That doesn't necessarily mean they'd find one.' said James. 'He'd covered his tracks well. Any evidence that pointed back to Theo had every right to be present. It was his museum, of course his DNA would be present. Anything that lay blame to Theo was properly disposed of. There was nothing to point the murder back to himself.'

'Do you think that this wasn't the first time that Theo had killed?' asked Drew.

'I suspect not. I'm told by my colleagues that the murky world of organised art crime inevitably gets ugly. It's likely that Theo has been called upon to steal and kill before, he certainly knew how to go about it.' said James.

'What about Finn?' asked Scott. 'He hadn't a clue what he'd got himself involved in, had he?'

'No.' said James. 'He thought that this was his chance to move up in the world, like you did, only he chose the dishonest route. He wanted to get one up on you, but not just by taunting you. He wanted to show you that he was still the boss, even in this new world. This was his chance to up his game and start working with the big boys.'

'Fool!' said Scott. 'I told you he was stupid. Now what will happen to him?'

'Of course he'll be charged with breaking and entering, and also with actually stealing the Constable, but he's being very helpful now and that will go in his favour. He's miraculously recovered from his amnesia. It's doubtful whether we can use his testimony in court but thankfully we don't need his evidence.' James looked gratefully at Beth as he made this remark.

'But why Sally?' What on earth did she do? She wasn't involved - I don't believe it!' said Hyacinth.

'Sally just got too close.' said James.

'Do you remember the evening together at my house, when we played the piano duet?' said Beth. 'We were talking about the tattoo that Rick had. Sally had obviously got to know Theo's body pretty thoroughly, if you consider their relationship, and showed off his shoulder tattoo.'

'I remember.' said Hyacinth. 'Conrad showed where he'd had his tattoo removed.'

'The coincidence of having a tattoo in the same place that Rick had one was astounding. Theo also has that same tattoo. Sally was annoyed at the prospect of Theo ending their relationship for the sake of a job in Amsterdam and so she goaded him.' said Beth. 'She knew that Theo's tattoo was the same as Rick's and showed Theo that she knew as much when she dared him to show it.'

'That's right!' said Conrad. 'She said we'd recognise the design but we all presumed it would be another Constable that we'd recognise but Theo knew she was telling him she knew that we'd recognise it as being the same as Rick's tattoo.'

'Sally knew too much, but she didn't understand the full extent of her knowledge. If she had she wouldn't have paraded what she knew. Theo silenced her quickly before she realised the full significance of his tattoo. She would undoubtedly have told someone eventually and would probably even have told the police. It may be that he could have explained it away but Theo was in too deep to risk drawing attention to himself.' said James.

'Poor girl.' said Drew. 'If I hadn't brought up the tattoo in the conversation that night she'd still be alive.'

'You can't go down that line of thinking, Drew. Down that road madness lies.' said James. 'You're not to blame, Theo is. You can't begin with "what if" with a murderer because there's no knowing what they may or may not do. Theo chose to kill, you didn't.' James spoke with an authority that made Drew see the sense in what he said.

'How did you know where to find the hidden sketch?' asked Scott.

This was Beth's part in the mystery and James looked at Beth to encourage her to explain her reasoning.

'We guessed it was Theo right at the start.' said Beth. 'I couldn't imagine Theo letting a Constable original end up mixed in with the general litter. He would be bound to keep it safely hidden away. I read up on historical art thefts to try and find a parallel that would help us. The most successful theft is still shrouded in mystery. The missing Ghent altarpiece has never been found but is thought to be tantalisingly close to hand, although nobody knows where. If a stolen car needs to be hidden the most effective place is amongst other cars. The most obvious place for a picture - or the least obvious, if you see what I mean - would be with other pictures. Of course the picture is instantly recognisable so it would need to be hidden. Why not behind another picture? Theo had never shown any interest in art outside of the museum genre before but now he was enthusing about the art of the common people. I wasn't convinced.'

'I remember that conversation.' said Hyacinth. 'I thought it was really inspiring. Theo convinced me.'

'I didn't really know what to make of it, but I was suspicious.' said Beth. 'When Theo kept harping on about wanting my embroidery I asked myself "why?" - apart from actually wanting an embroidery of mine, which was out of the question. What was there about my sewing to make Theo desire it so? The only thing I could think was the actual size and that it needed framing, so I did a test. I offered Theo the choice between two embroideries. Theo chose the poorer design with rough and untidy stitching because the size was right. Of course he couldn't choose anything smaller than the Constable as he wouldn't risk damage to the masterpiece by folding it or creasing it. Alternatively he couldn't choose anything much bigger because if he framed it behind a larger work it might cause a ridge or cast a shadow in the frame. In the circles he mixed in anyone with a critical eye would spot an inconsistency in the framing. The fact that he chose the exact size that he did, despite its lesser qualities was one indicator. The fact that he was suddenly so keen to get it was another clue and then the sudden desire to move to Amsterdam convinced us.' said Beth.

'I suppose you mean that he was trying to get it out of the country?' said Conrad.

'Not only that but particularly to Amsterdam. There's a specific legislation that suited Theo's purpose. Dutch law states that if you have a stolen item in your possession for more than thirty years, after that time the item is legally yours. If he sat tight on the Constable, he could legitimately enjoy owning it in his retirement. He could bask in front of his very own Constable original.'

'So even though we were told that art was never stolen for art's sake, that's precisely what happened!' said Maddox.

'In a very long winded sense, yes. I guess that's right.' said James.

'The whole charade the other night was an attempt to flush out the watercolour.' said Beth. 'I didn't know for sure that I'd guessed correctly and there wasn't enough evidence to justify an official police search. They need more than a guess before they will issue a search warrant. If Theo was happy to dismantle the embroidery then I'd know that I was wrong and we'd be back to square one. Mrs Malkin led the way beautifully, although she didn't know it, and I seized the chance.'

'And Scott and I were also put to the test.' said Conrad. 'You couldn't be sure which one of us it was and so you tested our conscience.'

'That's not the case at all.' said Beth. 'I didn't think it was either of you two but I needed you to lead the way.' Beth could have said that it was her brother who doubted their innocence and she had to prove to him that they weren't guilty but she let it drop.

'I'm glad I've cleared my name.' said Conrad. 'If you want to dismantle any of my other paintings feel free, but do be careful as some of them were very expensive.'

Everyone was surprised when Mrs Malkin stood up and commanded the attention of the room by speaking out.

'It was my mother who solved the case really then, wasn't it?' she said. 'She used to really annoy me, always mithering about keeping my stitches neat. I said I didn't care what the back looked like as long as the front was tidy enough. She'd lecture me about how disgraceful such an attitude was. But she was right! Because I followed her example, after much moaning, I had integrity in the details that nobody would normally see. But because of my mother I wasn't ashamed to show everyone my work and that cleared my boy's name. I'm right, aren't I?'

Beth laughed and soon everybody else laughed. There was an inarguably innocent truth in what Mrs Malkin said. If everybody cared more about what nobody saw then it was undeniable that the exterior would somehow reflect the difference. Drew remembered the croquet match. It was true that Theo had cheated. Although Theo didn't sew there was no doubt that his stitching was bad.'

Also Available by Sharon Bill
from Amazon in Paperback & eBook

A summer fête in rural Cheshire, organised by the Women's Institute of Mossleigh, holds the promise of an idyllic day out in the best British tradition. Everyone is enjoying the festivities until a beloved neighbour is found dead among the bins and refuse of the village hall which saddens the holiday mood. However, it is only when Beth Williams and her twin brother Detective Chief Inspector Benedict James join forces that it becomes evident that all isn't as innocent as it at first seemed.

Beth is a piano tutor and a member of the local WI. As such she has her finger on the pulse of the undercurrents of the village and is ideally placed to find all of the seemingly inconsequential domestic details which could give her brother the insight he needs. Together, if they each pool their own particular fields of expertise, they're bound to get to the bottom of the business. Sordid crime might prevail amid the pastries and preserves for a time but, in the end, the culprit will get their just desserts.

Also Available by Sharon Bill
from Amazon in Paperback & eBook

They say that truth is stranger than fiction. Nearly 30 years of teaching at the piano keyboard has taught me that this is an undeniable fact. My dear Gran said that the world would be a boring place if we were all the same and teaching piano and flute in various cupboard like practice rooms, week in and week out over the years, reassures me that there is no threat of humanity becoming dull. If I present a wry viewpoint of various past pupils it is only fair to say that I also take an equally droll approach to myself.

Letters From the Broom Cupboard was the given title to an actual correspondence from my piano teacher during her own periods of incarceration in the privation of various school practice rooms which served to fill the looming periods of pupil absenteeism. This literary offering continues the legacy and I now write to you, dear reader, in my own hour of need.

Also Available by Sharon Bill
from Amazon in Paperback & eBook

Taking your ABRSM Music Theory exam can be nerve wracking and nerves can prevent you doing your best in any exam. Good preparation and planning is always the answer to this problem. In this exam guide I give you tried and tested technique, not only how to prepare before the exam but also the best procedure for actually in the exam room.

I've been entering pupils for ABRSM Music Theory exams for nearly thirty years and it is not unusual for them to pass with DISTINCTION, some even scoring 100%!

Follow these simple steps and improve *your* chances of gaining TOP MARKS.

Coming February 2018 by Sharon Bill
from Amazon in Paperback & eBook

Check out **Sharon's YouTube channel** for a free accompanying series of music theory tutorials. You are guided, step by step, through the ABRSM Music Theory workbooks. Each video tutorial leads you through each exercise and free to download PDF information sheets give you everything you need to know.

There are lessons explaining all aspects of music theory and practical music topics which are simply explained so as to be easily understandable in 4k.

For everything you need to help you with your ABRSM Music theory visit....
http://www.bit.ly/SharonBillYT

& in the pipeline…

Death of a Diva

The third

Beth Williams Mystery

For more information about Sharon Bill's

Writing, Blog and Music Tuition &

Free PDF Downloads

www.SharonBill.com

Facebook @SharonBillPage

Twitter @SharonEBill

Instagram @sharonbill_ig

YouTube Channel showing Sharon's ABRSM

Grades 1-5 Music Theory and other Piano

tuition videos in 4k

New videos added weekly

http://www.bit.ly/SharonBillYT

All video & social media page links are also

available at www.SharonBill.com

23641318R00181

Printed in Poland
by Amazon Fulfillment
Poland Sp. z o.o., Wrocław